DANCE WITH DEATH

A British Murder Mystery

THE WILD FENS MURDER MYSTERY SERIES

JACK CARTWRIGHT

CP

CHESTNUT PRESS

DANCE WITH DEATH

JACK CARTWRIGHT

PROLOGUE

The summer sun was a welcome treat that seemed to silence the world around Myra, save for the bird song, buzzing insects, and the crunch of dry grass beneath her boots as she turned off Dunston Fen Lane onto the single track with a destination in mind, and the promise of a warm hand to hold.

Warm air licked at Myra's bare legs as her feet kicked through the long grass surrounding the field. She held her phone to her ear with one hand, and in the other, a limp dog lead hung, knotted and worn from years of use. Jambo, her working cocker spaniel, darted through the grass somewhere far ahead. She couldn't see him. But every so often, a family of lapwings would scatter from their nests and he would leap up to catch one. Inevitably he would fail and disappear from sight again.

"Where are you?" her daughter said over the phone. "Are you out with Jambo?"

"You know I'm walking the dog, Claire. I always come home to walk the dog at midday," Myra said. "Besides, Vince next door always cuts the grass at lunch time, and you know I can't bear the noise. Honestly, sometimes I think he does it just to annoy me."

"I just wondered how far you were into the walk, Mum. That's all."

"Halfway," Myra replied. "So we've got ten minutes or so to speak. Tell me about Kevin. What's he doing?"

"Are you in your usual haunt?" Claire asked.

"Of course," Myra said. "I always come here. There are plenty of other dogs for Jambo to play with usually."

"That's nice."

"And Kevin? Or are you avoiding talking about him?"

"Mum, do we have to go through this?"

"I just asked what he was up to."

"You were hoping I'd tell you that we're separating. That's what you were hoping for."

"Now you're putting words into my mouth," Myra said. "So? What's he doing?"

"Oh, you know. Working, as usual, I suppose. I haven't seen him since yesterday."

"Left you to do the housework, no doubt," Myra said, glancing out across the freshly harvested fields and using the break in conversation to listen and appreciate the silence.

"He does what he can," Claire replied. "He needs space to do what he can."

"It's not enough. He should be helping you more," Myra said, making her way towards the raised riverbank at the far end of the field, which was easily twenty feet high and stretched as far as the eye could see.

"He works, Mum."

"He sits in his study doing what he loves to do, while you have to clean that house all by yourself. I'm telling you, Claire, if you don't put a stop to it now, he'll walk all over you for the rest of your life."

"A rod for my own back. Yes, you've said that before."

"Is he listening? Is that why you're speaking quietly? Did you show him what I sent you?"

"No, Mum. He's not listening. He's gone away for a few days. Can you just leave him to me?"

"Gone away for a few days? After what he did? You should have kicked him out."

"Mum!"

"Leaving you to look after the house, no doubt?"

"Listen, Mum. We've been over this," Claire said. "I can't keep talking about it."

Myra stepped off the track and into the long grass beside the field, making her way towards the riverbank.

"Where are you anyway?" Myra said. "I can hear birds. Are you in the garden?"

"I'm just keeping on top of it," Claire said after a pause. "What about you anyway? Have you given your fancy man his marching orders?"

"He's not my fancy man. And yes, I have. Not that it's any of your business."

They shared a moment of silence, as they often did. Sometimes Myra just enjoyed having her on the end of the phone; it gave her a connection.

"Mum?" Claire said, her voice calm and thoughtful. "Mum, you wouldn't lie to me, would you?"

"Lie to you? No, dear. Why? Why would I lie?"

"It's just..." Claire started, then stopped. "Sometimes I think you twist the truth to get your own way, that's all. Like the whole thing with Kevin, and I just think that..."

"Think what, Claire?"

"Well, if you'd lie about that, what else would you lie about?"

"I am not twisting the truth," Myra said. "I would never lie to you. You're all I have."

"And you won't meet him again? Your fancy man, that is."

"For goodness sake, Claire. I promise, hand on heart, that I will not see him anymore. Why can't you just leave my private life alone?"

"Because he's married, Mum. You know it's not just your lives you're affecting?"

"I read his last book, you know?" Myra said, knowing it would tease her daughter back into a more amenable conversation.

Claire took a long breath. "You changed the subject," she said with a sigh. "And did you enjoy it?"

"Well, I say I read it. I skim-read it."

"You mean you read the last chapter to see who the killer was, then flicked through looking for mistakes?"

"You know I don't like surprises," Myra said.

"Then why read a murder mystery?" Claire said. "Why not read a romance or something, where you know the lovers will end up together?"

"I'm just showing an interest, that's all. It gives me something to talk to him about. Lord knows we have nothing else in common, him and I. I doubt I shall ever be able to look him in the eye again after what he did to you."

"You both have me," Claire suggested.

"We do, yes. But regardless of what he says, dear, you know that no man could ever love you like I do. Remember that, will you? There's no greater love than a mother's love."

"Yeah, I know," Claire said, although her voice was tinged with doubt.

"You *should* know, too. You need to stand on your own two feet more. Be independent. Show him you don't need him."

"I am standing on my own two feet, Mum."

"Well, stand taller. I shouldn't have to clean your house when I visit–"

"You don't have to–"

"There's dust everywhere I look. I wouldn't do it if I didn't love you. The bathrooms too. It's a shame that husband of yours can't put his books down for long enough to clean them. Although, I dare say he'd cut corners. Men just don't clean as well as women. It's a fact."

"Mum!" Claire said, and Myra sighed as she entered the shade of a large oak.

"I just want you to be happy, that's all," Myra said. "I won't always be around to watch out for you. I mean it, Claire. Just have strength. Stand up for what you believe in and be the best person you can be. Remember that and you won't go far wrong."

"The best person I can be?" Claire said.

"Just..." Myra began, and she stifled a tear, controlling her breathing and quelling the whimper in her voice. "I love you, Claire. That's all."

"Goodbye, Mum," Claire said, at last, her voice a faint whisper over the line.

"Goodbye," Myra said, hearing a footstep behind her in the grass. She inhaled, long and deep and found the smile she had buried somewhere inside of her.

"I didn't think you'd come," she called out, as she pocketed her phone, then turned to face him.

But instead of being met with a kiss, a strong hand clamped over her mouth and another gripped her throat before she was pulled to the ground.

The scent was familiar. The heavy breathing, even more so. But the strength was beyond what Myra had thought them capable of.

The last memory that passed through her mind as her world turned black was the day Claire had been born.

It was a beautiful memory. It had been a wonderful life.

And given the chance, she wouldn't change a single thing.

CHAPTER ONE

It was Freya Bloom's first summer in Lincolnshire. Since arriving in the county in mid-winter, she had faced snowfalls, icy roads, arctic winds off the North Sea, and rain to rival the storm Noah set sail in. On more than one occasion, she had questioned the move, which had been a secondment before it had developed into a full-time position leading a rural Major Investigations Team. But just when the weather had dropped her to her knees and she had been about to succumb, spring had raised a few daffodils in the roadside hedges. A few tantalising, blue skies had teased at what might be. Even the dull fields that surrounded her little cottage were full of life.

It was enough to quiet the questions of her decision.

The daffodils came, then the tulips and the poppies, and before she knew it, summer had arrived, and everywhere she looked, the country-side that, only nine months ago she hadn't known what it did or what it was for, was in full bloom.

And boy was it worth the wait.

She stared out of her bedroom window to the three houses across the fields with only a towel wrapped around her. With a smaller towel, she dabbed at her hair, then leaned back to catch her reflection in the mirror. She wondered if anybody would notice. In particular, she wondered if the man who owned one of those three houses would notice.

It was a subtle change. A splash of colour to emphasise her natural auburn and dull the predominant blonde. Her eyes were grey today. At least in the early morning light, they were. More than one person had commented that her eyes changed from grey to light blue. Some had even said they were green. But to her, they were grey. Dull grey, to be precise.

She sauntered over to her wardrobe and opened the pine doors. She knew what she was going to wear already, but still, she enjoyed flicking through her collection of designer dresses and trousers suits. Many of them had lain dormant during those harsh winter months. It was simply too impractical to wear a Versace dress with Jimmy Choos when warm trousers with wellington boots afforded her far more comfort and practicality. She had tried to dress a little more elegantly a few times during those colder months, but Ben, the owner of that house across the fields, had simply rolled his eyes, and grinned when she had trodden through the mud. Eventually, she had given in to the weather, but her sense of refinement was tenacious. She had insisted on buying a pair of expensive, warm boots, a Barbour jacket, and a selection of attire that could have been straight from the pages of *Horse and Hound*.

But it wasn't winter now. It was summer, and her leafy-green Versace dress was calling. Add to that said pair of Jimmy Choos and a hint of the fragrance she had picked up on her recent trip to Paris, and she could stroll across the fields like she was window shopping in Chelsea.

How she missed those days. How she missed London, with all its shops and restaurants. The days when an investigation would come to a close and she wasn't quite ready to return to her four-bedroom house complete with a needy husband and his son, she would peruse the little boutique stores, finding lingerie gems, overpriced and unappreciated. But still, she'd buy them, if only to feel good in herself.

She pulled the laden hanger from the wardrobe and slipped off the garment jacket she used to protect her finest clothes, before selecting lingerie that would do the dress justice. A few minutes later, she was dressed, and, as if a switch had been flicked, Freya Bloom was back. The old Freya. The Freya that had once strolled along Fulham High Street, turning the heads of men and women alike. In fact, she had prided herself on her ability to make an entrance. It was just a shame that the one man who, back then at least, could have her showed little interest.

Her phone vibrated against the tallboy where she had put it on charge, and knowing who it was, she glanced out of the window, wondering if he would be looking across the fields at the same time.

But she didn't reply. Not yet, at least. She would make him wait. Dressing was only part of her killer routine. There was still makeup and hair to be done, and all the while, she would be imagining his face when he saw her.

It would be a moment worth savouring.

That was when her phone began to vibrate once more and she saw the incoming call.

"Oh, Ben," she said to herself, "you really must learn how to play hard to get."

CHAPTER TWO

Across his father's fields from the little farmworker's cottage where Freya Bloom was preparing herself, in one of three houses that formed a horseshoe, Ben Savage gazed out of his bathroom window. He held his phone to his ear with his shoulder and zipped his fly. The call had rung off unanswered by the time he was washing his hands, and as he dried them, he glanced out of the open window once more.

"What's she doing?" he mumbled, then hit redial to call her again.

He was halfway down the stairs when the call was answered.

"Somebody ought to teach you a few things about women, Benjamin Savage."

"They did," he said, smiling to himself.

"Well, maybe I should extend your lessons to include effective communications. Namely, when and when not to call a woman."

"You said to call you," he argued.

"I did? When?"

"When you dropped me off the other night. You said to call you when I was ready."

"I said *I'd* call *you* when *I'm* ready."

"Did you?"

"Ben, for a detective, your memory is shocking sometimes."

"Ah, well. I'm ready. Who's driving? Me or you?"

"I'm not ready yet."

"Well, I can wait. How long will you be?"

"Lesson number two, Ben. Never hurry a woman when she's getting ready."

"Right," he said. "So, I'll just sit here and–"

"Wait. That's right," she replied. Her tone was curt but flavoured with humour. "I'll speak to you shortly."

She hung up before Ben could answer, and he stared at the phone in his hand, bemused. He checked the mirror again, although he doubted anything had changed since he had checked when he had arrived in the bathroom. He ran a hand across his face, undecided if he should shave or not. The truth was that he quite liked a few days' growth. Not a full beard, but stubble, or as his dad would call it, bum fluff, despite Ben's teenage years being long behind him.

He opened the door to the little cabinet and smiled to himself at the rudimentary collection of toiletries. There were some cotton buds, shaving foam, deodorant, and a razor. But behind those few items, tucked neatly out of the way, was a small bottle of cologne he'd received from somebody he had long since forgotten about, for either a birthday or a Christmas. He couldn't be sure.

Twisting off the lid, he sprayed it onto his wrist, just like he'd seen Freya do in Paris only a few weeks before. She'd let it dry on her skin, wafting it around, then she'd smelled it.

"Smells alright," he said. There were no markings on the bottle, save for a tartan pattern and some writing in French.

He sprayed three times, once on either side of his neck and once on his throat. Then, happy that he'd done everything he could to look and smell his best, he put the bottle back, closed the cabinet, and stared out the window again.

"Right," he said to himself, something he often did when he was about to take action. He strolled down the stairs, collected his car keys, and shut the front door behind him. If Freya was going to make him wait, he could at least wait in the car. At least then half of the process would be dealt with.

A few moments later, he was in his car. The engine idled quietly and the radio threatened to break the silence until he caught the button to turn it off just in time.

He tapped the steering wheel and stared at the other two houses. One of them, the centre house of the trio, belonged to his father, and the other was where his two brothers lived, both of whom worked for their dad on the family farm. Ben was the black sheep, the only Savage in generations who had ventured from their farming heritage.

Often, Ben wondered how his life might be had he stayed with his family and worked the fields, braving the cold winter winds and the searing summer sun for an uncertain future. The truth was that farming was as unpredictable as the criminals Ben dealt with. Sure, the day-to-day activities were wildly different. But the outcome – the harvest, the reward – was an unknown right up until the point the grain is loaded onto trucks. Damp weather, insects, the fluctuating markets, they all played their part and were an active threat to the lives of farmers. Not to mention the rising cost of fuel and the rising cost of labour. His father employed a team of Polish labourers. They were all good men, tried and tested to be honest and hardworking. They had families that needed feeding. Ben had seen the profit and loss accounts. The theory was the same as managing a personal budget, only the numbers were significantly larger.

Ben's challenges were different but in no way less arduous. Sure, getting to the bottom of a murder was a tough ask, but more significant was the risk of failure. Failure meant a killer walks free. Failure meant a murder goes unpunished. Failure meant endless suffering for the families of the victims. And just as insects, weather, and the markets could destroy a year's work for his father and his brothers, the risk in Ben's world was high, right up until the moment the judge passed sentence, when society, the victim's family, and Ben's team waited with bated breath for the gavel to fall.

Ben's thoughts were interrupted by a cloud of dust on the farm track ahead of him. In the distance, on the far side of some of his father's fields, was a small terrace of farmworkers' cottages, one of which was rented to Freya. The others remained dormant. The days of providing homes for farmworkers were long gone.

A glint of light flashed from the windscreen of Freya's black Range Rover as she tore across the track faster than usual.

"I guess I know who's driving," Ben said to himself, as he climbed from his car and closed the door. He was just checking his reflection in the window when Freya came to a stop behind him. He could feel the heat from the car's engine bay even though she'd driven less than a mile. She lowered the window. "You're in a hurry," said Ben. "The table isn't booked for another half an hour."

"I've had a phone call," she said, as she too checked her reflection, adjusting the few strands of hair that hung over her brow. "We're needed."

"Oh, you're kidding me? I can't go in like this," Ben said, and he opened his arms as if presenting his smarter-than-usual attire. Then he peered through the window to study Freya. She wore an emerald-green dress, expensive, by the look of it. She was wearing more makeup than usual, and even from outside the car, he could smell that perfume she'd bought in Paris. "Are you going in like that?"

"It's not an investigation," Freya replied. "DCI Granger called me. He said to rally the troops. He has some news he wants to share."

"Some news?" Ben said. "What kind of news?"

"I don't know, Ben. The type of news that requires us all to go in on a Sunday evening."

"Well, did he sound happy, sad, or angry?"

"I don't know, Ben. Judging by his tone, I doubt he'll be telling us we've won the lottery. But one thing is certain."

"What's that?"

"You'll need to cancel the table. I have an idea it'll be a long night."

CHAPTER THREE

It took just fifteen minutes to get to the station from the farm, during which time Ben cancelled the table he had booked. He ended the call as Freya was parking, then took a breath in preparation for what lay in store.

"What is it?" Freya said.

"I didn't say anything."

"Your breathing. You only do that when you're anxious."

"Do I?" he said, but the question was rhetorical. "Do you think he knows?"

"Who?"

"Granger. Do you think he knows?"

"Knows what?" she said.

"You know? About us."

"Us? What is there to know?"

"You know..."

"No, Ben. As far as I'm concerned, there's nothing to know," she said. "And if you're of a different opinion, then I suggest you think otherwise."

He stared at her, confused as she opened the car door and carefully stepped down to the ground in her heels. The way she carried herself was one of the things Ben admired in Freya. Had anybody else he knew tried to step from a Range Rover in those heels, they would have snapped an ankle and cracked their head on the side of DS Gillespie's car, which was parked beside them. But not Freya. She left behind more than a hint of her fragrance, and before she closed the door, she leaned inside.

"When we pass through those gates, there is no you and me," she said. "In fact, the moment we arrived back in the UK, the *us* that might have frolicked in Paris was left far behind."

"Right," Ben said, after struggling to process his emotions. He reached for the door handle. "How can you be so cold? What's wrong with you?"

"Do you know what Granger would do if he heard his two senior officers were..." She paused, unable to speak the words.

"Bunking up?" he offered.

"In a relationship," she corrected him, her tone sharp. "They'd kick one of us off the team, and you can bet your backside it wouldn't be me."

"Why not?"

"Because I'm senior. Because there are more openings for a detective sergeant in other units than there are detective inspectors."

"Ah, I see. I wondered when you were going to pull rank."

"I mean it, Ben. What happened happened. But I'm promising you if anybody finds out..."

"They won't find out," Ben said, rather too loudly as he opened the passenger door and dropped to the ground.

"Find out about what?" a voice said, a voice with all the subtleties of a Victorian docker's and a Glaswegian accent so strong that even Braveheart would have had trouble understanding it. "You two up to something, eh?"

"Gillespie?" Freya startled. She glanced at Ben then back at the tall Scotsman.

"Aye. I was in my car waiting for the pair of you. What're you whispering about? Do you know why we're here?"

"No, Gillespie, we do not know why we're here. But I'm sure all will become clear when we're inside," Freya said, and as if reading Ben's mind, she followed his gaze to Granger's parking space where a three-year-old Jaguar was parked. "In fact, I'm certain we will."

"Do you think we should be worried, boss?"

"Have you done anything wrong?" Freya asked.

"Me?" he said. "No, boss. Well, not today."

"Today is Sunday, Gillespie."

"Aye, I know. But you wait until tomorrow," he said, as he walked off, smiling to himself. "When I swap the coffee for gravy granules. I can't wait to see wee Cruz's face when he takes his first sip."

He turned at the fire escape door, punched in a code, then winked at her and slipped through.

"Sometimes I wonder how on earth he made DS," she said.

"Same way I did," Ben replied, making his way across the car park. "Hard work, thick skin, and bad coffee."

He felt her stare as he approached the door, and when he turned back, holding it open, he found her still standing beside the car.

"Come on, Freya. We don't want to be the last ones to the party, do we?"

"You don't think they know, do you?" she said when she got close enough to hiss a whisper his way.

"Know what?" he said, and he shoved the door open far enough for her to slip through. "There's nothing to know, is there?"

She turned on the staircase and stared down at him.

"One day, Benjamin Savage, you'll come to regret those words."

CHAPTER FOUR

"Thanks for coming in," DCI Will Granger said from the front of the incident room. He was standing where Freya usually stood by the whiteboard. But where she would have dominated the room with her personality and leadership, he seemed to shrink. It was as if he was about to fire them all and was searching for the right words. "There's no easy way to..."

The incident room doors burst open and DC Cruz, the youngest of the team, barged in, breathless from the single flight of stairs.

"Sorry I'm late," he said, blushing a bright red before even the doors had a chance to squeal closed. He dumped his bag on his desk and dragged his chair out. "My mum had the car. Had to call her and get her to turn around and come back. She only popped out for a new Sudoku book from the Co-op. Took bloody ages."

All eyes stared at him, waiting for him to shut up.

"What?" he said, and he checked their faces as if he was calling an internal school register in his head. "Blimey, has someone died or something?"

That was when it hit Freya. The truth. The reason they were there so late on a Sunday night. But before she could even turn to see Granger's reaction, he spoke.

"Well, I guess that was the introduction I was looking for," he said, his voice solemn and low.

"Guv?" Ben said. He'd known Will Granger the longest and had the best relationship with the old man. Granger had been DI when Ben was made a detective constable. They'd likely been through a lot together, Freya thought. If anyone was to broach the subject, it should be Ben. "Not…"

"I'm afraid so, Ben. Yes," Granger said.

"But how?"

"His heart," Granger replied, with a sad shake of his head.

"You've got to be kidding me," Gillespie piped up. "But he was alright the last time I saw him."

"Which was when?" DS Nillson said, causing him to stare at the ceiling while he thought about it. Nillson was a no-nonsense young woman, recently appointed the rank of sergeant. If anyone was to shut Gillespie up, Freya thought, it should be her.

"Oh, Jesus. Now you mention it. It's been months."

"Hold on, hold on," Cruz said. "Who are we talking about here?"

"Detective Superintendent Harper," Granger said, his voice low and calm, at a pace that was almost soothing.

"Arthur?" Cruz said, then blushed again when he realised he'd used the detective superintendent's unofficial nickname. He lowered his head, rather than spurting a feeble apology.

"Most of you will know that Detective Superintendent Harper was with the force for a considerable length of time. Longer than some of you have been in this world," Granger said. "So, it goes without saying that his death will have an effect on us, in one way or another. For some of us, the effect will be profound. It will consume us. It will change every aspect of our working lives. For others, the effect will be secondary. But mark my words, regardless of what you thought of him, regardless of how well you knew him, you should count yourselves as part of the former, not the latter."

He finished his monologue by folding his hands before him. For such a large man, he appeared small right there at that moment. He swallowed hard and held each of their gazes for long enough to convey his sincerity. He seemed to linger on DC Anderson, a young female officer who had recently followed Freya up from the Met in London. As far as Freya knew, Anderson hadn't even had the chance to meet Harper. He'd been off for months and she had only been with the team for a few weeks. Maybe that was for the best. Maybe her arrival would be the catalyst for a new start.

A new start.

New opportunities.

Something clicked in Freya's mind. An idea. A selfish and loathsome plan that should have been so far down on her mind's list of problems that she hated herself for even thinking it.

"I think that if this team is to continue then we should work under the same ethos Dennis Harper worked under," Granger said. "I was fortunate enough to work under Dennis for much of my career. You should have seen him. It was before the days of computers when we had to get down and dirty with the best and worst of them. But Dennis had a saying, a saying that he lived by, and it never saw him wrong."

"What was that, guv?" Ben asked, clearly moved by the news and the speech.

"He used to say that, when an investigation becomes so complex that you can't see the wood for the trees, strip it back. Strip it right back to its roots. The answer will usually be the simplest."

"That's sound advice, guv," Ben replied thoughtfully.

"DI Bloom?" Granger said, rousing her from the terrible promise of a positive outcome.

"Guv?" she said, correcting her body language as if she had been paying full attention.

"Well?"

"Well, what, guv?" she said, feeling the burn of her team's stares.

"I wondered if you might say a few words. You have a way with words that I'm afraid I do not. Not at this moment, anyway."

"Say something? Right," she said, clearing her throat. "Yes. Well, I met Detective Superintendent Harper so few times that if I counted them on my fingers and toes, I would still have at least two to spare. And I'd stick them up at the world for taking him from us."

Cruz's eyes widened and he fought to contain his grin.

Gillespie did nothing to hide his smile.

Ben rolled his eyes but was interrupted by his phone. He waved it at Granger and walked to the far end of the room to take the call.

Granger, on the other hand, seemed intrigued. Perhaps he wasn't expecting Freya to be so crude at such a sensitive time. But then, there were lots of things DCI Granger wouldn't expect of her.

"From the moment I arrived here in Lincolnshire, less than a year ago, he had my back. Do you remember, guv? Do you remember how confidently he placed me into the team, only a few weeks after losing DI Foster too? He saw in me a leader when the team needed steering. He saw in the team, in you all, warmth and support when I was on my knees. And he saw in us all a legacy. An image of himself. Of his life's work. He was proud. Proud of you all, and rightly so. Don't forget that. Don't ever forget that. He's the reason we're all here. It was his vision. This station. This team. It's all his vision," Freya said, and she cleared her throat to deliver the final sentence. "It's our job now, our duty, our commitment to his memory to bring his vision to life and damn well make a difference with it."

"Hear, hear," Granger said, and he clapped just once before a few others followed suit. But it wasn't a raucous applause. Such an act wasn't appropriate. Just a few of the team felt what Freya had said and displayed their thanks. "Now, like I said, expect change. Expect disruption. I'll do my best to ensure full transparency. But like DI Bloom just said, so eloquently, I might add, it's our duty to make a difference."

"Will you be stepping up, guv?" Ben asked.

"I'll assume command," Granger replied. "Until we hear if a replacement is to be sent in."

"Can we attend the funeral?" asked DC Gold, the most empathetic of all the individuals in the room.

"Of course," Granger said. "I'll keep everyone informed as soon as I hear anything."

Gold smiled a thanks and DC Chapman reached over to give her arm a gentle squeeze.

"In the meantime," Granger said, stuffing his hands into his pockets and clearing his throat, "I need a drink. Who wants to join me in the local?"

"That might have to wait, I'm afraid," Ben said, walking back from the far end of the room. Once more, he waved his phone at Granger. "We've had an anonymous call. There's a body in a field in Dunston. Uniform are there now."

Granger seemed to slump momentarily. Then his chest inflated and he raised his head high. Defiant, but sad.

"I suppose duty calls," he said and glanced over to Freya with eyes shining.

She nodded once.

"Gillespie, Cruz, and Ben, you're with me. The rest of you, go and have a drink," she said, then looked back at Granger. "Duty calls, guv."

CHAPTER FIVE

The ride out to Dunston Fen took a little over twenty-five minutes. Not because the distance was far, in fact, Ben knew it to take a little over fifteen minutes, but Freya was driving slowly, deep in thought.

"Something on your mind?" Ben said.

He leaned forward in the passenger seat to peer into the side mirror. Gillespie's car was close behind. To anybody who didn't know them both, the two men appeared as a father and son – the large-framed Gillespie in the driver's seat with his mass of matted and tangled hair, and Cruz beside him, with a much smaller frame and an excited look on his face.

"Should there be?" Freya said.

"No, it's just you seem a little distracted, that's all."

"Distracted?"

"Did the news upset you?" Ben asked.

She deliberated for a moment, biting down on her lip.

"No. I already knew he was ill. But still, it's sad news. And Granger is right. There will be some disruption."

"Left here," Ben said, guiding her through the Dunston village. "You knew he was sick?"

"Granger told me ages ago," she said. "Prostate cancer. I guess the treatment was too much for his heart to handle."

"He had cancer?"

"Nobody knows that," Freya said. "And I didn't tell you, alright?"

"Right," Ben said and signed for her to pull up on the side of the road beside a wide farmer's track. Three liveried police cars were parked in a line, and a little, white van was parked at the end. "I wonder who will be brought in to replace him."

"Why does anybody need to be brought in?" Freya asked, as she killed the engine and sat back in her seat. "We have the resources internally. And besides, I'm sure that's what he would have wanted."

Ben heard her say the words, and he saw the fake casual expression she tried to wear, without success.

"You're going for Granger's role, aren't you?" he said.

"What?"

"You are. You're hoping Granger gets bumped up to detective superintendent, so you can move up to DCI."

"Ben, I am not hoping to benefit from the death of—"

"Freya, I know you too well. I can see it on your face."

She stared at him briefly, then looked away.

"You want to progress. It's nothing to be ashamed of," he said.

"I know progression is nothing to be ashamed of, Ben," she snapped, then softened. "It's just... Alright, listen. Yes, I'd love to move up the ladder. Wouldn't you?"

"Of course."

"Right. I just wish that my mind wouldn't contemplate the idea until we've come to terms with Harper's death. Had time to adjust, you know?"

"You despise yourself, a little."

"A little, yes."

"I had the same thought," he said casually.

"You did?" she said, seeming surprised.

"Of course. I've known Harper for my entire career. He was up for retirement soon. I figured when the time comes, Granger will take his place. God knows, he's earned it. He's been doing the job for as long as I can remember."

"And?" Freya said.

He smiled.

"And you'd be moved up to Granger's position. Although, I kind of hoped you'd make it more of a field-based role," he said, then looked ahead at the field where half a dozen uniforms were waiting near an old oak tree, and two people in white suits were staring at the ground, presumably at the body. "No pun intended. I just like working with you. I'm not sure it would be so much fun if you were sat behind a desk all day."

"And you?" Freya said, cutting to the chase.

"DI," he said flatly.

"You have competition now," she said, glancing in the rear-view mirror.

Ben leaned forward to peer into the wing mirror and saw Gillespie and Cruz waiting by the side of Gillespie's old Volvo. Gillespie pointed into the dyke at the side of the road, and Cruz leaned over to see what he was pointing at, walking straight into Gillespie's trap. A slight shove was all it needed for Cruz to lose his balance. He cried out and flailed his arms in the air, but Gillespie grabbed his jacket just in time and dragged him upright.

Cruz then berated Gillespie, who laughed it off and leaned on his car, waiting patiently for Ben and Freya.

"I think I'll be okay," Ben said.

"And Nillson?" Freya replied. "She's a DS now too."

"She's been a DS for a matter of weeks. She's a good detective," Ben said. "One day, I hope she's my DI."

"Sounds like you've got it all worked out."

"I just need you to get out of my way," Ben said, and winked as he stepped down from the car.

"About bloody time," Gillespie called out. "What was it? A lover's tiff?"

"A what?" Ben said, feeling his face redden at the mention of him and Freya.

"We were discussing plans to remember Detective Superintendent Harper, if you must know," Freya said, as she walked to the rear of the car, hitting the fob to activate the locks. The indicators flashed once then faded. "I hope that's the last time I have to explain myself to a detective sergeant, Gillespie?"

"Eh?" he replied. "Oh, aye, boss. I was just playing."

"Well, the time for playing is over. We've got a dead body over there. So, let's stop acting like schoolchildren and do what we said we were going to do."

"What was that?" Cruz said, appearing more than a little confused.

"Make a difference, Cruz," she said. "We just spoke about it at the station, literally less than thirty minutes ago. Our duty?"

"Oh, yeah. Right. Yes, boss," he said, and before he could waffle himself into a corner, Freya shut them all down and focused on the job at hand, and the opportunity she had just discussed with Ben.

"Right, Gillespie, Cruz, have uniform put a cordon across this track. Then make yourselves useful and conduct a detailed search of the immediate area."

"What about you two?" Gillespie asked, then immediately regretted asking.

Freya stared at him. Her expression was neutral but her eyes told another story altogether.

"Detective Sergeant Savage and I, DS Gillespie, will be going to see the body, talking to CSI, who by the looks of things have already got to work. We'll then be arranging for uniform to conduct a wider search while we wait for the medical examiner to attend. Once that's complete, we'll arrange for the body to be transferred to the morgue, and for the pathologist, Doctor Bell, to confirm the cause and time of death," Freya said. "After that, we'll need to compose a report for DCI Granger to decide if and when a press release should be issued, and what information should be divulged to the public. And that's before we've even begun to think about who the murderer is."

"It's definitely a murder then?" Cruz asked. "We haven't seen the body yet."

"Over time, DC Cruz, you'll hopefully establish the power of sight and observation, which I might add, are two separate things."

"Eh?"

"Where are the crime scene investigators?" Freya tested.

Cruz looked into the field, scrunching his nose up as he did. The two white suits were kneeling over some tall grass under a huge, old oak tree.

"By the body, I guess?"

"And where are the uniforms?"

"Over there," he said, pointing to a spot fifty yards away, where the six uniforms were waiting as if an invisible fence prevented them from getting too close.

"Why do you think they're standing over there?" Freya asked.

"Ah, right," he said. "They don't want to ruin the evidence."

"Partially correct. The investigators shooed them off when they arrived for the purpose of preserving evidence and avoiding crime scene contamination," Freya said. "Now, why do you suppose they would do that if, say, the victim's death was anything but suspicious?"

"Don't know," he replied after a moment's thought.

"Exactly. Of course it's a murder," Freya said, straightening the collar of the jacket she wore over her favourite dress. "Now, what are we here to do?"

"Eh?" Gillespie said, and Ben rolled his eyes.

"Make a difference, boss," Cruz said. "Our duty."

"Good," Freya said. "At least one of you is switched on. Now let's get to it. I'm supposed to be having dinner with a friend tonight. I'd like to make it before the dessert menu is presented."

CHAPTER SIX

"What was that about the dessert menu?" Ben asked.

Freya didn't reply. She just glanced across at him as they strode toward the investigators.

"You were supposed to have dinner with *me*," said Ben. "How is the dessert menu supposed to be handed out when the other party is right here?"

"They don't know we were supposed to have dinner together, do they?" Freya said. "I was throwing Gillespie a curve ball."

"But look at us. You're wearing a fancy dress, which I might add, looks stunning on you," Ben said, leaning in for the last part of the sentence. He waved his hands over his own clothes. "And I'm..."

"Yes?" she said.

"Well, I've got my best jeans on."

"Exactly. I'm wearing clothes suitable for a nice evening out at a restaurant that serves food to die for and you look like you're heading out to catch a movie. On your own, I might add," she said and waved to get the investigator's attention.

"A movie? On my own?" Ben said. "I even–"

"Sprayed aftershave. Yes, I noticed," Freya said. "So did the wild roses at the edge of the field. Did you see them wilt when you passed by?"

Ben glanced back at the hedgerow at the edge of the field where there were, in fact, wild roses growing in abundance. But they were not wilting. By the time he began to question her opinion, Freya was calling out to Doctor Michaela Fell, the senior investigator, a woman who Ben had successfully admired, wooed, and lined up a date with in the past, only for his hopes to come crashing down in a series of embarrassing misfortunes involving Freya. Since then, the mood between them had been notably fractious.

"Michaela," Freya said. "So, this is how you spend your Sunday nights?"

"Well, it beats sitting on my own doing the crossword," Michaela called back. "Plus, of course, at least here I have an idea of what's going on."

"Unlike the crossword?" Freya replied. "Let me guess. You're a *Sunday Times* girl?"

"How did you know?" Michaela said. "Am I that transparent?"

"You're too well educated to be fulfilled by any of the tabloids. And you don't strike me as a *Telegraph* reader. You don't care enough about politics," Freya said. "No. You're a square."

"I'm a what?" Michaela said, appearing insulted.

"A square," Freya said again. "I'm a triangle. It's a–"

"Personality trait," Michaela said, finishing the sentence for her. "I get it. A square likes structure and organisation. The triangle represents leadership."

"What am I then?" Ben asked, edging his way into the conversation delicately.

"A circle," Michaela said, to which Freya nodded.

"Yep. You're a circle, Ben."

"What does that mean?" he asked.

"It means you're a communicator, an empathiser, someone who creates harmony," Michaela said.

"Right. So, you're a square, Freya's a triangle, and I'm a circle. Who's missing?"

"The squiggly line," Freya said. "A creative. Someone who thinks outside the box."

"That's you, isn't it?" he said. "You're not exactly known for your textbook methods. I still don't understand how you knew Michaela reads *The Sunday Times*."

"Because she's a square, Ben," Freya said. "She's analytical. Organised. No room for misinformation. Just the facts. Unbiased facts."

Ben looked between them, then settled on Freya. "So, what do I read?"

"You don't read the paper, Ben. You don't watch the news, and you don't listen to the radio."

He nodded his agreement, slightly disappointed at being described in such a dim light.

"But if you did read, I'd say you were a *Sun* man."

"*The Sun?*"

"We aren't tied to one trait. According to the theory, we have a primary trait and a secondary trait. So yes, I may consider myself first and foremost a triangle, but I might demonstrate the odd squiggly line here and there. You, on the other hand, are primarily a circle," Freya said.

"And my secondary trait?"

"A red-blooded male who enjoys looking at semi-clothed women," she said, then looked across at Michaela and nodded at the base of the tree where her assistant was still kneeling over the body. "May we see what we have to work with here?"

Michaela nodded. "It's not pretty, I'm afraid. Use the platforms, please. This whole area has been trampled already." She indicated to the aluminium steps they had placed down to prevent the scene from being further disturbed, which led from where Michaela was standing next to the body. It was like crossing a river on stepping stones. Except, instead of getting a wet foot should you slip off, you were likely to get an earful from Lincolnshire's finest crime scene investigator.

Ben considered the analogy and deemed quietly to himself that a wet foot was far more appealing. He'd been on Michaela's bad side before and didn't intend on returning there anytime soon.

The gaps between the steps closed to form part of a circle around the body. It was enough room for the four of them, including Pat, Michaela's assistant, to study the scene.

"Oh Lord," Ben said when he saw the remains of the woman lying in the wild grass. "Poor thing."

"That's the circle in you speaking," Freya said quietly. There was a joke in there somewhere, but it was feeble and spoken more out of flippancy than humour.

Ben replied with equal flippancy.

"And I suppose that's the type of thing a triangle would say?"

Pat, whose gender Ben had never managed to work out, looked up from where they crouched. His or her eyes were blurred by the goggles they wore, and the rest of their face and hair was covered by the mask and hood of the white suit.

"We think the killer followed her here from the lane," Michaela said, pointing at a path that had been trodden into the space between the two fields. "We think the area around us is just from that lot. We'll check, of course."

She nodded sideways to the uniforms, who were, at that moment, being corralled by Gillespie and Cruz.

"Where does the track lead to?" Freya asked, looking at the long mound that ran to the back of the field.

"The River Witham is on the far side of that bank. That's a flood defence," Ben said.

"We found the dog lead," Michaela added, pointing to a small, white flag protruding from a clump of grass a few feet away.

Ben turned away to find Gillespie and Cruz helping the uniforms. He took a breath, savouring the fresh air without the sight of the body before him. "Gillespie?"

The big Scotsman looked up.

"Aye, Ben. How does it look?"

Ben shook his head.

"Have Cruz look for a parked car further up the lane."

"Dog walker?" he asked, and Ben nodded. "Isn't it usually a dog walker who finds the body? They're not normally the bloody victim."

"Have him take down any number plates, colours, makes, and

models," Ben said, ignoring the humorous insight. "Chapman can run them through the database."

"Aye, Ben," Gillespie called back. Usually, he might have offered a witty remark. But there must have been something in Ben's expression that told him now wasn't the time for wit.

"Where's the dog?" Ben asked.

Michaela offered a grim expression, pointing to the far side of the tree. "In the grass over there. I'm afraid whoever did this paid more attention to the owner than the dog."

"Either that or the woman put up more of a fight," Ben said.

"No. There was no fight," Michaela said. "It's hard to tell from here, but it looks to me like she was dragged to the ground and strangled. Quickly, too."

"Whoever did this didn't plan it," Freya said. "This was emotional."

Michaela dropped to a crouch, using her pen to lift the sheet that was partially covering the victim's body.

"Bruising around the neck," she said. "It's not definite, but if I had to put money on it, this is how she died."

"Is that an ID card?" Freya said.

"Myra Dicks," Michaela said, reading the card that hung from a lanyard around the victim's neck. "Lincoln University."

"A student?" Ben asked.

"Lecturer, I'd say," Freya said. "Or admin of some description. But one thing is clear."

"What's that?" Ben said, trying to catch her eye so he didn't have to look down at the remains of the woman on the ground.

"This is about creative as it gets in our line of work," she said. "We've found our squiggly line."

CHAPTER SEVEN

A full hour and a half had passed. Uniform had cordoned off the field, Gillespie had set them to work searching the surrounding area, and Cruz had been on what looked like a Sunday afternoon stroll through a pretty field. He kicked at the grass as he returned, hands firmly in his pockets.

"Would you just look at him?" Freya said, and Ben, who had been watching the medical examiner from a distance, turned to look at what had upset her. "He's in a world of his own sometimes."

"Sometimes?" Ben replied. "That's generous."

"Did you find anything, Cruz?" Freya called out.

"Me?" he said, snatching a hand from a pocket to point at his chest. He glanced behind him, clearly hoping Freya's question had been aimed at another Cruz who just happened to be walking in his wake.

"All you need is a flat cap and a pair of wellington boots, and I'd have said you've come straight from the set of *Last of the Summer Wine*."

"Last of the what?" he replied.

"Give me strength," Freya sighed quietly to Ben, then raised her voice. "What did you find?"

"On the lane, you mean?"

Freya said nothing. There were no words she could use that would not trigger the frustration building inside of her.

"I found a car," he said and searched his pockets for his notebook. He found it and flicked to the right page. "A blue Vauxhall Corsa. Registration plate–"

"Don't tell *me*," Freya said, and he stared at her as if she was about to guess the number plate. She shook her head. "What do you do with the details, Cruz?"

"I normally give them to you, boss."

"Let me ask it a different way. Am I sitting at a computer right now?"

"No, boss."

"Do I have a radio on me?"

She opened her jacket to reveal her dress in all its glory, but he shied away, averting his eyes.

"No, boss."

"So, who do you think you should give those details to? Who has a radio on them, right now?"

"Ah," he said, eyeing the uniforms. "Cut out the middle man, you mean. Or woman, as the case may be."

He patted his pockets again and drew out his phone.

"Good," Freya said. "Let me know if the car belongs to our victim and we'll go from there."

"I'll ask them about the other one, as well."

"What other one?" Freya asked.

"The other car, boss."

"There's another car?" Freya said. "Why didn't you say that in the first place?"

"Don't know," he said. "I was, erm..."

"You were what, Cruz?"

"Scared, boss," he said.

"Scared?"

He nodded, and looked between her and Ben, then settled on staring at the ground.

"Are you scared of me, Cruz?" asked Freya.

"A little," he said. "It's just... When you're like this, I get all nervous."

"Like what?" she said, hearing the frustration in her tone.

"Like that," he said, nodding at her. "I'm sorry. I try so hard to impress you, I keep messing up. I say the wrong things. I don't know..."

Freya glanced across at Ben, then at the crime scene, which was a good hundred feet away.

"Give me a moment, will you?" she said, and Ben nodded, looking around to find the medical examiner discussing something with the crime scene investigators. "Talk to Doctor Saint, would you? There's nothing we can do here until the pathologist sees the body. He might be able to give an insight into the time of death. That'll give us something to chew on."

"Will do," he said and took his leave.

She put her hands in her pockets and strolled over to Cruz, but he couldn't look her in the eye.

"Walk with me, Cruz," she said.

"Boss?"

"I said walk with me. You're not in any trouble."

She made her way along the track and heard him run a few steps to catch her up.

"Sorry, boss. I didn't mean to offend you–"

"You haven't offended me, Cruz. In fact, your honesty is refreshing," she said, then slowed her pace to try and relax him. "Listen, I'm sorry I made you feel that way. I didn't know I was doing that."

"It's not all the time, boss. It's just when you get frustrated with me, I find it hard to get back on the front foot. That makes me try too hard, and that's when I overthink things and mess up again. It's a vicious cycle."

"So, what do you suggest I do?" she asked, and as predicted, he shrugged.

"Don't know, boss."

Freya took a breath and let it out through pursed lips as she considered what she might say in response. She knew what she wanted to say, and there was an opportunity here. But her choice of words and timing were crucial to its effectiveness.

"Did you hear what Granger said earlier?"

"About Arthur?" he said. "Sorry, Detective Superintendent Harper."

"It's okay. I think he knew we called him Arthur. And do you know what? I think he rather enjoyed the fact that we gave him a nickname," Freya said. "It'll have played to his ego."

"Do you think?"

"I do, yes. He had great aspirations for this team. Every one of us."

"Did he tell you that?" Cruz asked as they reached the lane. Freya took a good look around. The place was almost desolate with fields stretching as far as the eye could see, only the River Witham with its high bank blocking the view in one direction.

"Not directly. In fact, I didn't meet him very often. He's been off for, what, six months?"

"Something like that. I haven't seen him for ages. DCI Granger has been running things."

"Exactly. And what do you think will happen now? Who will replace..." She stopped herself from referring to the deceased by his full title, choosing instead to play to Cruz's humour. "Who will replace Arthur?"

"DCI Granger, I suppose," he replied.

"That's what I thought," she said. "But that would leave a hole in Granger's office, wouldn't it?"

"Oh, yeah. I suppose somebody will have to take his job if Granger gets promoted."

"Right," Freya said, leaving a silence for him to fill with his thoughts.

"Oh," he said. "You? You'd be next in line for DCI."

She stopped and stared across the fens, then turned to him, meeting him eye to eye.

"I suppose I would," she replied. "But then who would be DI?"

"Ben. It has to be Ben. I suppose DS Gillespie and DS Nillson are both the same rank. But Ben has the experience, after all. And he was supposed to get DI before you..."

He stopped and winced, fearing he had said something that might anger her.

"It's okay," she said. "You're right. He was about to be made DI when Arthur brought me into the team. It's high time he was moved up. So, we'd have Granger doing Arthur's job, me doing Granger's job, and Ben doing my job. That seems neat and tidy, doesn't it, Cruz?"

"It does, boss, yes. Makes perfect sense to me."

"That will make the team, what the top brass like to call, top-heavy. There's too much risk."

"Top-heavy, boss?"

"It's a term they use to describe a team that has more leaders than followers," she said, dropping to a careful crouch in her dress. She found a handful of large stones on the gravel track then placed the largest down with two below it to form a triangle. Then, beneath one of them, she placed a fourth stone with two more below that to form another triangle. Finally, beneath that triangle, she placed four more stones. To make her point, she started with the first stone. "Think about it. This stone is Granger leading myself and my counterpart in CID. I lead Ben who in turn leads Gillespie and Nillson, who respectively lead yourself, Anderson, Chapman, and Gold."

"Right?" he said, following but not really.

"Okay, so put it this way," Freya said. "Right now, we all work hard. We know there's the possibility of promotion. None of us are stupid, right? We all kind of guessed that Arthur wouldn't be coming back, didn't we?"

He looked up at her quizzically. But then agreed. "Well, yeah. I mean, it was obvious, wasn't it?"

"Right. But if Granger was to move up into Arthur's office, and I were to take Granger's office, Ben takes my desk, and what does that leave?"

She pointed to the lowest triangle formed in the rocks.

"Gillespie and Nillson," he said.

"Exactly. For how long? If the top brass decides to make those changes, which I have no doubt they will, then that leaves Gillespie and Nillson as DS for the foreseeable future. No chance of promotion."

"Do you think they'll leave?"

"Not Nillson. She's only been DS for a few weeks. But Gillespie, he's got potential, and he knows it."

"Gillespie? Potential?"

"He might come across like a great big mass of sweat and hair, Cruz, but believe me, that man is a good detective. And as soon as he realises he has no chance of promotion for at least five years, he'll be looking elsewhere. He has to. He's not getting any younger. That's where the risk is. And you can bet your backside that Granger is thinking the exact same thing."

"He is?"

"If he's any good, he will be, yes. It's called succession planning. He'll be wondering who he's got on the team to step up if Gillespie goes. I mean, Chapman has no aspiration to leave the office. She's a researcher, and she's bloody good at it too."

"Gold is focusing on her family liaison officer role," Cruz offered.

"Exactly. That leaves you and Anderson, and I know full well that Anderson will be all over that promotion. She's good too. She'd pass the sergeant exam with ease."

"She would?" he said, with more than a hint of disappointment in his voice.

"She would. I worked with her in London, Cruz. She can hold her own when push comes to shove."

"That just leaves me," he said. "I've been here longer than she has. She's only been in the team five bloody minutes."

"That's what I'm trying to get through to you, Cruz. Why do you think I chose you and Gillespie to come out here today, and not Nillson and Anderson?"

"Why?" he said, not following.

"Because if I get made DCI, and Ben gets made DI, then I want you to be ready to fall in behind us. I want you on my team, Cruz. Don't you see?"

"Right," he said unconvincingly. "What are you trying to say?"

"I'm saying that I want you to listen to what I said earlier back in the incident room. We need to make Arthur proud. We're *his* legacy, Cruz. You and the team are *mine*. I don't want to see Gillespie leave—"

"I do," Cruz mumbled.

"But I wouldn't be a very good manager if I didn't try to understand how my team are feeling, would I? Or how they might feel if things were to change. So, when I get frustrated at you, it's not because I'm trying to be nasty or to make you feel inferior in any way. It's because I want to see you do well. I want to bring out the best in you. You, Cruz, are the next generation of this team. I need you to up your game. Because if you don't, then the top brass will replace us all. It won't just be Granger, Ben, and me you let down. It'll be Arthur too. Everything he worked for. Everything he invested in us would be for nothing. Do you understand?"

He nodded, and for once, Freya thought he really was following.

"I need to be better."

"Not better. You're already a damn fine young detective," Freya told him. "I need you to be sharper. I need you to act before you've been asked. I need you to deliver results and information before it's been requested. I need you to be the best damn DC the station has ever seen. That way, when the changes come and Granger is looking for someone to nurture into a leader, there'll only be one obvious choice."

"Me?" he said quietly as if he'd only just realised the whole conversation had been about him. She collected up the rock that represented Cruz, and stood, straightening her dress.

"Yes, Cruz. You. None of us can move up in our careers without a solid team behind us. I need you to show me, show Gillespie, show Ben, and show Granger that you're not waiting to be told what to do. You can do this. You could go far. But you need to be switched on. Can you do that?"

He nodded, failing to hide his enthusiasm.

"Good," she said. "But listen. Anderson has come from the Met in London. She'll know how to play the game. She'll be working on her own plan. Gillespie too. He'll know that if Granger and I are moved up, my spot will be up for grabs. If he's got any sense, he'll be putting in the hours hoping to impress Granger."

"Gillespie?" Cruz said. "You said he would leave."

"Only if Ben makes DI. Gillespie still has a chance though, doesn't he?"

"Ah, no. He can't get promoted. My life would be hell. Not that it's not already. But you know? It would be even bloody worse."

"Exactly. So that's why we have to keep this to ourselves. You work hard. Show me what you can do. Show the team what you're made of. If not, in six months' time, things could look very different," she said, then met his stare to deliver her final point, placing the stone in his hand. "For all of us."

CHAPTER EIGHT

"How did it go?" Ben called out, as Freya returned from her walk with Cruz, who was as near as damn it skipping towards the group of uniformed officers and Gillespie.

"I just had a little chat with him. Pep talk, you know?" she replied, nodding a greeting to Doctor Saint, the local forensic medical examiner who waited patiently beside Ben.

"What did you give him? A pay rise?" Ben asked.

"No. Just a word in his ear. We all need a little motivation every now and then, don't we?"

"Ah, but we're each motivated in different ways," Doctor Saint added, then beamed at her. "Good evening, Inspector. It's been a while."

"It has," Freya replied, and Ben felt the shift in her demeanour. She was somehow more positive. Had it been anybody else, Ben would have enjoyed the turn. But experience told him that when Freya's mood became overly energetic, as it was now, she was either hatching a plan, or the plan had hatched, and a dozen little reptiles were snaking their way towards mischief. "I'm sorry to say that, on this occasion, I wish it had been longer."

"I couldn't agree more," Saint replied. "I've taken an in-depth look at the scene, and I've spoken to Michaela, who agrees with my theory. It seems our victim asphyxiated, very likely caused by somebody else."

"Time of death?" Ben asked.

"Eight hours at the most. Five or six at the least."

"That's around one p.m.," Ben said, checking his watch. "Somebody did this in broad daylight?"

"It would have taken a minute or more," Saint added and took a breath. "There's evidence to suggest the victim was dragged to the ground. She struggled, but not much. She was overpowered."

"Well, whoever did it was either brave or stupid," Ben said, and they both stared at him, waiting for him to embellish his statement. "The farmer will be wanting to get out here and do some baling before it rains again. Looks like the combine has been through here recently."

"You'll have to excuse Ben," Freya said to Saint. "He's from a family of farmers. Sometimes he forgets he's actually a police officer."

"I know," Saint said. "And I have to agree. Our farms are Lincolnshire's most prized assets. Farmers have a hard enough time trying to make ends meet as it is, without nonsense like this happening on their land."

"Hear, hear," Ben said.

"So," Freya said, "we have a mature female who was strangled to death, and we have two cars parked at the end of the lane. We need to inform the next of kin and begin the investigation, and we need forensics to find us something to go on. Thank you, Doctor. You've been a great help."

"Ah," he said, raising his giant hands in modesty. "I only wish I could tell you more. Michaela and the team seem to have the place all closed off."

"I think uniform and the farmer who found the body might have made a few unnecessary footprints," Ben said. "She'll be here all night logging them all."

"Well, I won't be," Freya said.

"Were you off out?" Saint asked her and nodded approvingly at her outfit.

"Nowhere special," she replied with a polite smile. "I just thought I'd air my dress."

"Well, you certainly brightened up the crime scene, Inspector," Saint said. "I imagine, whoever he or she is, they're feeling quite disappointed you've had to work tonight."

"It's a he," she replied. "And yes, I imagine he's feeling more than a little crushed right now."

"I know I would be," Saint added. In any other scenario, the conversation could have been deemed inappropriate. But Saint was a gentle giant and his compliments were anything but intrusive or sexually oriented. "What do you think, Ben? You'd be upset, wouldn't you? If you were the man in question."

Ben opened his mouth to speak but no words came out. Not for a moment anyway. He glanced between them, feeling his cheeks begin to burn.

"Devastated," he said and forced a smile. "Thankfully, I get to work with her. And I get to go home alone afterwards."

"Well, you're a lucky man, Ben. Somewhere out there, some poor bloke is crying into his pint."

"I believe he is," Ben said, more than mildly amused at the charade.

"Well, I better be off, or it'll be me who's crying into my pint. The wife did a joint of lamb earlier. It'll be lovely cold with a dollop of mint sauce."

"Thanks again, Peter," Ben said and reached to shake the man's hand.

"Always a pleasure," he said, as he extended his hand to Freya. "I'll send my report through as soon as it's written up. But my guess is that the lab results will point you in the right direction. Whoever did this is seriously disturbed. This was emotional. It wasn't planned."

"My thoughts exactly," Freya said. "Goodbye, Doctor Saint."

They watched him leave without uttering a word. It was only when he had exited the field and passed the group of uniforms that Ben spoke.

"That could have been awkward."

"As it happens, I tend to agree with what was said."

"About the attack being emotional?" Ben said.

"Well, yes. And that you're lucky to work with me," she said, and she turned and walked towards her car. She took a few steps before she called to him over her shoulder, "Then you get to go home alone."

CHAPTER NINE

It was a bright morning with a clear, blue sky. The type that, had Freya chosen a different career, she might have been walking beneath, barefoot across a freshly-mowed lawn with a cup of nice coffee and a plethora of flowering plants to admire. But she hadn't, and she wasn't. Instead, she was standing at the whiteboard in the incident room with a mug of terrible coffee insulting her senses from five feet away where it sat on her desk, untouched.

And instead of a dazzling array of summer flowers to admire, there were the faces of her team. Ben was quite obviously a rose. A climbing rose, to be precise. He was thorny where it counted, but sweet and quite charming when you got to the good parts.

Freya likened Chapman to a primrose, small and sweet. A flower that rarely took centre stage, but played its part beyond expectations. Anderson was, in Freya's mind at least, similar to a lily. For, most of the time, she was evergreen, consistent, and added variety to the textures among her plantings. But when the time was right, Anderson would spring up from nowhere and impress them all. It had to happen. It hadn't yet, not in this team, at least. But Freya had experienced the young woman's brilliance first-hand, and it was the reason she lived to tell the tale.

Somebody slurped at a coffee, and Freya turned to find Cruz
mopping up a spill with his jacket sleeve. A weed, Freya thought. Not a
mischievous perennial, but one of those plants you see emerge
between specimens that you know is a weed deep down, but you hope
might develop into something worthwhile.

"You clumsy oaf," Gillespie barked when he saw what Cruz was
doing, and he continued to insult the poor lad.

Ivy, thought Freya, strong, hardy, persistent, and unrelenting. That
was Gillespie. A wall of ivy. No matter what lengths you go to cut it
down, you just know it will be back next year, stronger than ever.

"Ah, come on," Gold said. The remnants of a soft Edinburgh accent
flavoured her voice, adding a purity. She was the orchid, delicate yet
complex, with a way of finding her way into people's hearts.

"You alright, Freya?" Ben asked, and she snapped back to reality, taking
one last glance around the room to consider what she had to work with.

"I'm fine," she said. They were the first words she had said to him
all morning. Normally, they would share a ride to work. But not today.
She had sent him a text explaining that she had an appointment after
work. But it was a lie. She knew it was a lie and he knew it was a lie.
She clapped her hands together once. "Listen up."

Cruz, who was turned in his seat arguing with Gillespie, faced
forward, and as if on cue, Chapman's fingers stopped dancing across
her keyboard as Gold snapped her laptop closed.

"Gold, how did it go last night?" Freya asked.

"Ah, as well as could be expected, ma'am," she replied. "I only
stayed for one. My mum had bingo, so she couldn't watch Charlie."

"I stayed the full course, boss," Gillespie said. "Went down there
when we were done at the crime scene. For the team, you know?"

"Naturally," Freya said. "And how is DCI Granger?"

"Well, the last I saw of him, he was banging on the florist door
asking them to open up and make him a quick kebab. I think he might
have been a little worse for wear."

"What time was that?"

"Pfff," Gillespie said, and Freya could only imagine how rank his
breath must have been.

"It must have been gone eleven. I left at closing time," Anderson said. "It was only you two left."

"Kebab shop shuts at ten-thirty," Cruz said, then sensed everybody's eyes on him and felt compelled to explain. "Hermione orders from there, sometimes. That is when she doesn't have an Indian. And by the way, the best Indian takeaway is in Woodhall Spa, according to her."

"According to her?" Gillespie said.

"Yeah. She decides what we eat and I have to go and pick it up."

"Sounds fair."

"Indian isn't too bad. But it's when she wants Chinese food that gets me. Branston."

"You go all the way to Branston to get Chinese takeaway?"

"Yeah. She won't go anywhere else. Says it's the best one for miles. I'd sooner have beans on toast, but no."

Freya watched the conversation with mild amusement. It was the beginning of a murder investigation. It was best to let them get it out of their systems before the real work began.

And right now, she needed all the votes she could get.

"Where do you go for Vietnamese?" she asked, and the team fell silent. Six wide-eyed faces stared at her. "What?"

"Vietnamese?" Gillespie said.

"Yes. Have you tried it?"

"Let me think," Gillespie said and placed an index finger on his chin as if in deep thought. "Nope. If it's not on the high street in my village, then I'm not having it. And by the way, Cruz, newsflash, the best Chinese takeaway is about two hundred yards from my house."

"No, we tried that place once. Hermione said she found a hair in her rice and the chicken still had bones in."

"Aye?" he said, and Cruz appeared a little confused.

"Well, she doesn't like hairs, or bones," he said.

"Never done me any harm," Gillespie said, sitting back in his chair and putting his hands behind his head. "The main thing is, when I eat my Chinese takeaway, it's still bloody hot. I haven't had to drive ten miles to get it."

"Well, that's good then, because you're normally drunk anyway. The less driving you do, the safer the roads will be."

"Alright, alright," Freya said. "We'll have plenty of opportunity to settle the argument over where the best Chinese food comes from over the next week or so."

"The investigation, boss?" Cruz asked.

It was a stupid question, but remembering her conversation with him yesterday and what he'd said, she chose to ignore it.

"Before we begin," she said, "I'd like to take a minute to give you an idea of what's going on in my mind. Detective Superintendent Harper was a career officer. He was well-known, and although some of you might think him a little lazy, he brought us together. His death will have severe consequences. Right now, we'll have eyeballs on us. Lincoln HQ will be wondering if we're worth keeping on, and if so, what the team might look like. So, when I say there can be no messing around on this one, I mean it. Is that understood?"

"Aye, boss. You won't find us messing about. In and out. Get the job done. We'll show them. Isn't that right, Cruz?" He kicked out under his desk and tapped Cruz, who sighed and held Freya's empathetic gaze.

"Everyone?" she said.

A melee of *ma'ams* and *bosses* filled the room, then silence fell once more.

"Right. Cruz, tell us about the cars you found."

"Yes, boss. The blue Corsa belongs to our victim, Myra Dicks," he said, then flipped open his notepad. "The Audi, which was the second car, belongs to a man named Adam Frost."

"Chapman?" Freya said. "Next of kin?"

"I checked this morning. Her daughter is a Claire Banner."

"Address?" Freya said, and Chapman whipped a slip of paper up from her desk. There was no smugness to her expression. It was her job, and she was good at it. Nothing else mattered. "Ben? This one's for you and me. After that, we'll go to the hospital to see what our friendly pathologist has to say. The rest of you, do some digging. Chapman, build a network of friends and family for us to question. Nillson and Anderson?"

"Yes, boss," Nillson said.

"Look into Adam Frost. See what you can find. Find out why he left his car there and what he was doing there in the first place."

"Yes, boss," Nillson said and gave Anderson a wide-eyed look as if to convey the difficulty of the task.

"Gillespie, Cruz?"

"Boss?" Cruz said, keener than usual.

Gillespie eyed him with suspicion, then refocused on Freya. "Aye, boss?" he said as if reinstating his seniority.

"You're door knocking."

"Eh?"

"It's okay," she said. "There are only about five houses in a mile radius. Oh, and while you're at it, walk the length of the lane, will you? See if you find anything suspicious. The killer may have tossed something into a field."

"Walk the lane? It's about two miles long, boss," Gillespie said, his face dropping into what she could only describe as utter dismay.

"It's okay, boss," Cruz said. "I was expecting this. I've brought my walking boots."

"Walking boots?" Gillespie said. "What are those you're wearing? Bloody sitting-down shoes? I suppose you have a pair of going-to-the-little-boy's-room slippers as well, don't you?"

"Walking boots. They're made for long walks," Cruz explained.

"Yeah, well, I'm a detective, not a bloody donkey."

The team stared at him, and if Freya was correct, each one of them was thinking the same thing as her.

She smiled at him, waiting for him to buckle.

"Aright, alright," he said, and he shoved himself out of his seat, snatched his jacket and bag, and made towards the exit. The double doors squealed when he shoved them, and he was just halfway through when he stopped and turned to glare at them all individually.

"Gillespie?" Ben said, without looking at him. Instead, he smiled at Freya, who knew exactly what was about to happen.

"Don't, Ben. Just don't. I'll wait in the car, Cruz," Gillespie said, swirling his keys on his finger then pointing at each of them. "And as for you lot, don't even think about it."

He glared once more then disappeared from view. But before Freya had even counted to three, the entire team erupted into a well-deserved and surprisingly accurate chorus of braying donkeys.

CHAPTER TEN

Freya was just fastening her suit trousers when somebody entered the washroom. She waited a moment, trying to guess who it was. Had it been Gold, she might have caught a whiff of the bouquet-like perfume she wore. If it was Nillson, then she might slam the door to the other stall and drop the toilet seat into place noisily. Chapman would have moved quietly, so as not to disturb whoever was in the other stall. But after a few seconds, it was clear who it was by the digital beeps of a mobile phone.

Freya opened the door, cleared her throat, and stepped over to the basins to wash her hands.

"How are you, Anderson?" she asked.

Anderson made a show of finishing typing a message on her phone as fast as she could, then slipped it into her pocket, sighing as if the recipient had been badgering her for something.

"Oh, you know? Monday mornings and all that," she replied, catching Freya's inquisitive stare in the mirror.

"Don't I just," Freya said. "Still, it could be worse. You could be in London still."

"Yep, I'm with you on that one. At least here there's no school-playground mentality to deal with."

"You've met Gillespie, right?" Freya said.

"You know what I mean. There's no boys' club here. I like that. I feel part of something."

"Good," Freya said, as she turned off the tap and reached for some paper towels. "So, you do plan on staying then?"

"Of course. That is if I'm welcome."

"You're welcome. In fact, you're a welcome breath of fresh air," Freya said, and she leaned on the basins, folding her arms. "But things are changing. I want you to be ready for that."

"Yeah, I get the sense that Harper was the glue holding this place together, even in his absence."

"He was. But listen, when I first arrived here, there were two teams. I had Ben, Gold, and Chapman, and there was another DI. A Steve Standing. He sat up in the dark end of the incident room with Gillespie, Cruz, Nillson, and a couple of others. I can't even remember their names. But the point is that I managed to stay and DI Standing moved on."

"So?" Anderson said, not quite following.

"This is an opportunity, Jenny. A real opportunity. It's an opportunity that just wouldn't happen in the boys' club back in the Met."

"You want Granger's job, don't you?" Anderson said, and Freya nodded, unabashed.

"I do. And I want Granger to have Harper's job. He deserves it."

"And what about the rest of us?"

"I want the best. I want the cream," Freya said. "I want you to move up. Either Ben or Gillespie will take my place. My money is on Ben, but Gillespie has a chance."

"What about Nillson?"

"She hasn't been DS long enough. But when my place is filled, there'll be a need for another DS. I'll need to fill that spot with someone from the team. But if you're not ready..."

"I'm ready," Anderson said.

"Are you sure? It's a big step."

"I'm ready," she said, with a little more defiance.

"There's competition," Freya warned her.

"Gold is too busy as an FLO and Chapman won't leave the office.

That leaves Cruz," Anderson said, with a sneer. "I don't want to blow my own trumpet here, but he's not exactly sergeant material."

"Isn't he?"

"Do you know something?"

"I have an idea," Freya said. "You see, if Gillespie is as smart as I think he is, he'll have worked out there's an opportunity. And if he makes DI, then you can bet your backside he'll want Cruz in under him."

"Cruz? Why?"

"Two reasons," Freya said. "First of all, Cruz and Gillespie both worked for DI Standing. They're cut from the same cloth."

"Yeah, I see that," Anderson said. "Now you mention it."

"Right, and who does Gillespie love to boss about? Who does he have control over?"

"Cruz. Right, now I see. Gillespie knows how to manipulate Cruz."

"Exactly. Do you see where I'm going?"

"Are you trying to split the team?"

"No, Anderson. In fact, I don't want to lose any of you. When I make DCI, I want the best team under me. This is my legacy. This is everything I've worked for. I'm not going to let the remnants of DI Standing ruin my chances of success."

"Was he really that bad?" Anderson said. "I mean, I've heard a few things about him."

"He was the worst. And you know what? He was the nearest thing this place had to a boys' club. Do you really want Gillespie in charge? Do you really want him to ruin all of this?" Freya said.

"No. Not now. I'm really enjoying it here."

"Me either. So, I need you to show me what you've got. You report in to Nillson. When she hands me her reports, I want to see your name shining, so that when I hand them to Granger, he can visualise what I can. I don't want my team to be a boys' club. I don't want the stain of DI Standing to taint every investigation we're handed. And most of all," Freya said, "I don't want you to be pushed out."

Anderson stared at her, her head cocked to one side.

"Do you really mean that?" she asked.

"Ask the girls how many times I've had pep talks with them in the washroom. You can count the times on one balled fist."

Anderson nodded and an embryonic smile formed in the corners of her mouth.

"I won't let you down, Freya."

"I know," Freya replied, as she tossed a paper towel into the bin. "If you do, then you'll be taking orders from Cruz. Just imagine that."

CHAPTER ELEVEN

Freya drove. There was a time when Ben had done all the driving, and Freya would occupy the passenger seat of his old Ford, which was a far more comfortable ride than the little rental she had arranged when she had first arrived in Lincolnshire. But that arrangement couldn't last forever. One of the promises Freya made to herself was that she would bring a little refinement to the team. A touch of class. As a result, she had opted for a Range Rover, and since then, it was rare that they used Ben's car. Besides, Freya preferred the higher driving position on the often winding and narrow lanes.

There had also been a time when Ben had to give directions for every journey they made. Being a local man, he knew the area like the back of his hand. But Freya's mental map had been populating with landmarks, turns in the road, and villages, and she could navigate to Metheringham village with ease, from the station at least.

Once they were driving through the village, Ben resumed his verbal directions.

"Princes Street," he said, and then gazed out of the window.

"Which one is that?"

"Turn right at the monument in the middle of the road," he said, and Freya added the road to her mental map.

A few minutes later, he beckoned for her to slow down while he studied the house numbers. A school and a large playing field took up most of one side of the street, overlooked by a row of terraced houses on the other side. They were of average size, Freya thought, and resembled a house that belonged to an aunt of hers in Essex. The sight of them conjured childhood memories, where she and her cousins would have to sit on the floor while the adults chatted.

They drove a little further, past the terraces of two-up-two-down houses to where the properties became a little larger, built at a different time. One in particular occupied an extremely large plot and was set back from the road.

"This is it," Ben said, and habitually looked in the rear-view mirror as if he was driving.

The road behind them was devoid of traffic, so Freya pulled to the side of the road and stopped. She considered reversing a little and parking on the long driveway, but given the lack of traffic and the news they had to deliver, she thought it best to leave the car on the road.

"Okay then," she said.

"Don't tell me, you'll do the talking?" Ben said.

"What makes you say that?"

"Because that's what you always say. Or words to that effect."

"No, I don't."

"Okay then, you don't," Ben said, then, rather dramatically, stopped with one leg out of the door. "Just remind me again. How many times have you asked me to deliver the news?"

"Once," Freya said. "When we first met."

"Right," he said, and he climbed from the car and waited for her on the footpath.

"What's that supposed to mean?" Freya said, as she closed her door and locked the car with the fob.

"Nothing."

"Do you want to tell her? Is that it? Do you want to be the one that delivers the news?"

"Not really, Freya. I was merely making light of how many times we've had to do this together. I know the routine, that's all."

"Yes, well, all that might be about to change."

"You're referring to the news about Arthur?"

"I am, yes. And given the changes that are likely to happen, perhaps it's best if you do deliver the news. It'll be good for you."

"Wow, you're really selling it. 'Hey, Ben, how about you go and tell a distraught daughter that we found a body that we think might be her mother? Then try and convince her to ID the body.'"

"You're such a child sometimes."

"You know what? When I woke up this morning, I had no idea my day was going to be so rich with experiences."

"Get on with it, Ben," she said, and as much as she tried to ignore his flippancy, she couldn't ignore his teasing smile. "Are you doing it?"

"Yeah, I'll do it. I haven't ruined anybody's day yet, so this'll be a good chance, won't it?"

Freya held back while Ben pushed the doorbell, and then stepped back to stand beside her. He fished for his warrant card and took an audible breath.

"Nervous?"

"No. But let's face it," he whispered, "if this job was advertised in the job centre, I'm pretty sure this bit wouldn't be in the description."

The door opened before Freya could respond, and a pretty, middle-aged woman stared at them. Her hair was a tired blond, and her clothes appeared to have been selected for comfort rather than appearance.

"Oh God," she said, holding onto the door, revealing recently manicured nails that had been picked at.

Ben held up his warrant card.

"Claire Banner?" he asked, and she nodded, wide-eyed and biting down on her lower lip. "May we come in?"

"Yes," she breathed. "Is he..."

She stopped as if there was no need to finish the sentence.

"May we come in?" Ben said.

"Oh God. Oh God," she said and stepped back to let them pass.

The hallway was bright and large, and the decor was akin to that of a grand, old manor house, rich with the oranges and reds of teak and oak. Freya waited beside Ben, keen not to interfere. It was vital that he built trust with the woman. Any effort to soften the impact on her behalf would only cause confusion.

Claire Banner closed the front door and lay against it, her palms flat on the wooden panels.

"Perhaps we could sit somewhere for a moment?" Ben said, and at that moment, Freya considered his tone almost perfect. If it had been her on the receiving end of the conversation, she would want somebody like Ben to deliver the news. There was a strength to his tone, yet it was calming. And the sheer size of the man created a comfort, knowing that he was on her side.

"Through here," Claire said, pointing to a doorway.

Freya led the way and had expected to enter a large sitting room with antique furniture and maybe even a stag's head mounted on the wall for good measure. But instead, she found herself in a snug. It was a small space, around fifteen feet square with a large L-shaped sofa and a brick fireplace. She took the end seat farthest from the door and settled in, leaving enough room for Ben to sit beside her, and for Claire Banner to not feel crowded.

"I'm afraid we've found a body," Ben said when Claire had settled down. She leaned forward and began picking at a fresh nail, then nodded anxiously. "We have reason to believe it's your mother. Myra Dicks."

"My what?" she said, a little confused. "Did you say my mother?"

"I did, yes. I'm sorry. There's no easy way to break the news."

"I don't understand. I thought you had found..." She stopped. "I thought you'd found Kevin. My husband."

"Is your husband in any trouble?" Ben asked.

"No. Not at all. I just haven't seen him since Saturday," she said. "My mother? You're sure it's my mother?"

"Well, we found a woman's body wearing her university ID," Ben explained. "Until somebody such as yourself formally identifies her, we won't know for sure."

"Oh God. Oh God," Claire said, covering her face, then pulling her hands away to fan her reddening eyes.

"I'm sorry," Ben said.

"How?" she said, apparently numbed by the news. That was normal. People handled the news in different ways, and being numbed was perhaps one of the easiest to deal with. "I spoke to her yesterday. How on earth is she dead?"

"She was walking her dog."

"Oh God," Claire said, and she fumbled as she pulled a tissue from the box on the coffee table. "I spoke to her. I spoke to her yesterday. When she was on her walk, I called her."

As if there was a chance the body may not be her mother's, she pulled her phone from her pocket, found the list of recent calls, and held it up.

"Look. Look, I spoke to her. She was walking Jambo. I was in the garden. We..." She broke off again, apparently reliving the call.

"Your mother owns a blue Vauxhall Corsa. Is that right?" Ben asked.

"Oh God, it is her. That's her car."

"We have to be sure, Miss Banner–"

She blew her nose. "I know it's her. Who else could it be?"

"Let's not be too hasty. We need you to identify her. Do you think you could?"

"Me? Identify her?"

"We have to be sure, Miss Banner."

"It's Mrs Banner," she said. She held up her left hand, which still had five intact, manicured nails, and a wedding ring on her third finger. "I'm married."

"Mrs Banner, can you tell us when you last saw your mother?" Ben asked.

"A few days ago. Thursday, I think. I usually see her twice a week. Once in the week, depending on what day I can get off, and at the weekend. She'll come here for dinner or we'll go to hers."

"Claire, I know this is a difficult time. But we need some facts. We have to be sure the woman we found is your mother."

"You mean, there's still a chance she could be alive?" Claire said, through stifled sobs.

"It's just procedure. The more detail you can give me, the easier it will be," Ben explained. "Did she say anything else, Claire? Anything unusual? Or did she perhaps mention where she was going after the dog walk?"

Claire wiped her eyes, sniffed, and dabbed at her top lip. She had enough grace about her for Freya to judge her as a woman who moved in wealthy circles. Her mannerisms, the house, and her etiquette were all indicators of somebody who habitually behaved correctly, regardless of circumstance.

"No," Claire replied, then sucked in a breath, but shook her head as if she was dismissing an idea.

"What is it?" Ben asked.

"Nothing. I'm just being silly."

"Any detail, Claire. No matter how small."

She folded the tissue in her hand then enclosed her fist around it so that the skin around her wedding ring turned white.

"She told me she loved me. That's all," Claire said softly, then puffed her cheeks, as people experiencing regret often do.

"Is that something she would normally tell you?" Ben asked, and Claire stared at him like the question was rhetorical or inappropriate.

"No. She always tells me. Every time we speak," Claire said. "But this was different. It wasn't off the cuff, as it normally is. It was like she was making a point of making sure I knew. I asked if she was okay and she told me she was. So I left it. I should have pressed harder. I knew something was wrong."

"Claire, what time was this?" Ben asked, expertly bringing the distressed woman back to reality. It was a tactical move, playing on the human desire to help or be useful in a situation such as this.

She glanced back at her phone and navigated to the recent calls.

"Twelve fifty-one p.m."

"And where were you when you made the call?" Ben asked.

"I didn't make the call. She called me."

"And where were you?" Ben said, pressing the matter but bordering on the verge of implied accusation.

Claire stared at him as if she might explode at any minute with a series of 'How dare you?'

"Here," she said. "In the garden. I was just pottering really. Having a bit of a tidy up."

"And your husband?" Ben asked, and Claire's expression sagged visibly.

She shook her head and unfurled the tissue.

"Like I told you," she said, "I haven't seen him since Saturday."

CHAPTER TWELVE

DS Jim Gillespie parked his car in a small car park at the end of the long lane, denoted by a little sign that read, *Stepping Out*.

"What do you suppose that is?" he said to Cruz, who had spent the entire journey reading something on his phone.

"Eh?"

Gillespie nodded at the sign. "What do you think 'Stepping Out' is?"

"It's a walk."

"A walk?"

"Yeah, a walk. A route."

"Ah. That's a wee bit weird."

Cruz lowered his phone, clearly becoming annoyed.

"And why is that weird?"

Gillespie stared in the mirror at the lane that ran at least two miles in a dead straight line. It was a single-lane track with fields on either side and seemed, from Gillespie's perspective, to run on forever.

"Well, it's not like you could get lost here, is it?" he said. "The bloody road's so straight the Romans could have built it. There's no turns, no side roads, and no footpaths. You can go that way or you can go the other way. Hardly needs a bloody sign, does it?"

"You're such a Philistine," Cruz muttered.

"A what?"

"A Philistine. It's like everything is black and white in your mind. It's either one thing or the other. There's no room for deviation, is there? There's no possible chance that people might drive here to go on a walk, or, God forbid, arrange to meet a friend here to go on a walk? No. To you, it's just a straight road. You can't put yourself in other people's shoes."

Cruz straightened his collar, pocketed his phone, and climbed from the car, leaving Gillespie pondering not only his words but his tone. He climbed from the car and closed the door to find Cruz using the rear bumper to tie the laces of his walking boots.

He watched him for a moment, fascinated by the young DC's attitude and sudden shift in demeanour.

"You alright?" he asked him.

"Yep, why?" Cruz said, pulling his trouser legs down over his ridiculous boots.

"You're acting weird."

"Nope," he said, and made a show of looking himself up and down. "It's just me."

Gillespie sensed something was amiss, but he couldn't quite put his finger on it.

"Shall we?" Cruz said, and jabbed his thumb over his shoulder, indicating that they should begin. "I'll take the left side, you take the right."

"Whoa, hold on," Gillespie said. "I'm the boss here."

Cruz stopped but didn't turn. He waited for Gillespie to catch up.

"I'm the DS. You're the DC. If there's a plan to be made, it'll be my plan."

"Okay," Cruz said. "So, what's your plan, boss?"

Gillespie looked at the long road ahead and withheld a sigh that was just dying to get out. "I'll take the left and you take the right."

Cruz shrugged. "Okay then."

"What do you mean, okay?"

"I mean, okay. I'll take the right and you take the left."

"No argument?"

"No argument," Cruz said.

Gillespie eyed him with suspicion.

"Those comfy, are they?" he said and gestured at Cruz's boots.

"When you've been sent on as many door-knocking exercises as I have, you get to know the drill," Cruz replied.

Gillespie stared down at his own shoes. He'd never polished them. Not once. He couldn't even remember how long he'd had them. But one thing was for sure. They weren't made for walking, and they certainly weren't made for Stepping Out, or whatever the hell the route was called.

"Well, thankfully somebody with some brains recognised my abilities and made better use of my time," Gillespie said, as he overtook Cruz and stepped out onto the lane. "Right then. We'd better get on with it. And no dilly-dallying. I want to be back at the station for lunchtime. It's too bloody hot to be stuck out here."

"It'll take as long as it takes," Cruz said, and Gillespie stopped again.

"You what?"

"I said, it'll take—"

"I heard what you said," Gillespie said. "I was referring to your tone and the fact that you seem to have forgotten who's calling the shots here."

"Okay," Cruz said, with another of his annoying shrugs.

"What's got into you? You're..."

"I'm what?" Cruz said.

"Different."

"Nope. I'm still me."

Gillespie took a moment to study the little idiot, then resigned to the fact that even if Cruz was up to something, he was clearly unlikely to say anything. He'd have to trick him into talking. That was easy enough. The lad wasn't exactly Stephen Hawking.

"You first," Gillespie said.

"Okay," Cruz agreed, then paused. "Did you say I was to go on the right or the left? I can't remember what you said, and I'd hate to disobey your instructions, Your Lordship."

Now he came to think of it, Gillespie couldn't remember either.

"The left," he said. "You take the left and I'll take the right."

So, Cruz took the left side of the road and Gillespie took the right. Each of them scanned the fields on either side in silence.

"Ah, this is like a bloody bad dream," Gillespie said after a few minutes. "Like one of those nightmares where you're running, but you're not getting anywhere."

It wasn't Cruz's lack of conversation that was annoying Gillespie. It was the persistent, cheerful, tuneless humming. It was almost as if the lad was enjoying it. Either that or he was enjoying seeing Gillespie suffer.

"You know what?" Gillespie said.

"What's that?" Cruz said.

"I'm looking forward to when we get to that wee farmhouse up there. A little door knocking will be a welcome break in this monotony."

Cruz hummed again, repeating the same melody over and over.

"Ah, for crying out loud, Cruz. Will you stop that?"

"Stop what?" Cruz said lazily. He had his hands in his pockets and was ambling along the roadside, peering into the field.

"The humming. The bloody humming. You're driving me mad."

"Okay," he replied cheerfully, and the humming ceased, just to be replaced a few moments later by a whistling even more tuneless than the humming.

"Alright, that's it," Gillespie said, and he pointed back towards the car. "Go. Just bloody go."

"Go where?" Cruz said, calmly and without the usual childish, defensive retort.

"To the car. Just go to the car," Gillespie said, hearing the frustration in his own voice. "I can't stand it. I'd rather walk the bloody road to hell on my own than deal with you in this mood."

"What mood is that?" Cruz asked, again calmly. It was as if the lad had swallowed a tub of Valium before work. There was no way into him.

"This," Gillespie said, and his voice had reached a pitch reminiscent of his pre-pubescent days. "This calm lack of reaction. What's the matter with you? It's like you're dead or something."

"What, because I'm not rising to your pathetic behaviour?"

"Yes," Gillespie said before the words had actually made sense. "No. But you're not yourself. You're all serious and–"

"Professional?" Cruz asked, with a single cocked eyebrow.

Gillespie sighed.

"Yes. I don't bloody like it. I preferred it when you were all–"

"Unprofessional?"

"Yes. Exactly. Where's that Cruz? Bring him back. It's like you're a career officer or something."

"I am a career officer. You don't think I come to work with you every day because I enjoy being teased and taunted, do you?"

"Eh?"

"I want to make something of myself, Jim. I don't want to be a DC forever."

That was when it clicked. When the whole charade made sense.

"Right," Gillespie said. "Now I get it."

"Get what?"

"You, and this whole behaviour thing."

"Professionalism," Cruz corrected him.

"Yes, that. You think you're in with a chance of promotion, don't you?"

"No, what makes you say that?"

"You think that there's going to be a shift in the team. That, somehow, the stars will align and a space will open up for you, DC Gabriel Cruz, to move up in the world. You do know you'd have to pass the sergeant's exam, don't you?"

"Yes, I do know, as it happens."

"Ah, so I'm right," Gillespie said, and then lowered his voice to a grumble and jabbed an index finger at Cruz. "You're hoping to cash in on the demise of poor Arthur."

"No–"

"You are, and it's despicable."

"No–"

"You're planning your move. You're hoping DI Bloom gets promoted, which means that..."

He stopped, and an idea struck him. But before he could put the pieces together in his mind, Cruz had caught the shift in his expression.

"You okay, Jim?" he said, and that calm, professional tone had returned.

"Aye," he said.

"I know that look. You're planning something."

"I'm thinking," Gillespie said.

"Ah, I see," Cruz said, and he turned to continue scanning the adjacent field for anything unusual. But then, just when all the pieces had come together in Gillespie's mind, Cruz turned back to him, and everything made sense. "You're not planning on cashing in on the team's recent loss, are you? Because, well, I mean, that would be a terrible thing. Despicable, in fact."

"No. No, I wouldn't dream of it," he replied, then, buying himself a few moments to think, he pointed at the first of a handful of houses that were dotted along the lane. "There's bugger all here, Gabby. I'm going to knock on that door. See if the owners saw or heard anything unusual yesterday."

"You do that," Cruz said, calm and patient when he would have normally protested. "You never know, they might have seen the killer, and you could come away with a vital piece of evidence."

"What are you trying to say?"

"Nothing," he said, peering through the long grass. "Except that providing a crucial piece of evidence in the investigation might demonstrate your competency. It might just be enough to sway a decision in your favour."

"What decision?"

"The decision to promote one of our existing detective sergeants to DI Bloom's position," Cruz said. "You've got some fierce competition. You're going to need people on your side. I mean, Ben has Gold supporting him. Those two are old school buddies. He probably has DI Bloom as well. Let's face it, they're inseparable. It's like a political campaign. You're going to need backbenchers. You're going to need support. Someone who will put in a good word for you. Big you up in front of Granger."

"Support?" Gillespie said. "Like who?"

"Like me," he replied, and then plunged his hands into his pockets. "But let's get one thing straight here, Jim. If I do this, there can be no more little jibes at me. No more petty one-liners in an attempt to make me look stupid.'

"You do that on your own..." Cruz raised his eyebrows, assuming control, and Gillespie silenced. "Aye. You're right. We should work together. You and me, Gabby."

"No more bossing me around like I'm a teenager on work experience," Cruz said. "If you want my help, you'll treat me as an equal. Is that clear?"

Gillespie stared at him. The wee squirt was as annoying as they came. But one thing he did have was intelligence.

"Aye. Crystal," Gillespie said, and he stepped across the lane to shake Cruz's hand. "I go for DI, you go for DS. We help each other. Truce?"

"Truce," Cruz said, and he shook the hand of the man that took delight in making his every working day a complete misery.

CHAPTER THIRTEEN

"We'll need to speak to your husband, Claire," Freya said, and Ben caught her sideways glance. "Will he be home soon?"

"He's out somewhere. I don't know where exactly."

"Where does he work?" Ben asked, his pen poised, ready to note the name of the business.

"He works here, mostly. He has an office in the garden. He writes. That's what he does."

"He's a writer?" Ben asked.

"Yes," Claire said, and she looked up from wiping her eyes with a tissue, and nodded at a small bookshelf. "Those are his."

"Your husband is Kevin Banner?" Freya said. "*The* Kevin Banner?"

Claire nodded like it wasn't the first time she'd had the conversation, and her accompanying smile, though brief, was borne of politeness and appreciation.

Freya inhaled a deep breath, and Ben, not being much of a book reader, guessed that Kevin Banner was well-known, and that would add complications to the investigation.

"He goes out sometimes. To write, you know? He likes to visit the locations so he can write the stories true to form. He says the realism allows him to bring the senses into his writing. You know? The sounds of the birds, the smell of the flowers, the feel of the grass, or whatever."

"So, he's out now? On location?" Ben asked.

"You could call it that. But I don't know where. I'm sorry to say I haven't read his latest books. And I haven't a clue what he's writing now or where it's set. But it'll be around here somewhere," Claire said, then changed the subject. "Do I need to..."

She stopped and seemed to consider how she might phrase her question.

"See her?' Freya said, her voice soft.

Claire nodded. "To make sure it's her? I mean, this could all be some huge mistake. The woman you found could be somebody else's mum." Her voice trailed away and she bit her lower lip in a sign of regret. "That sounds horrible, doesn't it?"

"Well," Freya began, "here's how the process works. When a body is reported to us, the Major Investigations Team, that's us, attend the scene along with a forensics team and what's known as a forensics medical examiner. His or her job is to, first of all, pronounce and record the death, plus they give us all sorts of insights that might help us to outline an investigation."

"Outline?" Claire said. "I don't understand. Sorry."

"We can't start an investigation officially until we have a positive ID. We can't interview suspects for a murder if the victim hasn't been confirmed."

"That makes sense," Claire said. "So, what are you supposed to do? Wait? Are you saying you can't find who did this until you have a positive ID?"

"That's exactly what I'm saying, Claire. I'm sorry, it's just how the force works. We'd be sued left, right, and centre for wrongful arrest. We prefer to be sure that the individuals we investigate have a motive, means, and–"

"Opportunity," Claire finished, with a hint of a brief smile, which she explained with, "My husband. He's always talking about this stuff."

"I see," Freya said, with another of those sideways glances at Ben.

"So, I'll see her. If it helps, I mean, then I'll do it."

"Are you sure, Claire?" Freya said. "Is there anyone else we can ask? A family friend, perhaps?"

Claire buried her face in her hands and Ben waited for the awkward silence to finish. It was during those moments that the true horrors of their job were evident. He recalled how he'd had to turn away, and even Freya, with all her experience, had distracted herself from the scene.

But then Claire's breathing stopped and she pulled her hands away from her face, suddenly enthused with an idea.

"I'll do it," she said. "When?"

"This afternoon?" Freya asked. Claire looked between them, hoping that either Ben or Freya would make a revelation to put her mind at rest.

"I'm sorry you have to go through this, Claire," Ben said, and in the moment's hesitation that followed, she filled in the blanks. The hope that had raised her expression sank, taking with it any strength she had. "We'll send somebody to be with you, our family liaison officer. She'll help you through all of this."

"And in the meantime?" Claire asked.

"In the meantime," Ben said. "We need to find your husband."

CHAPTER FOURTEEN

"Are you sure you're ready for this?" Ben asked when he and Freya were at the entrance to the mortuary. He held his finger poised over the button to alert the pathologist of their arrival and smiled at Freya.

"It's just a body, Ben," she replied. "Just another body."

Ben rang the bell and stood back.

"I wasn't talking about the body, Freya," he said, as the door opened and a familiar face appeared.

Doctor Bell was what Ben's dad would have described as well-fed. In all the times the two had met her, her bobbed hair had been dyed a different colour, not because she was wild or because she was a new-age hippy; she did it to raise money for her dying mother's treatment.

Protruding from her cuffs were the tell-tale signs of large tattoos, and her nose, lip, eyebrows, and ears were so full of piercings that Ben had always wondered how she got through airport security.

"Now then," the pathologist said, her thick Welsh accent adding a certain curiousness to the words. "If it isn't Cagney and Lacey."

"They were both women," Ben said.

"I knows," she replied flatly, still blocking their entrance. "But what I really want to know is, which one of you had me up in the middle of the night?"

"If you're looking to pin the blame, Doctor Bell, then perhaps I can arrange for you to meet the killer when we find him or her," Freya said. "One-on-one in a locked interview room. How does that sound?"

"That sounds like my type of party," Doctor Bell replied, then smiled at her. "How are you, Freya?"

"Not as good as I was yesterday," said Freya. "And if I'm honest, my day is getting worse by the minute."

"Ah, well, that's good news then. Ben?"

"Yes?" he replied.

"How have you been?"

He looked at Freya for support, waiting for some kind of punchline.

"Even better for seeing you, Pip," he said. "How about our friend? Have you managed to get around to her yet?"

"Ah," she said, and stepped back, holding the door to them. "She reminds me of when I was training. Had to watch an autopsy in London, we did. Chap stepped out in front of a train. His body was battered and burned from the electricity. Terrible sight, it was."

"How is that similar?" Ben said, gesturing at the double doors to the lab room. "Our victim has been strangled. At least, that's what we're led to believe."

She stared at him and licked her lower lip, leaving it glistening in the fluorescent lights.

"Because I had to get up in the middle of the night to attend, Ben," she said. "Just like last night."

She slipped through the doors, which closed behind with a swish, and a breath of chilled air greeted Ben's legs.

"She gets weirder and weirder every time I see her," he said, as he tossed Freya a mask and a gown, each individually wrapped in cellophane.

"Who would you rather have? Her, or an anorak with the personality of a wet sock?"

Ben considered the question and stared at her.

"The first pathologist I ever worked with," she explained. "No sense of humour. No conversation. Just fact after tedious fact. I swear you don't know how lucky we are, having her working here."

"I suppose I should count our blessings," Ben replied, and he turned to let Freya tie his gown. He felt her grab at the strings and smiled to himself. "Does this remind you of Paris?"

The strings suddenly pulled tight, tighter than he had hoped for, and the accompanying knot that followed gave little breathing space.

She leaned into him, speaking quietly over his shoulder, "No, Ben. In fact, I'm doing everything I can to forget about Paris, and if you value your career, I suggest you do the same."

By the time he had turned to look at her, she was pushing her way through the double doors, tying her own gown as she walked. Ben followed behind, growing ever more concerned that he had said, or done, something to offend her. But now was not the time to find out.

"Right, then, Pip. What do we have?" Freya called out, as she approached one of the stainless steel benches where Doctor Bell was waiting. Ben had just stepped up to the bench, adjusting his mask, when Pip pulled back the sheet that covered the body.

"I've given her the once over," the Welsh pathologist replied, speaking slowly as if every syllable held more importance than the last. "No physical signs of abuse or violence except for the bruising on her neck. No puncture marks and no deformities."

"What about self-defence?" Ben asked. "Have we checked beneath her nails?"

"First thing I did," Pip said. "The lab will confirm if they find anything. Me? I'm not hopeful."

"What about the bruising?" Freya asked. "Are there fingerprints? Can we determine the size of the killer's hand?"

"No and no, I'm afraid. Whoever did this wiped her down when they were done, and the nature of the grip doesn't really tell us much."

"How so?" Ben asked.

Pip opened her mouth to reply but thought better of it. She walked slowly around the bench to stand beside Ben then reached up and grabbed him by the throat.

"See, when we think of strangulation, we think of a grip like this," she began, stretching her hand around Ben's throat and holding him tight with her other hand on the back of his neck. "My fingers are stretched. Can you see, Freya?"

She squeezed tighter and Ben felt his face begin to redden.

"I see," Freya said, seemingly amused at the charade.

"However," Pip said, and she lowered her voice to an eerie grumble, made even more conspicuous by her Welsh accent. She adjusted her grip to a single pinch of Ben's windpipe, which if anything was far more painful. "Our killer didn't stretch their hand around the victim's throat. They did this. See?"

Ben pulled away, but Pip, whose strength was surprising, held him close.

"I see," Freya said. "I get it."

In a flash, Pip let Ben go and, while he recovered, she strolled back to her position on the other side of the bench, taking her time to ditch her gloves and don a new pair.

"That pretty much aligns with what Doctor Saint had to say," Freya said. "Well, what else do we have? Left-handed, right-handed? Tall? Short?"

Pip waved her pen around Myra Dicks' neck.

"See here?"

"The bruise?" Freya asked.

"The bruising on the right side of the victim's throat is smaller than that of the left."

"The killer was right-handed."

"Brilliant," Ben muttered. "That narrows it down to ninety per cent of the population."

"They were also taller," Pip said. "Stronger, fitter, more physically capable in nearly every way."

"How tall was Myra?" Freya asked.

"Five foot four."

"Great," Ben said, once more resorting to sarcasm. "So we're looking for somebody who is right-handed, of average height, and is younger than Myra was. I'll have uniform keep an eye out."

"How tall are you, Ben?" Pip asked.

"Six foot something," he replied, rolling his eyes. "But I have an alibi."

"Oh? Do tell," Pip said. Freya's eyes widened above the mask and the crow's feet beside her eyes marked a smug smile forming beneath it. "Who is she?"

"Nobody you know," he replied, then moved the subject on. "Time of death?"

"Anywhere from midday yesterday to two p.m.," Pip said, off-hand. "So, come on. Where did you meet her?"

"It's nothing," Ben said. "Just some woman."

"Tinder, was it?"

"Tinder?"

"The dating app. Did you meet her online?"

"Oh, come on, Pip. Ben can barely open an email, let alone set up a Tinder profile."

"It was not an online dating app. I met her..." He paused, feeling both of their inquisitive stares and recognising the thrill in Freya's eyes. "She's an old friend. That's all."

"An old friend, eh?" Pip said. "With benefits?"

"I am not going to divulge my sex life with you, Pip. Especially across..." He waved his hand across Myra Dicks' body. "This."

"Shall I cover her?"

"No. Can we just move on? This is a bloody murder investigation. Not an analysis of the women in my life."

"Women?" Pip said. "As in plural?"

Freya laughed. "Oh, come on, Ben. We were only saying a while ago how nice it is to have a pathologist with a personality."

"Well, yeah. But–"

"Did you really say that?" Pip asked.

"We did, as it happens," Freya replied.

"Oh, that's sweet."

"Can we just talk about Myra?" Ben said, and both women shared amused expressions before Pip waved her pen over Myra's eyes.

"What do you see here, loverly?" Pip said.

He shook his head. "Nothing. Her eyes are closed."

"Ah," Pip said, accentuating her remark by stabbing her pen in his direction. "Closed."

She made her way around the bench once more and came to stand beside him. Then once more, she reached up, but this time, he backed away and gripped her wrists.

"Did you see that?" Pip asked, staring at Freya. "Did you see what he did?"

"He stopped you from throttling him?"

"And?"

"His eyes widened," Freya said.

"Right. His eyes widened with fear."

"I'd hardly call it fear—"

"You were scared, Benjamin Savage. And so would have our friend been. Terrified, in fact. Mortified," Pip said, her voice not unlike an actor reciting a child's bedtime story. "So why then are they closed?"

"The killer closed them," Freya said, and Pip spun on her heels, jabbing her pen at Freya.

"The killer closed her eyes. They took the time to lay our friend at rest."

"Either that or they couldn't stand being stared at by a dead body," Ben said.

"Why? Why would they be stared at?" Pip said. "You've just killed somebody. You're in the middle of nowhere. There are no signs of sexual interference. Why would you stay?"

"It was emotional," Freya said. "They hadn't planned on killing them. Otherwise, they would have taken a weapon. Strangulation is commonly associated with emotional homicides. It's a spur-of-the-moment thing."

"So our killer stayed there for a while?" Ben said. "And they closed Myra's eyes."

"And that's why the body was wiped down," Freya said, and Pip raised an eyebrow. "Tears. The killer shed a tear, but had the foresight to wipe it off her."

"The killer knew her well? Loved her even?" Ben said.

"Not necessarily," Pip said. "Not if this was their first time. In fact, studies show that first-time killers undergo a huge amount of remorse. They're scared of the consequences. They're ashamed of what they've done. The tears that were wiped from Myra's body may not have been tears of loss. They could have come from a deep self-loathing, a hatred of themselves, and the fear of the unknown."

"So, we're looking for somebody taller than five foot four, younger, fitter, and stronger than Myra, and who seems to be a little bit tearful," Ben said. "Oh, not to mention was in the area on Sunday around lunchtime."

"Sounds like a profile on an online dating app," Pip said, as she covered the body with the sheet. Then she felt Freya's glare. "Just kidding. You said you liked personality."

Freya was silent for a few moments, then nodded at her.

"Personality," she said, turning to leave the room. She called over her shoulder, "That's it. Come on, Ben."

"Where are we going?"

"We need to find out who Myra Dicks really was. We need to speak to her friends."

"Her friends?" Ben said. "And where do you suppose we'll find them?"

"At the university. She was an academic. She was smart. Who do smart people talk to?"

Ben shrugged. "Librarians?"

"Other academics, Ben. Nobody else can keep up with their conversations."

"So, we're going to the university now, are we?" he said, but she ignored him and addressed Pip.

"Thanks for your help, Pip," she said, as she held the door open.

"You're welcome. There aren't many people I'd get up in the middle of the night for, Freya. Consider yourself part of my inner circle."

She formed a circle with the fingers of both hands, then winked at Freya, who took a breath, glanced at Ben then met Pip's uncomfortable stare.

"That's good to hear," Freya said, without conviction.

"Maybe now I can go and get some breakfast," Pip said, snapping off her gloves. "Absolutely famished, I am."

"I wouldn't go too far," Ben said, happy for the opportunity to get one back on her.

"Oh? And why's that then, Benjamin?" she said.

Ben waited until he was at the door Freya was holding open before he replied, feeling the security of the heavy doors.

"Because we're arranging for Myra's daughter to come and formally

ID the body," he said. "With any luck, she'll be here this afternoon sometime. Enjoy your breakfast."

CHAPTER FIFTEEN

The call was routed through the Bluetooth system in Freya's car, and a voice, lightly fringed with a soft Edinburgh accent, answered.

"DC Gold," she said.

"Gold, it's DI Bloom. What are you doing?"

"I was just helping Chapman with a report for DCI Granger. He's going to need a press release."

"Right, well, that can wait. I need you to put your family liaison hat on and get down to the victim's daughter's house."

"The victim? Have we identified her?"

"Not yet. That's what you're going to do. I want you to stay with her. Escort her to the morgue, and just be a shoulder for her. I don't think she has anyone else to lean on."

"Right," Gold said, making notes as they spoke.

"We've seen the pathologist already and are pretty certain. So, this is just a box-ticking exercise, but any insights you can get us might help build a picture of who Myra Dicks was. I want to know if she had any grievances with anybody, and anything else you think is relevant. I'll have more questions as the investigation develops, but in particular, I want to know more about the daughter's husband, Kevin Banner."

"Kevin Banner?" Gold said, then gave a little laugh. "Not *the* Kevin Banner?"

"Yep," Freya said. "The very one."

"The crime writer?" Gold said. "Surely not?"

"He has to live somewhere and I suppose he has a family just like everyone else."

"Bloody hell," Gold said, then cleared her throat. "Sorry, ma'am. I'm just a bit shocked."

"Well, do try not to be a fan girl if you meet him. Just ask him to attend the station for an interview. We need to eliminate him from our investigation. That's all he needs to know."

"Yes, boss," Gold said, and even over the call, Freya could imagine Gold mouthing the news to Chapman.

"Gold?" she said.

"Ma'am?"

"Transfer me to Chapman, will you? And call me when we have a positive ID."

"Yes, ma'am," she replied, and the line clicked once before Chapman's voice came over the line. "Yes, ma'am?"

"Is DCI Granger in yet?"

"He was, but he's gone out, I think. I said I'd have his report by close of business."

"That's fine. Keep it vague. We're working off a visual ID right now. Do not disclose any names until Gold gives us the go-ahead. Is that clear?"

"Yes, ma'am," Chapman replied.

"Good work. We'll be in touch when we've been to the university."

Freya ended the call as she joined the new circular road that ran from the southern edge of the city to the north.

"Now," said Freya, more to herself than to Ben, "what we need is for DC Gold to do what she does best."

"And what's that?"

"To get Claire Banner to open up. There's more to that family than she's letting on."

Freya's phone rang through the speakers and Freya watched Ben turn away as she answered the call.

"DI Bloom," she said.

"Boss, it's Gillespie," came the reply, heavy and gruff when compared to both Chapman and Gold's light voices.

"What have you found?" she said.

"Ah. Not much, if I'm honest."

"Are you calling to tell me you haven't found anything?"

"Aye, well, no. Not really. I spoke to the owner of one of the houses on the lane. A bloke named Edward Rose. He's the farmer who owns the land where the body was discovered. Lives in the first house on the right. Nice guy actually. He was in the fields baling on Sunday," he explained. "He said that the lane is quiet. There's a pub and an Airbnb at the end of the road, up by the river. But barely anyone goes up there."

"Right. So?"

"So, when somebody does go up there, he often notices. Especially if he's out on his tractor."

"And did he happen to notice anybody on Sunday lunchtime?"

"As it happens, yes," Gillespie said. "A van. A blue van. He didn't see the make or the model. But he did see a van. He said he knows all the other residents' vehicles and none of them have a blue van."

"Did he happen to see the driver?"

"No. He said it was probably a dog walker. The area's quite popular. Apparently, there's a path that runs beside the river and walkers often tread his crops."

"Anything else?" Freya asked.

"No, boss. I thought I'd mention it, you know? Could be useful."

"Right. And where's Cruz?"

"Ah, I left him down by the lane checking the fields."

"On his own?"

"Aye, boss. I went ahead and left him to catch me up."

"How is he supposed to check both sides of the lane, Gillespie?" Freya asked.

"Ah, well. He's a bright lad."

"He's a bright lad with one pair of eyes," Freya said. "The way I see it, you got bored looking in the fields, so you went ahead to talk to the neighbour, hoping that you might learn something useful that will impress me."

"Eh?" Gillespie said, after a pause.

"I suggest you get back to helping DC Cruz, Gillespie."

"Aye, well, I'm actually on my way back there now," he replied, his breathing growing heavier as he walked a little faster.

"This is important, Gillespie. We need to demonstrate teamwork. I want you both to search the fields, and I want you both to talk to the neighbours. That's a two-mile stretch of lane and we don't have the resources to put a dozen uniforms on the search. Not unless we find something."

"Aye, boss. Sorry. I was just thinking outside the box."

"Well, I suggest you keep your thinking inside of the box for the time being. Search the fields. Report back to me."

"Aye, boss," Gillespie said, with more than a hint of dejection. But in the distance, a smaller voice could be heard calling Gillespie's name.

"Who's that?" Freya asked. "Is that Cruz?"

"Aye, boss," Gillespie said. "He's waving at me."

"Has he found something?"

"Hold on."

A scratching sound came over the call as Gillespie ran along the lane, and Ben looked across at Freya, curious as to what the pair were doing.

"He's found something. A patch of tall grass."

"Grass? In a field?" Freya said, and she sensed that Ben's sarcasm must have rubbed off on her somehow.

"It's the dyke at the edge of the field. The area has been flattened. Someone's been lying here. Hiding maybe?"

"Does it look recent?" Ben asked. "Could it have been a badger or a deer?"

"If it's a badger, Ben, then it's a damn big one. I wouldn't want it to hit my car, that's for sure."

"We'll need photos," Freya said. "And I want the area cordoned off."

"Should I call CSI back?" Gillespie asked.

"I've done it already," a distant, boyish voice called.

"You've called CSI already?" Gillespie said, engaging with Cruz while Freya and Ben listened in.

"Yeah, of course. We need this place photographed. It might have been the killer."

"Boss?" Gillespie said, breathing heavily into the phone only moments later.

Freya and Ben stared at each other, mouths open, both thinking of the next course of action. But then they turned away, focusing on the road as they made their way through the city. A wry smile crept onto Freya's face.

"What do you want me to do, boss?" Gillespie said. "Are you heading back here?"

"No," she replied, as she pulled into a parking spot. "No, it seems to me that Cruz has everything under control."

He inhaled loudly over the phone. "Aye, boss."

"Ask him to call me when Michaela and her team arrive," she said. "Are you able to, at least, follow that simple instruction, DS Gillespie?"

CHAPTER SIXTEEN

The University of Lincoln was spread across several buildings in the city. According to Chapman, the building they were looking for was one of a few close to Brayford Pool, where, only a couple of months before, they had questioned a man on the riverboat that he moored there.

A sign bearing the university crest, a pair of swans on either side of a shield above a scroll bearing the words *Libertas per Sapientiam*, had been fixed to the wall beside a pair of large double doors.

"Through wisdom, liberty," Freya muttered.

"Eh?" said Ben, holding one of the doors open for her.

"The motto. Through wisdom, liberty," she repeated. "There doesn't seem to have been much liberty for Myra Dicks."

"Ah right," Ben said, following her gaze to the sign. "Study Latin, did you?"

"I went to public school, Ben. It was part of the curriculum."

"Right, and here's me thinking that the time I spent dissecting mice and playing with Bunsen burners was a complete waste of time."

"Wasn't it?" Freya asked.

"How many times have you had to call upon your Latin so far in life?"

She shrugged, which was rare for Freya. She normally had an answer for everything.

"How many times have you called upon your dissecting skills and your experience with a Bunsen burner?" she replied.

"A few," he replied. "We've just been to see Myra Dicks being dissected, and I experiment with boiling water every day."

He smiled and ushered her through the door, and she left a waft of alluring perfume in her wake as she passed.

"You can't honestly find a similarity between a mouse and a dead human being, Ben."

"Why not?" he asked. "It's all biology. Granted, a mouse is smaller, but the organs are the same."

"Had any of your mice been strangled to death?"

"Well, not as far as I could tell."

"There's no similarity, Ben. And as for your experiments with boiling water, I presume you're referring to the act of making coffee?"

He grinned.

"Life is one big science lesson, isn't it?" he said.

"Are you looking for somebody?" a voice called out from the stairs that led up to the first floor. It belonged to a man who wore a tweed jacket, a yellow bow tie with red dots, and a pair of tan corduroys.

"Oh, Christ," Ben muttered under his breath. "It's the love child of every teacher I ever had."

The comment threw Freya off what she was going to say, and she looked down at the tiled floor long enough for her grin to subside.

"We're looking for Myra Dicks," Freya explained, retrieving her warrant card from her pocket and letting it hang open for him to inspect, which he did by peering down the length of his nose, seemingly scrutinising every minute detail.

"You're police?' he said finally. "What's this about?"

"I think it's best if we talk to Mrs Dicks—"

"I'm afraid she's not here," he replied. "Can I help at all?"

"Are you friends with Mrs Dicks?" Freya asked.

"I am," he replied, eyebrows raised in waiting. But Freya left a silence for him to fill. She found that, paradoxically, it was often the most effective way to move a conversation along. The man swept the hair on one side of his head across a rather shiny bald patch, as if it might convince them both he still had a full head of hair. "Is she okay?"

"Is there someone close to her?" Freya asked. "Her line manager, perhaps?"

"I asked if she was okay?"

"And I asked if there was somebody who might know her well enough to answer our questions," Freya reminded him.

"Perhaps we can talk in my office?" he said after a time.

"And you are?" Freya asked.

"Jeffery," he replied. "Jeffery Steel. I work with Myra."

"Lead the way then, Mr Steel," Ben said, with a tone that left scant room for argument.

"I've got a lecture in fifteen minutes, so it'll have to be quick," Steel said, as he led them along a corridor. He stopped at a door near the rear of the building, and with one hand poised on the handle, he stared at them both in turn, as if he was trying to fathom what had happened to Myra ahead of them making any kind of announcement. The sign on the door read *Prof. Jeffery Steel*.

"Is this your office?" Freya said. The question was rhetorical, and he pushed open the door, flicking on the light as he entered. It was a habitual move, one he must have done a thousand times. And if that wasn't proof enough that he was indeed the tenant of the office, the photos dotted amongst the hundreds of books and the name plaque on his desk confirmed it.

He took the seat behind the desk, placing his keys with care beside a pot overflowing with pens and pencils. He gestured at the two guest chairs. "Please," he said.

Ben took one of the chairs then turned to find Freya browsing the book titles.

"Myra Dicks," Freya announced from her spot beside the bookcase. "A friend of yours, you say. Are the pair of you close?"

"Myra? Well, yes. She's..." He paused. "Look, can you just tell me what this is all about?"

"What can you tell us about her, Mr Steel?" Freya asked.

"About Myra? Well, I, erm... She's nice. Lovely, in fact. Extremely intelligent. Is she in trouble? I'm more than happy to offer a character reference if that's what you're—"

"She's dead, I'm afraid," Freya said, watching every muscle in the man's face for some kind of sign he was lying. But if there was, Ben hadn't seen it. Jefferey Steel sat with his mouth and eyes wide open, clearly struck dumb by the news.

"Dead?" he said, retrieving a pen from his breast pocket, which he began to fiddle with as if he needed to occupy his hands. "I don't understand. I spoke to her yesterday."

"Do you need some time, Mr Steel?" Ben asked.

"Eh?" he said, staring at Ben while he processed the question, which he then shrugged off. "No. No, I'm okay. I'm afraid the news has caught me off guard. That's all."

"Did you know her well?"

"Yes. Yes, I did," he replied as if he was remembering a specific moment they had shared. "Look, I'll have to find somebody to cover my lecture. Do you mind?"

"We just need a few more minutes," Freya explained. "How close were you and Myra?"

He shrugged. "As close as you can be to somebody you've worked with for more than ten years," he said, then seemed to consider those words with a disbelieving shake of his head. "Ten years. Are you sure it's her?"

"Right now, we're establishing the facts, Mr Steel," Freya said. "Her car was found close to the crime scene along with her dog."

"Jambo?" he muttered, and he fiddled with the cuffs of his shirt. "Her dog. Jambo."

Ben watched him with interest. People processed information in a number of ways, and their initial reactions were often indicative of their relationship with the deceased.

"Hold on. Crime scene?" Steel said. "What the hell happened?"

"I'm afraid Myra was the victim of an attack, Mr Steel," Ben said, and just as Freya had done, he searched the man's eyes for some sign of previous knowledge. But there was none.

"What kind of attack?" Steel said, slowly and quietly, as if he didn't really want to hear the truth. "How did she die?"

It was Freya who spoke, making the decision to be frank with him while Ben was still deliberating on how much information they could justify giving away.

"She was strangled to death," she said, and the man's face paled. His mouth seemed to downturn as if he might break down at any moment. "By somebody close to her, we think."

There was barely any detail of Myra's injuries in Freya's explanation, but it had been enough to convince the contents of Steel's stomach to make a sudden appearance. He leaned over to one side, panting, as he spat into a plastic bin, and Freya came to stand beside Ben, then dropped into the second chair.

They waited a moment, while Steel caught his breath, and in contrast to her description of events, Freya slid a box of tissues towards him, which he used to clean himself up.

"I'm sorry," he gasped. "I wasn't ready to hear that."

"I did try to keep to the facts," Freya explained. "I'm afraid we're dealing with a serious crime, Mr Steel. Is there anything you can tell us that might help our investigation?"

"Like what?" he mumbled, still leaning over the bin.

"Do you know of anybody who might have wanted to hurt Myra? An argument, perhaps?"

Steel shook his head but stared down at the polluted bin.

"What exactly did she teach?" Ben asked.

"Teach?" Steel said, seeming almost outraged at the term. "She was a professor of cultural heritage, not a bloody teacher."

"Cultural heritage?" Ben replied, pretending that actually meant something to him.

"Conservation," Steel spat, as though he could see through Ben's feigned understanding.

"Conservation of what?"

"Architecture, archaeology, art. All of it. She's written papers on it. She wrote half the rulebook on who can dig up what, why, and when," he said, and then stared between them both. "She was a brilliant mind. She's done more to protect our heritage than anybody in history. Anybody that I know of anyway."

"So, she taught students how to conserve artefacts? Is that right?" Freya asked.

"Amongst other things, yes. She was also on the Heritage Advisory Board. A very privileged position."

"What do they do?" Freya said. "And please, excuse our ignorance. This isn't our field of expertise."

"I can see that," Steel said, throwing a brief look of disdain in Ben's direction. "The Heritage Advisory Board is the committee that essentially manages our heritage. The Tower of London, Hadrian's Wall, you name it, Myra worked on it. Typically she would be involved in the decision to go ahead with an archaeological dig, or not."

"So, if a group of archaeologists want to dig something up, they'd have to go through this board?" Ben asked.

"If the dig is thought to be of historical value, yes," Steel replied. "The group would submit a proposal, outlining what they expect to find and how they would manage the finds."

"Value?" Freya said.

"Not monetary value. Historical value. Will the dig fill in any gaps in our knowledge? Will the finds help us break through in other areas of history? Will the dig destroy evidence for future generations?"

"Academic stuff?" Ben said, and Steel swung his head around to look at him.

"If that's how you choose to describe it, yes. It's research. We can't just have any Tom, Dick, or Harry digging up our past. There'd be nothing left for future generations. The entire countryside would be full of holes and our history would be sold for a few quid on websites like eBay."

"But it's okay if the board has given it the go-ahead? Is that right?" Ben asked.

"Yes. It's okay if the board has given the dig the go-ahead. But believe me, it isn't easy, and even if permission is granted, you'll find it covers only a small percentage of the proposed area."

"So, if a site was, say, the size of a football field, the diggers would only get permission to dig up, say, the eighteen-yard box?"

By purposefully limiting his language, Ben had evoked the exact reaction he had hoped for. As expected, Steel shook his head at Ben's comment and put his confidence in Freya for his reply, perhaps swayed by her public schoolgirl accent.

"If the site was, as your colleague suggests, the size of a football field," he began, "then the archaeologists might hope for two to three trenches, no more than three yards in length. The aim of an archaeological dig is not to unearth the entire site, but merely to understand what is beneath the ground and preserve what remains."

"Most of your books are on history," Freya said, by way of a reply. "You seem to be well-versed in the practises of heritage."

"We talked," he said, with more than a trace of indignity in his tone. "I think you'll find all the professors in this building know a little about the other's field of expertise. It's what we do. We speak. We learn."

"Through wisdom, liberty?" Freya said.

"Something like that. Now, if you'll excuse me. I really must find somebody to cover my lecture."

"Had Myra made any enemies through her work with the board?" Freya asked.

"Archaeologists can be a tenacious bunch. When they get an idea in their heads, that is. Though I doubt any would go as far as to call themselves Myra's enemy. They are quite an amenable collective."

"We'll need access to the requests for archaeological digs," Freya said.

"Then I suggest you contact the board," Steel replied, and he unlocked his phone, searched for a number, and slid it across the desk. "Marianne Levitt-Ellis. She worked with Myra on a few research trips. She's also on the board."

Freya slid the phone to Ben to copy the name and number down, then addressed Steel for the last time that day.

"You didn't answer my question," she said.

"I believe I answered everything you asked," he replied.

"My first question. Do you know of anybody that might have wanted to hurt Myra Dicks?"

He softened again as if the question had reminded him of the loss of a colleague.

Ben finished copying the number down and slid the phone back to him, which he pocketed with a curt nod of thanks.

"Talk to Marianne," Steel said. "Now, if you'll excuse me. I really must rearrange my day."

"Just one more question," Freya said, and Steel spat into the bin before sitting up straight. "Where were you yesterday lunchtime?"

His eyes widened in disbelief and a look of utter indignation spread across his face.

"How dare you?"

"It's standard procedure, Mr Steel," Ben said. "We're just following protocol."

"Protocol? Accusing me—"

"Nobody is accusing you of anything, Mr Steel," Freya said. "Of course, the longer it takes for you to answer, the more reason we might have to pursue another line of questioning."

He sat with his mouth open for a moment, then relented.

"I can assure you that will not be necessary," he said, standing from his seat and presenting the door with a curt wave of his hand. "I was home. With my wife. Now, if you'll excuse me."

CHAPTER SEVENTEEN

Keeping one eye on the road, Anna Nillson watched Anderson check her makeup in the sun visor mirror from the corner of her eye. She flicked her fringe to one side in a final flourish, then closed the visor.

"Looking good, Jenny," Anna said.

"Just because we're police officers, doesn't mean we can't make an effort," Jenny replied.

"You do realise it's very unlikely that archaeologists look like Indiana Jones, don't you?"

Jenny gave a little laugh.

"A girl can dream, can't she? They don't give us handcuffs for nothing."

"Oh, stop it," Anna said, then thought about what she had said. "You haven't, have you?"

"I see, now you want all the gory details."

"You have, haven't you?" Anna said. "You've used your handcuffs outside of work. That's abusing police resources, that is."

"That wasn't the only thing that was abused, I can tell you," Jenny said with a wicked and infectious laugh that got Anna going.

"Absolutely shocking," Anna said, as she turned off Monks Road into Devon Street. "What number are we looking for?"

Jenny peered at the houses on her side then leaned forward to see the house numbers on Anna's side.

"That one," she said. "Red door."

While Anna found somewhere to park, Jenny checked her pockets for her notepad, pen, and of course, her handcuffs.

"Ten pound says he's wearing corduroys or a cardigan," Anna said, as she yanked up the handbrake.

"Facial hair?"

"A beard."

"Anything else?"

"Ear hair," Anna said, and Jenny pulled a disgusted face.

"If you're right about one of those things, you can have him."

"Who said I wanted him in the first place?" Anna joked as they climbed from the car, and while Jenny wasn't looking, she checked her reflection in the car window, thinking that she really ought to make more of an effort.

The houses were terraced and opened directly onto the pavement with no front garden. It was similar to the house Anna had grown up in, and she remembered how she and her friends could each walk into each other's houses through the back door, accessed via a network of alleyways. There was no need for knocking, not in those days when the only form of security was the tightknit community.

Anna reached up and rapped on the door a few times.

"Mid-forties, slightly unshaven, blue eyes," Jenny whispered, and Anna had to control her smile as the front door opened, and a man stood there, gawping at them.

"Can I help you?" he said, after a few moments of silence.

He was near as damn it six foot tall, with the broad shoulders Jenny had been hoping for. His facial features were masked by a few days' growth and his hair was both wild and jet-black. His eyes also met Jenny's expectations, being ice-blue, the type Anna could stare at for hours on end.

However, in those few brief moments of appraisal, those were the only redeeming features Anna could spot. Below a dolly cardigan, he wore a check shirt that needed a good clean, and on his legs were a faded pair of green corduroys.

"Adam Frost?" Anna said, and she let her warrant card fall open for him to see. "Lincolnshire Police. We wondered if we might have a word."

"Wow, that was quick," he said and stepped back to invite them inside with a sweep of his hand.

"What do you mean?" Anna said once she was inside the cramped hallway. Inside, it was almost identical to the house her parents had owned.

He closed the door and ushered them through a galley kitchen into the living space.

"You've come about my car, haven't you?" he said.

"We have, yes," Anna said. "But–"

"Have you found it then?"

"I'm sorry?"

"The car? Have you found it?" he pressed.

"Yes. Yes, we have found it. A black Audi," Anna said, and she read out the number plate.

"That's it," he said, with a smile that faded as quickly as it had arrived. "Don't tell me it's smashed up?"

"Not as far as I know," Anna told him.

"Thank God for that. That's the last thing I need."

"Can you talk me through what happened?" Anna said, testing the water. She had an idea of where he was going with the story but didn't want to influence his narrative in any way.

"I don't know, really," he said, and he gestured that they should sit at a dining table that was piled high with books and paperwork.

"We'll stand," Anna said, looking around the room. As she had expected, there were a few artefacts dotted around, and no doubt each of them had a lengthy and dull story behind them about someone in history doing something new for the first time, or dying horrifically.

"I came down this morning and it were gone," he said, his local accent shining through.

"Your car?" Anna said for clarity.

"Of course. What do you think I'm talking about?"

"Where was it parked?" Jenny asked, with her pen held ready to make a note of everything he said.

"Just out front where I always park. I mean, you hear about it, don't you? But you never think it'll happen to you."

"And when was the last time you saw your car?" Anna asked.

"Saturday. Saturday night, to be precise. I popped out to get some supplies."

"Supplies?"

"Food shopping. I've been locked away in here for weeks. It's the only time I get out."

"You don't work?" Anna asked. "I was led to believe you're an archaeologist."

"I am, yeah. How did you know that?"

"We ran some checks," Anna explained.

"I've had my car stolen, not robbed a bank."

"I understand that, Mr Frost—"

"Do they always send plain clothes to investigate a car theft?"

"We're part of the Major Investigations Team," Anna said, and she let him digest that piece of information for a moment.

"Major investigations?"

"We're investigating a murder."

"A what?"

"A murder, Mr Frost. In fact, your car was found close to the crime scene. Hence our visit."

"I'm sorry, I don't quite understand," he said. "Are you suggesting that my car was involved in a murder?"

"I wonder if you could tell us where you were on Sunday at midday?"

"Sunday?"

Anna nodded, watching his face for the slightest sign he was lying.

"Here," he said. "I just told you."

"Doing what, exactly?" Jenny asked.

"Working on a proposal. We're making a documentary."

His voice had risen at least two octaves since Anna had mentioned the murder investigation, and his hands, which had been firmly in his pockets, were now being put to use with wild gestures to support his story. He pointed at the table.

"I can show you if you like?"

"I'm sure that won't be necessary," Anna said. "I just need to talk to somebody to corroborate your story."

"To what?"

"I need proof you were here, Mr Frost."

"Proof? How the bloody hell am I supposed to prove it?"

"Did you talk to anybody?"

"No. Nobody."

Jenny closed her notepad and Anna caught her stare in her peripheral.

"Mr Frost," Anna said, "your car was found near the scene of a major crime. You failed to report your car stolen until Monday morning. You can see why we just need somebody to back your story up, can't you?"

"Back me up?" he said. "I was here."

"Okay," she replied with a sigh. "I am going to need you to come to the station at some point."

"To the station? I haven't done anything. I haven't murdered anybody —"

"Just to provide a sample of your fingerprints and DNA, Mr Frost. I'm sure if you weren't there, as you say you weren't, then there shouldn't be a problem and we can eliminate you from our investigations. How does that sound?"

"How am I supposed to get there?"

"I can arrange for you to be collected if you can confirm a time."

"No. No, that won't be necessary," he muttered, and he stared at the floor. "I'll find my way."

"Good. I suggest you do so at your earliest possible convenience, Mr Frost," Anna said, as she beckoned for Jenny to lead the way back to the front door.

"And why's that?" he said, as Anna walked through the kitchen. She stopped at the front door and stared back at him, as he stood once more with his hands in his pockets.

"Because despite what we have just told you, you haven't once asked if you can have your car back," she told him. "It doesn't look good if you ask me."

"But..."

"Have a nice day, Mr Frost," she said, as she pulled the front door closed behind her. "I'm sure we'll be seeing you soon."

CHAPTER EIGHTEEN

Freya burst through the incident room doors, which squealed as they always did, sharp and loud like a wounded animal. They closed slowly behind her and Ben with a soft whine, as if that same beast was injured, dying, or just plain sad at her arrival.

"Right, listen up," Freya said, while both the sound of the doors faded and the heads in the room all raised from laptops and note-books. "If you need coffee or the washroom, go now. Briefing. Two minutes. We need to move fast on this."

It was Cruz who moved first, but not without a cautionary glance at Gillespie, who seemed to be inspecting the rest of the desks to see how much hard work a round of coffees would be.

"Where are you going?" Freya asked Cruz.

"Khazi, boss," Cruz replied, one hand gripping the door handle.

"The khazi?"

"The toilet," he said, with a jab of his thumb in the direction of the washrooms.

"Be quick," Freya reminded him before turning to Gillespie, who was just pushing himself out of his seat. "And you?"

"Me?" he said.

"Are you going to help him or something?"

"Aye, well. No, actually. I was going to..."

"Make a coffee?"

He stared at her, and Freya felt the rest of the team's stares boring into them both.

"Aye."

"Good. I'll have one, too. Black, no sugar. Ben?"

Gillespie's expression sank like an old boot in thick mud, pulling every muscle in his face along with it.

"White, no sugar," Ben said.

"Anybody else?" Freya asked, and she turned to find Nillson, Anderson, Chapman, and Gold, each with their mugs held up ready for collection.

"Oh, for God's sake," Gillespie muttered.

"You may as well make Cruz one while you're in there," Freya said. "I don't want any disruptions once we get started."

"Aye, right. Might as well lace it with strychnine, too," he grumbled as he approached the double doors. "That'd be one less coffee I'd have to make in future."

He yanked open the doors and slipped through, leaving the remaining members of the team to wince at the awful racket made by the hinges.

The whiteboard had been cleaned and a fresh pack of pens had been brought from the stationery cupboard.

"Thank you, Chapman," Freya said, without looking at her; only Chapman would have the foresight to make such a worthy preparation.

She withdrew the black pen from the packet then tossed the rest onto her desk. In a few minutes, she had written every name they had collated so far, and just as she clicked the lid back on the pen, Gillespie returned with a tray full of coffees. He set them down on Cruz's desk, grabbed his own mug, and then announced that everybody could help themselves.

He avoided Freya's glare, doing his best to busy himself with his phone.

The doors burst open again, and Cruz entered, wiping his hands on the sides of his trousers as he made his way to his desk where the coffees were.

"What's this?" he said.

"What does it look like?" Gillespie said, and foreseeing exactly what was about to happen, each of the women in the room, Freya, Gold, Chapman, Anderson, and Nillson, all shared a horrified expression.

"Coffees?" Cruz said.

"Aye. I made them. You hand them out."

"Oh," Cruz said. "Alright, then."

"No," Gold said, a little over-zealously. She shoved her chair back and sprang to her feet.

The sudden outburst clearly alarmed Cruz, who stopped, his hands poised ready to collect two of the mugs.

"I'll do it," she told him, beating him to the drinks. "You've done enough today. What with all that walking you did."

"That's right," Anderson said, gratefully accepting the drink from Gold. "From what I heard, you did a great job."

"I did?" he said, glancing at each of them in turn with a little more than mild suspicion.

"Aye, he did?" Gillespie said, looking as confused as Cruz.

By the time Gold had delivered all of the drinks except Cruz's, the moment had passed, and all eyes were on Freya, leaving Cruz standing there perplexed.

"Are you going to sit down, Cruz?" Freya asked.

"Right," he said slowly and dropped down into his chair. He collected his drink from the tray and took a loud sip as Freya turned to the whiteboard.

She stabbed at the name in the centre, which she had circled with the pen.

"We have a positive ID. Myra Dicks. Sixty-three years old. Female. University lecturer and expert in the conservation of cultural heritage. According to Doctor Bell, the pathologist, Myra died from asphyxiation. She was strangled."

A hiss of whispers behind her caused her to stop, and she tuned to find Cruz and Gillespie arguing over where the tray should go.

"Is there a problem?" Freya asked.

They both looked up at her sheepishly.

"Aye. I was just telling Cruz here that the tray should go back in the kitchen, boss. You know? In case somebody else needs it."

"We're the only team on this floor," Freya said. "CID are upstairs, uniform are downstairs, DCI Granger is out..."

She stopped mid-sentence, unsure if she should say any more.

"And we all know about Detective Superintendent Harper..." she said quietly. "So, I doubt anybody will be looking for the tray."

"Aye, well," Gillespie said. "You may as well keep it then, Gabby, eh?"

"I don't want it on my desk. It's got coffee all over it."

"Well, I don't want it on my desk. I'm taking notes."

"Just," Freya snapped, then took a breath. "Just put the tray on the floor, Cruz, and let's just do our jobs."

Cruz pulled the tray from Gillespie, who held onto it a moment too long and then let go, causing the spilt coffee to flick on Cruz's shirt and face.

"Oh, for God's sake," he cried out, wiping his cheek with his shirt cuff. "What did you do that for?"

Freya held Gillespie's stare, shaking her head with utter distaste. But instead of berating him, she chose to move on.

"May I continue?" she said.

"Aye, boss. Ready when you are."

She studied him for a few more moments, then turned back to the whiteboard.

"Claire Banner. Myra's daughter, spoke to Myra on the phone while her mother was walking the dog, which must have been just moments before she was attacked."

"What about the husband?" Ben asked.

"Exactly," Freya replied, tapping the name linked to Claire Banner on the whiteboard. "Kevin Banner."

"Kevin Banner?" Nillson repeated, speaking up for the first time. "*The* Kevin Banner? The crime writer?"

"Do you know him?" Freya asked.

"Not personally," she replied. "But I've read all his books. They're brilliant."

"Kevin Banner," Chapman cut in, again flicking through her notebook to find her notes. "Forty-five years old. Drives a blue VW Transporter."

"A blue van?" Gillespie said, and the team all turned to him. Mirroring Chapman, he flipped through his own notepad to find his notes. "The bloke in the house I knocked at, Edward Rose, he's the farmer who owns the fields down there, he said he saw a blue van around lunchtime yesterday."

"Make and model?" Chapman asked.

"He couldn't tell. But it's a start. I mean, that lane isn't exactly the M1. It's a dead end and hardly used."

"Gillespie's right," Freya said. "If we can place him near the scene, all we'd need is a motive to bring him in for questioning."

"He has a motive," Gold said, and all heads spun to stare at her. Unlike the others, Gold didn't need to flick through her notepad. She stared at Freya solemnly. "When I was with Claire earlier, she mentioned some disagreements between Kevin Banner and her mother."

"An argument?" Freya pressed.

"No. It was more of an ongoing thing. She said they had never seen eye to eye."

"Right," Freya said. "Let's talk to him to see what he has to say."

She turned back to the whiteboard.

"It's too obvious," Nillson said, and Freya turned to find the young DS wearing a serious expression.

"Too obvious?"

"His mother-in-law dies in suspicious circumstances and he's the lead suspect?" she said, shaking her head. "It's too similar to one of his books, *Dance With Death*."

"*Dance With Death*," Gold said. "You're right. I've read that one. That's the one where the author kills his mother-in-law and frames her lover, isn't it?"

"And how does he kill her?" Freya asked.

Gold and Nillson exchanged concerned looks, before turning to Freya.

"Asphyxiation," Nillson said, and Gold nodded. "He strangles her."

CHAPTER NINETEEN

"Chapman, I want ANPR checked, please. Find me Kevin Banner's blue van. Ben and I will talk to him," Freya said, and she eyed him from across the room before turning to the whiteboard again to write their initials beside the lead.

Ben enjoyed watching Freya give briefings. She had a confidence that he likened to his old DI and mentor, David Foster. It had been David's death that had created the space for Freya to enter the team, and he often wondered if those circumstances, as painful as they might have been, were all meant to be. In Ben's mind, there were two Freyas – the one standing before the team now, leading the beginnings of the investigation, and the one he had seen in Paris, not so long ago. The one who had writhed beneath him after months of torturous longing.

But right then, the passion he had seen in her eyes was gone, leaving only scars of a flame amidst the focus and drive for her career.

"Nillson, how did you get on with the Audi owner?" Freya asked.

"He reported the car stolen, boss. Claims he was at home all day working on a proposal."

"What type of proposal?"

"Something about a documentary," she replied. "He's an archaeologist; not exactly Indiana Jones, but close."

"Is that objective or subjective?" Freya asked.

"Sorry, boss."

"You said he was an archaeologist," Freya said, and Ben caught her giving him a sideways glance. "Look into him. Find out more. And while you're at it, talk to Ben. He's got the number of a woman who worked with Myra Dicks at the Heritage Advisory Board."

"The what?" Gillespie said.

The Heritage Advisory Board," Freya repeated. "Anybody care to hazard a guess as to the purpose of such an organisation?"

Cruz raised his hand tentatively.

"Cruz?" Freya said. "Always a source of information."

"Aren't they the ones who decide if historical sites should be dug up, boss?"

"They are indeed. Nice work, Cruz."

"How the bloody hell do you know that?" Gillespie said.

"I watch *Time Team*," he replied, straightening his collar with pride.

"*Time Team*? You mean the show with Baldrick?"

"I think you'll find he's done a lot more with his career since those days, Jim. He was even knighted a while back," Cruz said. "Anyway. The Heritage Advisory Board are responsible for our history. They work with the National Trust to decide if people like Adam Frost should be digging up stuff or leaving it alone for people later on."

"Why would they leave it for someone else?" Gillespie said.

"I wondered that myself," Freya said. "Cruz?"

"Well," he began, enjoying the limelight, "let's use an example—"

"Oh, for Christ's sake," Gillespie muttered. "Here we go. Another lecture from Professor Pissy-Pants."

"DS Gillespie, I'm asking Cruz for some insights into an area that, quite frankly, none of us seems to know anything about other than him. Unless you can demonstrate that either you know more on the topic than he, or that his information is useless, please do us all a favour and keep your bloody mouth closed for once."

"Aye, boss," he said, sucking in a lungful of air to quell the retort that no doubt was ready to spill from his lips.

"You were saying, Cruz?" Freya said.

"Right. Well, let's take the discovery of tombs within the pyramids," he began.

"The what?"

"Gillespie, will you shut up?" Freya snapped, and even from the other side of the room, Ben could see her nostrils flaring. She nodded at Cruz, urging him to continue.

"Well, the tomb of Tutankhamun was discovered in the nineteen-twenties," he said. "Nineteen twenty-two, if I'm not mistaken. Which is fine. They did a good job, apparently. But what did they miss? What do we know now that could have made the dig more successful? What technology do we use now that could have preserved the site or provided more value?"

Freya shook her head, not quite following.

"That's the point, boss. What technology or methods will archaeologists be using in a hundred or two hundred years' time that differ from what we use today?"

"Right, so they don't dig *everything* up so that future generations can glean better insights with more advanced methods and technology?"

"Partly, yes," he said. "That's why we need organisations like the one Myra Dicks worked for."

"Fascinating," Freya said, and she seemed to study Cruz in a new light. "Nillson, work with Chapman, please. I want to know everything we can find on Adam Frost. Find out if he's working on any digs right now. If so, I'd be keen to go and take a look."

"On it, boss," Nillson replied.

"Right, then. You two," Freya said, addressing Gillespie and Cruz, "let's hear it."

"Well..." Gillespie started.

"Not from you," Freya said. "As I understand it, Cruz made the discovery."

"Aye, well..." Gillespie said quietly.

"DC Cruz, if you could please share the news of your findings with the team?"

"Me?"

"Do you remember what I said, Cruz?"

"Oh," he said. "Yes. Well, erm, whilst performing a detailed search of Dunston Fen Lane, I endeavoured to–"

"Just plain English will suffice," Freya said with the slightest of eye rolls.

"Right," he said, taken aback a little. "I found a patch of flattened grass in the dyke beside the lane. I thought it looked like someone had been hiding there. You know? The killer maybe?"

"And what did you do about it?" Freya said, coaxing him on.

"I called Michaela. The pretty one. You know? The one that fancies Ben."

"Excuse me?" Ben said.

"Oh, come on, Ben," Gold said. "It's obvious she likes you."

"Shall we get back to Cruz's discovery?" Freya said. "We'll keep the gossip for the pub, where possible."

"Right," Cruz said. "Anyway, she turned up. Her and her assistant, Pat. By the way, does anyone know if Pat is a bloke or a girl?"

"Nobody knows," Gillespie said. "One of life's mysteries, that is."

"Yeah, I couldn't work it out either," Cruz said.

"And what did they find?" Freya said. "Michaela and her assistant?"

"Oh, nothing much really. The dyke was too dry for footprints. But they did agree that somebody had lain there. Recently too."

"And why would somebody lie in a dyke?" Freya asked. "Anybody?"

"It's wide open there," Ben said. "There's nowhere else to hide for miles."

"Why would you want to hide?"

"Well, if you were the killer, for example, and you were leaving the crime scene. You might want to hide if, say, a vehicle came along. There's only one way in and one way out of that place."

"Right. So we're saying the killer left on foot, are we?" Freya suggested.

"Maybe they parked their car in that car park?" Cruz said. "You know? The one where Myra Dicks' car was, and that Audi. The killer could have been walking or running back down the lane to their car. Someone might have come along and dived in to take cover. I think what Ben said was right. There's so little traffic there, if you see some-body, you're bound to remember them."

"I agree," Freya said. "However, that theory does rather push our blue van man out of the equation. Does anybody have anything useful to add?"

Freya glanced around the room and Ben watched her, internalising his amusement. Chapman waited with her hands poised above her keyboard, Gold looked like a deer in headlights, Nillson and Anderson were both itching to get started on their tasks, while Gillespie sucked on the end of a biro, leaning back in his chair with his legs crossed. Cruz was the only one who also followed Freya's gaze around the room.

"Nobody?" Freya said.

Once more, Cruz raised his hand sheepishly.

"Thank heavens," Freya said. "What is it?"

"There's something I can't work out," he said. "According to what Gillespie said, the farmer was in the field baling straw when he saw the blue van."

"Right?"

"But when we went to the crime scene on Sunday, I don't remember seeing any bales in the field," he said.

Freya's expression morphed into one of realisation, and contempt for herself.

"Chapman?" she said.

"I'm checking the photos now, ma'am," she replied almost immediately.

The team all looked to Ben, who, as a farmer's son, had the greatest knowledge of farming practises. Ben waited for Chapman's response.

"No bales," Chapman said, spinning her screen around for the team to see. "Just an empty field with lines of hay."

"Straw," Ben said. "Hay is cut grass. Straw is the stems of crops the combine harvester leaves behind. And the lines are called windrows. The combine leaves them behind to dry in the wind."

"Why's that?" Chapman asked.

"If the stems are damp or moist, the bales will rot. My dad combined his fields on Saturday. He didn't start baling until this morning. I'd wager nearly every farmer in the area did the same."

"Bloody hell, I feel like I'm at school," Gillespie said. "Have I come to the wrong place?"

"That's a question I ask myself every day," Freya said, throwing his remark back his way. "It looks like we need to talk to the farmer. Good work, Cruz."

"Aye, well, any of us could have spotted that," Gillespie said.

"The point is that none of us did. I'll make sure DCI Granger hears of your good work, Cruz."

"Thanks, boss," he replied gleefully.

"In the meantime, I suggest we hit this with fresh minds tomorrow. Nillson, Anderson, you're both looking into Adam Frost and the society Myra belonged to."

"The Heritage Advisory Board, boss," Cruz added.

"Yes, them. Use Chapman where you need to. Ben and I will be looking for Kevin Banner. Chapman, we'll need your help as I've already stated."

"What about us?" Gillespie said. "What delights have you got in store for the dream team?"

"I want you to go to Jeffery Steel's house."

"Who the bloody hell is Jeffery Steel when he's at home?"

"A friend of Myra's," Freya replied. "He also works at the university, and he told us he was at home with his wife when Myra was being attacked. I want his story corroborated. Clear?"

"Crystal," Gillespie grumbled.

"Good. Chapman will give you the address," she said. "Gold, when are you going back to the daughter's house?"

"I was going to pop in on my way home. I only came back for the afternoon briefing."

"Good. Don't let her out of your sight, please," Freya said. "As for the rest of you, stay close, stay in touch, and most importantly, stay safe. Tomorrow, I want names checked off our list and I want to take a plan to DCI Granger. Understood?"

A few mumbled acknowledgements were all Freya received, but that was okay. They had enough to think about.

"Good," Freya said. "Get yourselves home and get some rest. I'll see you all in the morning."

CHAPTER TWENTY

"For somebody who had a great deal to say in the incident room, you're awfully quiet," Ben said from the passenger seat of Freya's car. He pulled on his seatbelt as she accelerated out of the station car park, checking her mirror briefly, then her speedo, before she slowed a little and cleared her throat.

"I'm thinking," she said quietly, her voice barely audible above the rumble of the Range Rover's V8 engine.

"About what?" he said.

There were times when Freya could be as warm as a fireside rug, as welcoming as a plush, wingback chair, and as charming as a chocolate box cottage. And there were times when she could be as cold as ice and sharp as steel, and as uninviting as a prison shower block.

Today, she was the latter of the two.

"About a blue van, a dead body, and a missing person of interest, Ben," she replied with a quick lash of her tongue. "I suggest you do likewise."

"Is that all?" he said. "Just the investigation?"

"Yes, Ben. The investigation is consuming every cell of my grey matter. However, by your tone and persistence, I can only assume you have something else on your mind you'd like to share."

"Paris," he said.

"Is there any particular aspect of Paris you'd like to discuss, Ben?" she said, letting each word ride a single, bored exhalation. "The architecture, perhaps? The Louvre? Or maybe that delightful creme brûlée we had on the Rue du Louvre? One of the finest I've ever tasted, I have to say."

"No," Ben said. "I had something else in mind."

"Ah, then you must want to discuss Notre-Dame? It's a shame you couldn't have seen it before the fire," she said, and a wry smile grew on her face, as a lily might open with the morning sun.

"No," he replied, sensing he had worked his way through her cold exterior. She was toying with him, as she would have done only a few days before. "What are you smiling at?"

"Me?" she said. "Smiling? Am I?"

"You know what I mean."

"I was just remembering something, that's all," she said.

"What? Tell me. It feels like ages since we had a proper chat. Ever since Arthur died, you've been..."

"I've been what, Ben?" she said, as she pulled out onto the main road into Lincoln.

"Different. Cold. Like nothing happened."

It seemed like an age passed before she said anything. She stared through the windscreen, refusing to meet his gaze. In the end, Ben resorted to watching the world go by out of the passenger window.

"I've got a lot on my mind, Ben," she said finally.

Ben gave those words some thought. She always had a lot on her mind. It wasn't a new concept for her.

"What made you smile?" he said.

"Did I smile?" she said eventually. And the corners of her mouth upturned, threatening to reveal her true thoughts.

"Come on. I had a great time with you in Paris. We came back and I thought everything was going well, and now it's like you're keeping me at arm's length. What is it? What's wrong? And why are you bloody smiling?"

"Do you really want to know?"

"Yes," he said. "What are you smiling about?"

"Do you remember Notre-Dame?"

"Notre-Dame?" he said. "Of course, I do."

"Do you remember the views from the top of the tower?"

"Is that it?" he said in disbelief. "I'm sitting here thinking about you and me, and you're smiling at the memory of the view over Paris?"

"No," she said, navigating a roundabout and then gunning the engine as if she was growing tired of the conversation and wanted to get home quickly.

"Well?" he said, as she pulled into the single track that led to his dad's farm, his house, and Freya's cottage, which she rented from his father.

Freya waited until she had brought the car to a stop outside his house. She put the car into park and hit the button to kill the engine. Then she sighed and sat back in her seat.

"If you must know, Ben, I was thinking of that gargoyle we saw. Do you remember? It looked just like you."

"Oh, for God's sake, Freya."

"You asked," she said, reaching for the door handle.

"Hold on. Hold on," he said, catching hold of her arm. She glanced down at his hand with her eyebrows raised, and he let go. "I'm sorry. I just thought—"

"You thought that because we had one weekend together in Paris, somehow we'd come home and play happy families?"

"No," he said, shaking his head. "Is that all this is to you? One weekend in Paris?"

"Well, what else is it?" she asked, the tip of that sharp tongue finding its way to the centre of Ben's heart.

"This is nine months of pushing and pulling. This is nine months of us being close, growing close, and almost but never quite becoming something. Nine months ending in what was possibly the best weekend of my entire life. And we come home to this? Whatever this is. It's like it never happened. Well, I hope I don't need to remind you, Freya. But it did happen. You and I. We happened. We got close. Closer than is humanly possible. And if I'm honest, I loved every second of it. Sod Notre-Dame. Sod the museums and the cafes. Yes, they were nice, lovely, in fact. But the highlight for me was waking up next to you and seeing a real chance of something that, until that moment, had been out of reach, unattainable. It's like the Freya I knew so well, the Freya I fell–"

"Don't say it, Ben," she said, unable to meet his stare. "Don't say those words."

"Fell head over heels for..." he continued. "She's gone. She's still in that fancy hotel suite on Opera Street, or whatever it was."

"It was the Avenue de l'Opera, Ben," she sighed.

"Whatever it was, I don't bloody get it," he said. "And you know what?"

"What?"

"I don't deserve it. *You* know I don't deserve it. *I* know I don't deserve it. And anybody who knows me knows I deserve better. If you're going to carry on like this, then maybe it's for the best."

He reached for the door handle, and this time it was Freya who grabbed his arm. But he didn't glare at her or her grip. In fact, his body warmed at her touch.

"Wait," she said softly, and there was a hint of that warmth he had come to know and relish. She nodded as if his words had only just permeated her mind, and she agreed. "You're right. You don't deserve this. I'm sorry."

"I just want an explanation, Freya. That's all."

She was silent for a few moments, staring through the windscreen, but then Freya spoke, and the words came like spent air from a balloon.

"A week ago, I could see it. I could see us. We could have made it work. If a senior officer found out about us, they would have moved one of us to a different team. They would look at the positions available and make a judgement call, which we would just have to swallow. But I think between the two if us, we could have kept a relationship below the radar."

"So, what's different?"

"Everything, Ben," she said. "If Granger moves into Harper's role and I'm moved up into DCI, we couldn't make it work. Don't you get it?"

"No," he replied. "Not really."

"It means that, should anybody find out about us, it'll be you who gets moved, not me. And if I know the force as I think I do, you won't just be moved to CID on a different floor, you'll be moved to another station. HQ maybe? Imagine that? You'd be working under DI Standing."

"But at least we'd be together," he said.

"No, Ben. You have to think bigger picture. Imagine how the team would react if I was the reason you were sent away. They love you. I don't know if you see it, but every one of them adores you. They have a massive amount of respect for you, and so do I. How am I supposed to lead a team who all hate me for being responsible for that?"

He considered the prospect of transferring. Even to work under Steve Standing. It would be a change. A significant change. He probably wouldn't enjoy the role as much as he did now, but at least they could make a go of it. He said nothing while he chewed the facts, imagining how life might be for both of them.

"I've spent my entire career," she continued, "working my way up the ladder. I've worked the hours, I've put myself through hell, Ben. I've been the victim of verbal abuse, I've endured sexist comments from the neanderthal males in London, and I nearly died trying to make a name for myself. And do you know what, Ben? In all my life, I've never known a friend like you."

He turned to stare at her. He'd known her long enough to recognise sincerity, and he waited for her to finish what she'd begun.

"I can't do it," she said. "I can't risk destroying all my hard work when I'm this close to promotion. I can't risk throwing away all those hours, all that hardship, and the bloody tears."

He nodded, seeing where she was leading the conversation.

"And I can't risk you," she said finally. "Even if we made a go of it, there's no certainty it would work."

"Oh, come on–"

"I mean it. I want you in my life, Ben. I need you in my life. You've helped me through so much," she said. "I'd rather have you as a friend than not have you at all."

Ben inhaled long and hard. He turned to stare out of the passenger window for a moment, then returned to find her still watching him, waiting for a response.

He nodded once.

"That's your decision? You'd rather save your career–"

"Our careers," she corrected him.

"You'd rather save our careers, the team, and our friendship than make a go of it?"

"If you must summarise the facts with brutality, then yes. Your friendship means more to me than anything. The team is one of the best I've ever known. And this is our chance, Ben. Don't you see? This is our chance to move up. To get what we deserve. Side by side."

"And Paris?" he said.

"Was the best night of my life," she finished, and they both smiled.

"Alright. I understand," he said, and he clicked open the door. "But if you're really going to move up to DCI, you're going to have to work on a few things."

He climbed from the car and closed the door, meeting her across the car bonnet as they often did to share a final thought or two.

"Such as?" she said. Ordinarily, Freya would have resented any suggestion of self-improvement. But the relief of airing her thoughts was evident in her expression.

"You need to get yourself a man," he said, as she clicked the fob to lock the car. He turned away and made towards his house, feeling her watching him, waiting for him to finish. "Paris was mediocre at best. I've had far better nights."

He shoved the door open, savouring the shocked expression she wore, and the glimmer of amusement that woke her crow's feet. Freya hesitated halfway through her autopilot walk to Ben's front door.

"Are we at least having dinner together?" he said. "For old times' sake?"

She glanced across his father's fields to where the cottage she rented stood in the distance.

"No," she replied, and walked slowly back to the driver's door, looking back at him with an apologetic smile. "I don't think that's a good idea, do you?"

"It's just dinner, Freya."

"It's just dinner, and then it's dessert," she replied. "You need to get over this, whatever this is."

"Me? *I* need to get over it?"

"And the best way to do that," she replied, as she climbed into her car, "is to get under somebody else."

"Freya? It's just dinner."

"And if you can't do that..." she replied, as she closed her door. She fired up the engine again and lowered the window. "Then perhaps you should have some alone time."

"Some what?"

She put the car into drive and began to roll away, leaning from the window to offer him another pearl of wisdom.

"Do whatever it is you men do when you're all alone," she said with a wink. "Goodnight, Ben."

And with that, she put her foot down and left him standing outside his house, utterly bemused.

CHAPTER TWENTY-ONE

In his office adjacent to the incident room, Will Granger heard the squealing doors open and then slam closed. A few moments later, the aroma of expensive perfume wafted through his open door, and the hum of the team fell silent.

He checked his watch. They would be going into overtime soon, and with the funeral looming, there was scant room for error.

The voice on the other end of the phone stopped and Will pulled himself back into the now.

"Are you there, Will?" it said.

"Yes, sir. I'm here, and you're right. There is a lot to think about."

"And the team? How did they take the news?"

"As well as can be expected, sir. DI Bloom and DC Anderson are both new to Lincoln. I think that's worked in our favour. They didn't know him like the others did."

"You mean he didn't have long enough to upset them?"

"I wouldn't say that, sir. They all had an affection for him, in their own ways."

"And moving forward?" he asked. "There'll be some changes, you know?"

"I've made the team aware of that, sir. But if I can just add, they are a good team. They work well together. As much as change is inevitable, disruption could be detrimental."

"What are you saying?"

"Off the record, sir?"

"Will, I've never known you to speak on the record."

"I don't want anybody new brought in. They need familiarity right now. They need, dare I say it, hope, sir."

"Hope?"

"They work hard. They deserve a break. If the plan is to kick them when they're down, then I'm afraid I'm going to do my best to stand in the way."

"You've made that clear in your recommendations. Are you sure this is what you want?"

"Positive, sir. I know them well. No disruption. That's what they need."

"And hope?"

"Yes, sir. Plenty of it. The recommendations I've laid out play to everyone's strengths. I think we're moving the right people up, and providing a chance for the others to prove themselves. If we bring anybody new into the team, then we stand a good chance of losing someone. And right now, there isn't a member of the team I would do without."

Deputy Chief Constable Kelly listened. He was the type of man that could actually listen, and although he said nothing in reply, to begin with, Will knew his considerations would be complex and effective.

"This is an opportunity for you too, Will," he said. "This is the move you've been working for all this time."

"I know, sir."

"I might also remind you that you could have had it a lot sooner."

Will smiled at the thought.

"I know, sir," he said. "I'd like to think my progression has been based on merit, and not telling tales, to date at least."

He could picture the old man smiling at the other end of the line.

"You're a stubborn old fool, Will. You always have been."

"Always will be," he replied, as cheerfully as he could.

"And this investigation they're working on. The Dunston lady. What was her name?"

"Myra Dicks, sir. Big name in the cultural heritage world, apparently. They're making progress. It's early days, but we have some leads."

"I'm sure," he said. "What about Bloom? Is she up to the job?"

"She's hungry, sir. Very driven."

"Driven is one thing, but what about leadership? The ship needs steering, Will."

"I think she can do it."

"Think?"

Will knew what he was getting at. He wanted something tangible.

"I'll make enquiries," he said.

"Good, I want to start clean. I want the right person at the helm. I'll be making my decision over the next few days. If we're going to start clean, then I want things wrapped up."

"I've already put the pressure on, sir. The funeral is on Friday. Monday morning will be a new beginning. A new chapter, as it were."

"In that case, you'll have my decision before then," Kelly said. "Until then, Will."

"Goodnight, sir," Will said, and he ended the call before they ventured down another tangent.

He set his phone down on his desk, then almost immediately scooped it up and tossed it into his desk drawer. It wasn't only the team who could do without distractions. He collected up his pen, a rather elegant Montblanc that Detective Superintendent Harper had given him for his fiftieth. It seemed like an age ago. If he knew then what he knew now, would he still be sitting there writing that letter?

It was the second letter of condolence he had written to the family of a team member in under a year. The first had been David, and in a way, it had been more challenging to write. Perhaps it was because David had been so much younger? Or perhaps it was because they had been closer?

He read through what he had written, using Harper's voice in his mind's narration. He hoped the anecdote would raise a weary smile while reminding them that their treasured father, husband, and grandfather was never alone in his work; there were people by his side who would miss him.

He considered adding another line, but then stopped, his pen poised above the stationery. Sometimes, the power doesn't come from the words that are spoken, or written, but from those that are not.

With all my heart, gratitude, and sympathy,
Will Granger.

He replaced his pen lid and laid it flat on his desk, clinging to it for a moment then letting it go.

He folded the letter into thirds then slipped it inside the matching envelope, which he placed atop his files to be taken to the funeral. He hoped that Dennis' wife would read it alone, perhaps when the funeral was over. Maybe then she could share it with her mourning family.

Either way, there was very little else he could do. All that had to be said had been, and the next chapter of the team hung in the balance.

CHAPTER TWENTY-TWO

It was one of those moments when a man stands at a urinal hoping for a few moments of peace and quiet. But no sooner had Gillespie begun than the door opened and a familiar figure came to stand beside him.

"Cheer up, Gillespie," Granger said. "You look like you're carrying the weight of the world. That's not like you."

"Aye, well. It's nothing, guv."

"Come on. You can tell me," Granger persisted, but Gillespie said nothing. "Are you concerned about the future?"

"The future, guv?"

"You know? What with the funeral and such."

"The funeral doesn't concern me. I'm just sorry I didn't get to tell him thanks, you know? It was Detective Superintendent Harper that brought me into DI Standing's team. If he hadn't done that, I dread to think what I'd be doing now."

"Ah, come on. I'm sure you'd be doing well wherever you ended up," Granger said. "Do you sometimes wish you'd transferred with DI Standing?"

"With Steve?"

"Yes. You know? Like the others did? I hear it on good authority that at least one of them has been promoted to sergeant."

"I enjoy Major Investigations, guv," Gillespie said, as he finished what he was doing and turned to wash his hands. "It's different now Steve's gone. But I guess I need to stick it out."

"And how do you find working for DI Bloom?" Granger asked, as he too finished the job and moved to the washbasin as Gillespie stepped up to the hand dryer.

"Ah, well. You know?"

Granger gave a little laugh and finished with a sigh. Then the smile faded.

"No. No, I don't. Tell me," he said. "How do you find working for DI Bloom?"

The dryer finished and Gillespie's hands, though still damp, found the pockets of his trousers, and his fingers jingled the loose change.

"She's okay, I guess," he said, which did nothing but raise one of Granger's spidery eyebrows. He finished washing his hands and the two shared an awkward moment where Gillespie had to shuffle sideways to allow Granger access to the dryer. "I mean, she's different. Aye, that's it. She's different."

"Different to who?" Granger asked. "DI Standing? If I remember rightly, you made several complaints about Steve Standing while he was here. Do you remember, Jim?"

"Ah, aye, well, I might have said one or two–"

"You were ready to quit," Granger said, speaking over his shoulder to be heard above the dryer.

"Well, I might have overreacted a wee bit."

"And DI Bloom?" Granger said. "Does she make you feel like that?"

"No, no, of course not."

"But you're unhappy? I can see it in your face."

The dryer stopped, leaving both of them with no more errands in the cycle. They were just two men standing awkwardly in the men's bathroom – one waiting for the other to speak, the other wishing he had held on for a few more minutes.

"She's a good leader," Gillespie said, thinking on his feet.

"I agree," Granger said.

"Everything she does, or says, is for the benefit of the team," Gillespie said, believing it more as he spoke the words.

"But?" Granger said. "I feel a *but* coming."

"Well, let's just say that not all of those things that are good for the team necessarily translate to us as individuals."

Granger seemed to be digesting the statement, appraising Gillespie as he mulled it over.

"That's a nice way of saying it," he said.

"Saying what?"

"Saying that you're unhappy because of the way DI Bloom treats you."

"I didn't say I was–"

"It's okay, Jim. I understand. You don't want to be the one to badmouth your boss."

"No, I didn't–"

"There's change coming this way, Gillespie. But I'm sure that if DI Bloom hasn't mentioned it already, you're probably experienced enough to recognise that, right?"

"Right, aye. It goes without saying. I mean, with Detective Superintendent Harper and all..."

"Correct. I remember when I was a sergeant. It seems like an age ago now."

"It's hard to imagine, guv. If you don't mind me saying."

"Not at all. I've sat in every one of those seats in my time. I know what it's like to be handed the bum deal in an investigation. It always feels like the others are getting the good jobs, doesn't it?"

"Well, aye, it can do. I won't lie."

"Dennis Harper was a DI back then. He never suffered fools, let me tell you. If you think DI Bloom can be hard on you. You should have seen some of the things we had to do. Anyway, maybe those little anecdotes should be saved for the funeral, his eulogy even. For what it's worth, our chief inspector was a man named Kelly. DCI Abel Kelly."

"Kelly? As in Deputy Chief Constable Kelly, guv?"

"That's him. Did well for himself, didn't he?"

"Aye, boss. I never knew that."

"And just like you all referred to Dennis Harper as Arthur, as in Half-a-job Harper, we had a nickname for Kelly. Unable Kelly, we called him, mainly because we never saw him do a day's work in his life."

"Very good, guv," Gillespie said.

"Not quite as catchy as Arthur, but it worked. We all got on with him. We knew the lines we could and couldn't cross, and when push came to shove, we knew he had our backs."

"That's what counts, guv. That's what really counts."

"It is. And he was good too. If you did what he asked, he'd back you even if he knew you were in the wrong. It's hard out there. You have to make split-second decisions, and we don't always get them right, do we?"

"No, guv. It's impossible to get it right every time."

"I know that. You know that. The only people who don't realise that are the general public, and quite often it's them who have the loudest voice."

"Them and the media, guv."

"Exactly. But one day, Unable Kelly came to me and asked me something similar to what I'm asking you now."

Gillespie hesitated. "Like, an informer?"

"No. Far from it. I just want to be closer without crowding DI Bloom. What I'm looking for, Jim, is a team player. Someone I can rely on. Someone who isn't afraid to tell me the truth. I mean, I'm not out there on the ground. I'm not privy to what goes on in the team. All I see is the investigations begin, I get a few updates, and I see them coming to a close, or not, in the case of DI Standing. I'm just looking for a way to make sure people, like you, Cruz, and Gold, and the rest, are looked after."

"You want me to spy on the team?"

"No, no, no. I just need somebody I can rely on," Granger said. "Somebody who wants to take the next step up the ladder. Who isn't afraid to tell the truth, good and bad. Is that you, Jim? Are you the man I'm looking for? Or have I got you all wrong? Because from where I'm standing, I see a sergeant who is ready to become an inspector. Am I wrong, Jim? Have I read the situation wrong? Do you want to stay a sergeant forever and watch people like DC Cruz and DS Nillson climb that ladder, while you spend your life knocking on doors and doing the grunt of the work?"

Gillespie said nothing. He'd heard every single word loud and clear but was fighting with the multiple meanings.

"Change is coming, DS Gillespie," Granger said, placing a large, soft hand on his shoulder. "You either see the opportunity, or you don't."

He moved toward the door, edging past Gillespie and coming a little too close for comfort. But with one hand on the door handle, he had one more thing to say.

"I'll be in my office if you want to talk," he said. "No pressure."

"Guv?" Gillespie said as Granger was halfway through the door.

He turned and his eyebrows raised in question; even the few extra-long hairs seemed to fall in line.

"What did you say? To Kelly, I mean. Did you do it?"

Granger peered along the corridor, then looked back at Gillespie with a smile, sincere and broad.

"I'll let you work that one out for yourself," he said, then nodded once. "You know where I am."

"Aye, guv. I do."

"Good. Get some rest. You look like hell," Granger said. "Good-night, Jim."

CHAPTER TWENTY-THREE

The morning sky was nothing short of fabulous. Streaks of reds and oranges spilled across the blue, and the warm horizon promised glorious sunshine. Still, Freya took her light jacket, tossing it onto the back seat because, she heard her father say, you just never know.

Barely a drop of rain had fallen for days, and as she tore across the track towards Ben's house, a cloud of dust formed in her wake. She honked her horn once and turned around outside his father's house, which stood between Ben's and his brothers' houses to form an arc.

By the time she had made the turn, he was at the passenger door, and he climbed inside before she'd even come to a full stop.

"Morning," he said, which was surprising. She'd been expecting some kind of hostility given the way she had left him the night before.

"Good morning," she replied with a smirk. "How was it?"

"How was what?"

"You know? Your alone time," she said. "Man stuff."

"I had dinner with my father," he replied. "Then I went home and went to bed."

"Oh yeah?"

"And went straight to sleep," he said. "For God's sake. Can't you think of anything else? I bet you've been dying to ask me that."

"Oh, lighten up. I'm just trying to raise a smile."

"Well, that's all you'll be raising," Ben said. "What news do we have?"

"News? About what?"

"Dead body? Missing suspect? Remember?"

"Oh, right. We have Myra Dicks, strangled to death. We have Kevin Banner still missing, apparently on a research trip. We have Adam Frost, who I'm not convinced is wholly innocent in this. And we have Cruz's miraculous observation."

"The straw bales?"

"Exactly. Somebody, somewhere, isn't being honest."

"Aren't they always?" Ben said. "I called you last night, by the way."

"Oh, did you? Sorry, my phone was on silent."

She pulled her phone from her pocket and saw four missed calls from Ben, plus two from Chapman's desk phone, and one a few minutes ago from Nillson.

She clicked it off silent mode and hit the button to return Nillson's call, and the dashboard screen lit up.

"Morning, boss," Nillson said, after just one ring.

"Morning, Nillson. I missed your call."

"You asked us to look into Adam Frost. I think we have something. I want to bring him in."

"Go on," she said, intrigued. She glanced across at Ben, whose ears had been pricked.

"I spoke to Marianne Levitt-Ellis yesterday after you left," Nillson explained. "She couldn't go into details, but she did say that Adam Frost and Myra Dicks have had professional disagreements for some time."

"Was that normal?" Freya asked.

"Well, it was for Myra. From what I can gather, she had a habit of rubbing people up the wrong way. Marianne couldn't say too much, obviously, but reading between the lines..."

"So, it's nothing against Adam Frost personally? Just a clash of personalities?"

"Something like that, yeah. Jenny did a bit more digging on him. It turns out he's in financial difficulty. He's missed his last three mortgage payments, his bank accounts are depleted, and the TV documentary series he had been working on fell through."

"Now that is interesting," Freya said, musing aloud. "Do we know why?"

"Not yet. We're working on it."

"How did you find out about the production company? Please tell me it was by ethical means."

"Marianne spoke to him. He called her a few weeks back for their backing."

"And his car was found at the scene," Freya said. "Okay, bring him in. Talk to Sergeant Priest. He'll give you all the resources you need, and if Granger needs to talk to me before he signs a warrant, have him call me."

"Thanks, boss," Nillson said. "I'll keep you posted."

The call ended and silence resumed.

"Do you know what bothers me?" Ben said. Freya raised an eyebrow but didn't look up. She was busy checking her emails before they reached the main road. "Other than using your phone while you're driving?"

She set the phone down in the centre console and gave him a questioning look.

"You were married, right?"

"Right," Freya said, elongating the word to convey her curiosity.

"If your husband—"

"Ex-husband," Freya corrected him.

"Okay, if your ex-husband's mum died. What would you have done?"

"I'd have gone to him."

"Even if you'd been arguing?"

"Yes, of course."

"And even if you didn't get on with the in-laws?"

"I'd still have gone. Sometimes, you have to put things to one side. That's what marriage is about. An argument doesn't mean you don't care."

"Even if you were in the middle of a murder enquiry?"

She nodded.

"Arrangements can be made for those occasions."

"So why hasn't Kevin Banner gone to be by his wife's side?" he said. "We know he gets caught up in his writing, but you'd think he'd be there for her."

"Maybe he has been?"

"We asked Claire to tell us if he showed up. Or at least tell Gold."

Freya met his stare, translating his furrowed brow into deep suspicion. With a few clicks of her phone, she'd found a contact and hit dial. The call tone sang out over the car's speakers.

"Ma'am?" the voice said when the call was answered. It had a faint Scottish accent and the tone was gentle.

"Gold, where are you?" Freya asked.

"I'm with Claire," she replied. "Is there a problem?"

"Any sign of Kevin?"

"No, none at all. He hasn't been home."

"Do you find that a little strange considering his wife's mother has died?"

"I said that to Claire. But she said he often does this when he's writing. He'll go off in his van. He could be gone for days."

"Jackie, it's me," Ben called out. "We need to find him. Can you ask Claire where he might be?"

The line quietened, and Freya imagined Jackie burying the phone into her shoulder. Muffled voices could be heard but without detail.

"She's not sure," Gold said. "He could be anywhere."

"What's he writing?" Freya asked. "His books are all set here in Lincolnshire. What's he working on now?"

Again, Gold buried the phone into her clothing, this time for a much longer. Eventually, her voice returned, loud and clear.

"We're checking his office," Gold said, amidst the sound of papers being ruffled.

"Can you put us on loudspeaker?" Freya asked, and the ambient noise altered. "Claire? Claire, it's Freya Bloom. We met yesterday."

"Hello," the voice said. "I really don't know what I'm looking for here. I don't often come in here."

"Anything," Freya said. "Anything at all. Notes, scraps of paper, any help at all."

"You can't think he had anything to do with it?" Claire said. "He wouldn't. I know they didn't get on, but–"

"We just need to eliminate him from our enquiries, Claire," Freya said. "It's standard procedure. I'm sorry to ask you to do this."

"I found something," Gold said, and Freya heard herself gasp with relief. "It looks like a brainstorm. Like he noted down ideas."

"What does it say?" Ben asked.

"Magna Carta. That's what's written in the middle, anyway. Then there's loads of things connected to it."

"Like what? Read them out, Jackie," Ben said.

"Edward the First. Twelfth century. Little Saint Hugh."

"Saint Hugh?"

"That's what it says," Gold said, then carried on reading out the brainstormed notes. "Imp. Robert Chesney. Harold Swain. That's it. That's all I have."

"I'll have Chapman run those names," Freya said. "Thank you, both."

"Ma'am?" Gold said as Freya was about to end the call.

"Yes?"

"Claire wants to visit her mum's house," she said, then waited for Freya to speak. Freya imagined her looking at Claire, biting down on her lower lip as she waited for permission.

"As long as you don't touch anything, I don't see a problem with it," Freya said. "CSI have been in there already. Just use common sense."

"I think Claire just wants to check her paperwork. You know? The funeral arrangements and such."

"Well, make a note of what is taken and supervise her at all times, please," Freya advised. "And that's for her own protection as much as ours. The last thing we need is a defence lawyer suggesting something was planted later down the line."

"Will do. Thanks, ma'am."

"And Gold?" Freya said, hoping that Jackie had heard her.

"Ma'am?"

"Have a word with the neighbours while you're there. See if they spotted anybody coming and going."

"I'll try," Gold replied. "Although I wouldn't hold your breath."

"And why's that?"

"My mother and the man next door didn't see eye to eye," Claire said, saving Jackie from having to think about how she worded the fact.

"Is this something you were going to tell us about?" Freya asked, then winced at her poor selection of tone.

"He's an old busy body, Inspector Bloom. The most he's capable of is cutting back her overgrown shrubs."

Freya gave it all some thought, then replied softly, "Okay. See what he has to say, Gold. And stay in touch, please."

"Will do, ma'am."

The call ended, and Freya turned to find Ben staring through the windscreen deep in thought.

"Thoughts?" she said.

"Lots of them," he replied, just as Freya's phone began to ring. Chapman's name flashed up on the car's screen, above the words, *Incoming call.* "Chapman," Freya said, after the first two rings, and she eyed Ben, trying to read his expression. "Give me some good news."

"Hi, ma'am. We've picked up the van on ANPR. It passed through two cameras. The first one was Bunkers Hill heading into the city, and then four minutes later, it passed through another camera near the Northgate."

"And then where did it go?" Freya asked.

"That's it, ma'am," Chapman replied. "No sign of it since."

"Then it's still in the cultural quarter, somewhere," Ben said. "Parked up."

"Parked up?" Freya said. "What's he doing?"

"Thanks, Chapman," Ben called out. "Talk to Sergeant Priest for me. Get a couple of uniforms in the area, will you?"

"He might have ditched the van and gone on foot," Freya said.

"No," Ben replied, and a grin began to form on his face. "I know exactly where he's gone. Chapman, if I said to you, Edward the First, Robert Chesney, and Harold Swain, what would you say?"

"What would I say?" Chapman said, then puffed out her cheeks, which was audible over the line. "I'd say if this is a quiz, then you'd be better off asking Cruz. He's the quiz night legend."

"What about if I said Little Saint Hugh and an imp."

"An imp?" Chapman repeated, and in the background, they could hear her typing the words into her keyboard.

"What's the common denominator, Chapman?" Ben asked, smiling as he waited for her reply.

"Oh," she said to herself, clearly reading the results of her internet search. "He's gone to the cathedral. Edward the First was the king who accused the Jewish community of killing Little Saint Hugh. Some say he was fictitious."

"And the imp?" Freya asked.

"The imp is nothing. It's just a sculpture in the ceiling. Tourists like to try to find it," Ben said. "Apparently it's part of some legend about an angel and two imps. The angel turned one of them to stone while the other got away."

"So, why is that pertinent?" Chapman said.

"It was in Banner's notes," said Ben. "My guess is he was noting down relevant points of interest for his story."

"Hold on, I've got something else," Chapman said. "Harold Swain is the Dean of Lincoln. Don't tell me he's gone there to do some research when his mother-in-law has just been killed?"

"What if he doesn't know about the murder yet?" Freya asked, voicing what she and Ben had discussed only minutes before. "What if he's just getting on with his everyday life?"

"There's only one way to find out," Ben said. "Chapman, we have an eyewitness stating Banner's van was seen at the scene, and we have a statement from his wife to say that he and Myra Dicks didn't get along. We're going to see if he'll come for a voluntary interview."

"Haven't we got enough to arrest him?"

"Probably," Freya said. "But if we do, we'll only have twenty-four hours to charge him. We need enough on him to get CPS behind us and I don't think we're there yet. If he refuses to come for an interview, then we'll have no choice, and then the pressure will be on."

"In that case, uniforms are on their way," Chapman replied.

"Thank you," Ben said, and he ended the call before turning to Freya. "Are you ready for this?"

She nodded.

"Let's try to do this without causing a scene, eh?" she said. "The last thing we need is our pictures in the papers."

CHAPTER TWENTY-FOUR

An introvert by nature, DC Jackie Gold always found small talk challenging. This was accentuated by the fact that Claire Banner, numbed by the death of her mother, sat bolt upright in the passenger seat, staring dead ahead, almost statuesque.

As the team's dedicated family liaison officer, Jackie was all too aware of how individuals processed death. Some people broke the moment they were told. Others, like Claire, needed time. It wasn't that the latter were mentally stronger, or had greater emotional intelligence. It was just how it was. The human mind has developed a keen sense of survival. Often, when other factors are in play, the brain will delay the emotion caused by loss until such a time when the tertiary factors have been dealt with. The fact is, everybody breaks eventually, and Claire had yet to do so.

Jackie had learned how to read the signs during the intensive FLO course she had attended. She had discovered a whole new side of policing that she hadn't seen before. To help people through grief, acting as the conduit between the investigating team and the victim's family, reading the signs to help them all, was what Jackie loved. Often, the role was passive, as opposed to the active roles of sitting in interviews with hateful individuals or scouring information searching for lies and deceit. Sometimes, all she had to do was listen, processing the information and waiting for something new, something fresh that could spark a new lead.

But as she navigated her way through Metheringham in silence, all she could think about was the other factor on Claire's mind. What was it that was preventing her from breaking, delaying the mourning process?

"It's just here," Claire said, and even without looking at her, Jackie knew that tears had begun to form. "It's the one with the brown door."

Jackie eased the car to a stop outside the house and appraised the property. It was a detached building which stood a good fifty feet from the neighbours' houses on both sides. The garden was lined by tall trees that hung over the fences, and the grass in the front garden was at least knee-high.

It was no surprise to Jackie that the neighbour to the left of Myra Dicks' house had a *For Sale* sign at the front, although it had clearly been on the market for some time as the bold colouring from the well-known local estate agents board had faded in the sun.

Claire had fished a set of keys from a pocket on the inside of her handbag. She inhaled hard, then climbed from the car.

"Do you mind if I go in alone?" Claire said, leaning back inside the car. "I just need a minute. You know? To remember."

"You heard what DI Bloom said," Jackie replied sympathetically. "You can't."

Claire gave a disappointed nod, then smiled the setback away with a stiff upper lip.

"I understand. I suppose you have to follow orders."

"It's just..." Jackie began, seeing a face at a window of the neighbouring house with the *For Sale* sign. The curtain fell back into place. "If you go in alone, I can't vouch for you. There might be something inside that could help us identify who did this, but if a defence lawyer found out you'd been in alone, we wouldn't be able to use it as evidence. Do you see, Claire? It's for your protection."

"But if you come with me?" Claire said.

"If I come with you, I can testify that the only items you touched were the documents."

Another of those tight-lipped half-smiles emerged on Claire's tired face. She looked up at the house as if Myra was about to walk out the front door. But she didn't. In fact, the only movement was the front door of the neighbouring house opening. A man stepped out, pulling on a check shirt.

"Now then," he called out, and he nodded at Claire, a sign the two were at least familiar with each other. "You alright, duck?"

"Oh God," Claire mumbled under her breath.

"Who's this?" Jackie asked, as the neighbour made his way out of his property and approached them.

"That's Vince Hodges, Mum's neighbour," she replied, then turned to meet Jackie's stare. "He can be a bit full-on. I don't know if I can cope with him right now."

"Would you like me to handle him?" Jackie asked, and the last of Claire's half-smiles formed, only this one was laden with gratitude.

"She's not in," Vince called. "Hasn't been home for a couple of days now."

Claire turned her attention to the house, trying her hardest not to make eye contact.

"Hi. Vince?" Jackie said, and she fished her warrant card from her pocket and let it hang open for him to see. "Detective Constable Gold. Lincolnshire Police. Can I have a quick word?"

"Police?" he said, studying Jackie from her boots all the way to her hair. "What's going on? Claire? You okay, duck?"

"Mr Hodges, perhaps you and I can step over here?" Jackie said, reaching for his arm to redirect him away from Claire.

"What's happened?" he said. "Claire? What's going on, love? She's not home, I tell you."

Claire ignored him.

"Is she alright?" he asked Jackie. "I don't understand."

They had reached the far border of Myra's property when Jackie finally stopped and addressed the man. Over his shoulder, Jackie watched Claire walk slowly along the garden path, seeming to run her hand through the mass of thorny shrubs that lined the overgrown as if she might feel some connection with her mother.

"Mr Hodges, how well do you know Claire and her family?"

"Claire?" he said, and his eyebrows seemed to unite as his brow furrowed. "Years. All her life, I dare say. Watched her grow up, I did."

"So, you knew Myra Dicks?"

"Of course we knew," he began. "Hold up. What do you mean *knew*?"

"I'm afraid Mrs Dicks has been found dead, Mr Hodges."

"Dead?" He glanced over his shoulder at Claire, who had crouched to inspect a rambling rose that filled the corner of a flower bed. Dark, red, velvet flower heads hung heavily on their stems, drooping as if the news had reached them already. "But how?"

In the distance, Claire stood upright, and with a glance back at Jackie, she made for the front door.

"Wait for me, Claire, please," Jackie called, then returned her attention to Vince. "When did you see Myra last, Mr Hodges?"

"Me? Pfff," he said, sucking in a deep breath and glancing across to his left as if trying to recall the moment. "Couple of days."

"Did you talk to her?" Jackie asked.

"Talk to her?" he said and gave a little laugh that was cut short with immediate effect. "No. No, Myra and me don't talk. Didn't talk. You know?"

"Oh?" Jackie said. "Why was that?"

"Long story. I won't bore you with the details," he said. "But she went out a couple of days ago. With her dog, you know? For a walk."

"She left to walk the dog?"

"Yeah. Always the same time. About lunchtime," he said, then turned towards the house, and Claire. "She's not going in there, is she?"

"I've asked her to wait for me," replied Jackie. "Why?"

He took a few steps away from Jackie. "Claire? Claire, don't go in there, sweetheart."

"Mr Hodges?" Jackie said, sensing a rise in tension. But he ignored her, and Jackie saw Claire raising her key to the door.

"Claire, don't do it. Not yet, love."

"Mr Hodges, is there a problem?" Jackie asked.

"You can't let her go in there. It'll destroy her."

"Destroy her?"

"They were close. Claire and Myra. I don't want her getting upset, is all. Myra was a very private person. There could be all sorts lying around. Things Myra might not have wanted Claire to see," he said, then called out again to Claire. "Claire, don't do it, love. Come away from there."

A part of Jackie wanted to call out to Claire to advise her not to open the door. But Vince was walking towards her now, and the last thing she needed was for him to enter the house.

"I'm just going to look," Claire called back, and she twisted the key in the lock.

"No," Vince called, and he seemed to be waiting for something to happen. Claire shoved the door open and turned back to them, making a point of staying on the doorstep. "Whatever you need from inside, love, I'll get it for you. Trust me. When my mum died, I thought I was okay until the day I stepped into her house. Then it all came at once. Flattened me, it did."

"He's right, Claire," Jackie said. "At least let me go in and have a good look around first."

Claire said nothing. She turned away from them and stared into the gloom of the house. From where Jackie was standing, she could have sworn Claire inhaled a breath, savouring that house smell that is unique to the owner.

She bent to collect some post from the doormat inside, then glanced at Jackie.

"Can I?" she asked, holding the post up, and Jackie nodded.

"Thank you, Mr Hodges," Jackie said. "I'll take it from here. Somebody will probably be in touch to get a formal statement. So, if you could make a few notes of what you remember, it might help us."

"Aye, right," he said, tearing his eyes from Claire briefly to acknowledge Jackie's request. "You alright, Claire?"

She nodded and flicked through the pile of letters. Jackie watched him return to his own home, offering furtive glances over his shoulder as he left.

"He seems to care for you," Jackie said, as she approached the house. She stood at the garden gate and Claire sauntered towards her. "I have a neighbour like that. She watches over my son like his second mother."

Claire let the letters fall to her side and stared at Jackie.

"He's okay. I just..."

"Go on," Jackie said.

"I feel bad for it," she said, "but I just get a bit creeped out by him. Cares a bit too much, you know?"

"Has he ever—"

"No. No, nothing like that. God knows, my mother would have killed him," she said, then looked away. "Sorry, that was poor taste."

"It's okay. I suppose you've earned a few comments in poor taste, after what you're going through," Jackie said. "Shall I go in first?"

Claire looked back at the house, the front door standing open. It was lifeless as if its soul had been taken when Myra had been killed.

"No," Claire said. "No, he's right. You were right. And your boss. It's too early. Besides, if there is something inside that could help..."

"Then we don't want to lose valuable evidence," Jackie said, holding her arm out to escort the grieving woman away.

"I'll just lock up," Claire said, and Jackie took a slow walk back to her car, giving her a few moments to remember. She watched Claire with admiration and wondered how strong she would be if it was her mother that had just died as Myra had. The truth was that Jackie would fall to pieces without her mum.

Claire used the key in the lock to pull the door closed, but just as the dark hallway disappeared from view, she stopped, like something had caught her attention. She opened the door again, holding onto the key.

"What is it, Claire?" Jackie called out, fearful that she might just go inside after all.

It took a few moments for Claire to respond. Her head was cocked like she was trying to figure something out.

"Claire?"

"I'm not sure," Claire called back, glancing at Jackie for a split second before returning her attention to the hallway.

"Leave it," Jackie called. "Whatever it is, leave it."

But Claire wasn't listening. She took a step inside.

"Claire?" Jackie called.

She reached up to feel along the wall, and for a moment, time seemed to freeze. A light flickered on in the hallway then flashed off before Jackie could see any detail. Claire stopped in the doorway, flicking the switch on and off a few times. Then, as quickly as she had entered, she turned back, pulling the door closed behind her. She pocketed the keys and shrugged at Jackie.

"I guess it's nothing," Claire began, but she had barely finished speaking when the downstairs windows burst in a shower of glass, and the front door was torn from its hinges by a raging fireball.

CHAPTER TWENTY-FIVE

"Are you hoping he catches you with his whip and drags you close to him?" Anna asked as they pulled into Devon Street again. She drove past the red door and found a place to park fifty yards away, tucking her little hatchback into a space between two vans.

"Yeah, right," Jenny replied. "He's like a hybrid of Hugh Jackman and Michael Fish, with more essence of the latter. What are we doing anyway? You could park outside his house."

"I don't want to frighten him off," Anna replied. "How long until uniform get here?"

"They're on their way. A few minutes."

"Right, come on. Let's do this," Anna said, and she climbed from the car, noting that even though Jenny hadn't checked her make up and hair this time, she still looked good. She was just one of those women. "Do you have the warrant?"

Jenny tapped her breast pocket.

"Hopefully we won't need it," she said, as Anna reached up and rapped on the door three times. She stepped back and looked up at the house, just as a curtain in the front twitched.

"Did you see that?" Anna asked. "Knock again, will you?"

She peered through the window as Jenny knocked again, three times to mimic Anna's.

"He's going out the back door," Anna said, with her hands against the glass to block the sunlight. "Round the back, now."

Immediately, Jenny was on her toes, sprinting towards the end of the road. Anna watched a few seconds longer to make sure he didn't turn back, then ran in the opposite direction, hoping to head him off at the other end of the alleyway. By the time she reached the end of the road, her heart was pumping wildly. She turned the corner to find two uniforms in a liveried car idling along. She waved to catch their attention, and when the passenger lowered his window, she screamed for them to go to Jenny, pointing in the direction she had come from.

The blues and twos were switched on and the driver put his foot down, leaving Anna alone. It was times like these that she prayed he was going her way. A little action was good for the soul.

She ran the few steps to the back alley, slowed, and then stopped to peer around the edge. But Adam Frost was not hot-footing it towards her. Nor was he anywhere in sight. The only person Anna could see at the far end of the alleyway was Jenny, rolling around on the ground, clutching her stomach.

Anna was beside her in seconds. She dropped to her knees as Jenny rolled onto all fours, severely winded.

"Which way?" Anna said, visually appraising Jenny for signs of further injuries.

"I don't know," Jenny said, and she forced a lungful of air into her body as the liveried car passed on the road a few metres away, sirens and lights blaring. The driver slammed on the brakes, bringing the car to a halt. The passenger door opened.

"Get after him," Anna screamed. "Male, mid-forties, cream top and jeans. Go."

The passenger hesitated for a second as if deliberating whether or not to offer help. But one more look from Anna set him on the right path, and a few seconds later, the sirens could be heard echoing off the nearby houses.

"I'm okay," Jenny said. "I'm sorry. He came out of nowhere."

"Don't worry, he won't get far," Anna said, and she dragged her to a nearby wall to lean on. "Call it in. I'm going to check the house. Will you be okay for a moment?"

Jenny nodded and let her head drop between her knees.

Anna stood, glanced at the back gates to the row of houses on Devon Street, and then saw that one was open. It was the rear entrance to Frost's house. If they didn't get him, she'd find something in his house to get him for, in addition to assaulting a police officer.

She stepped through into a small rear yard, which she gauged to be twenty feet by fifteen with a small shed in the corner, presumably a converted coal bunker. The back door to the house was open and Anna took a step inside. He'd been cooking and the stove was still on. Some cheap sausages were spitting fat across the hob, and on a wooden chopping board, two slices of bread were ready to butter.

Anna turned the gas off and moved back into the living space where the dining table was still covered in paperwork, exactly as it had been during her previous visit. She leafed through a few documents. Areas in nearby Washingborough and Heighington had been circled in highlighter pen on printed maps, and there were letters, printed emails, and endless copies of historical nonsense, in addition to stapled proposals marked with a red stamp bearing the words *Not Approved*.

She tossed the paperwork back down onto the table and scooped up a selection from another pile. It was more mind-numbing drivel. But then something caught her eye. Another printed map, but this time it was somewhere a little more familiar. The map was of Dunston and Metheringham, and the area that had been highlighted was just two or three hundred yards from where Anna estimated Myra Dicks body had been found – a small space on the raised bank of the River Witham. She flicked through the pile of papers beneath it, and among the printed correspondence, she found a stack bound with a staple.

The front page read *Proposal for Investigative Excavation - Location: Dunston.* But of interest was the red ink stamp in the top right-hand corner.

Not Approved - Heritage Advisory Board.

The stamp had been authenticated with a signature running through the ink.

Myra Dicks.

Anna collected the papers of interest into her own pile, using the last of the free space. She had just tapped the edges on the table to straighten the pile when she heard a noise from upstairs. It was slight and, had she been in her own house, she might have considered the sound to be the building settling.

But she wasn't in her own house and the noise was alien in the near silence. Slowly, she moved through to the hallway and peered up the stairs. A gentle sobbing sound could be heard, then a sniff, wet and thick.

As quietly as she could, Anna ascended the stairs. The first door was a bathroom, which was empty, save for a wet towel on the floor along with a pile of clothes. There were two other doors, one of which was closed, the other ajar. She pushed the second door, and there sitting on the edge of the bed with his head in his hands was Adam Frost.

She waited a moment, studying him with curiosity and wondering what dilemma was going through his mind, and what on earth had made him run.

Then, with her feet planted, she announced her presence.

"Adam Frost," she began, and he sat up in surprise and edged away from her. "I'm arresting you on suspicion of assaulting a police officer. You do not have to say anything. But, it may harm your defence if you do not mention when questioned something which you later rely on in court. Anything you do say may be given in evidence."

"I'm sorry," he said. "I'm so sorry. I didn't mean to hurt her–"

"Save it," Anna said. "You've got some explaining to do, Mr Frost. Down at the station."

CHAPTER TWENTY-SIX

"Do you know, I haven't been in here since I was a boy," Ben said, as they entered Lincoln Cathedral's nave. The air was cool, and even his breathing seemed to echo from the eaves far above. He took a moment to take in the scene. It was just as he remembered it from all those years before. The gentle hum of voices somewhere beyond the choir, at the presbytery. The way the light from the dean's window caused the hundreds of sculptures to appear as if they were dancing, grinning, or following his awestruck gaze.

He glanced across at Freya, who for once in her life, seemed to be struck dumb. "Beautiful, isn't it?"

She licked her lips and swallowed, taking a brief moment to conceal her true thoughts.

"It's wonderful," she said dryly. "How do we find the dean?"

Ben looked along the length of the cathedral, realising that he had absolutely no idea.

"I suppose he'll be the one wearing the big hat," Ben replied, hoping to catch even the beginnings of a smile creep onto Freya's face.

But no smile came.

"He's the Dean of Lincoln, Ben. Not the bloody Archbishop of Canterbury," Freya replied. "And it's not a hat. It's a mitre."

"Actually, it's called the Canterbury Cap," a voice said from behind them. They turned to find a pleasant-looking, mature lady with rosy-red cheeks, and the type of perfume that, in Ben's opinion, wasn't too dissimilar to the smell of the little, yellow blocks found in the Red Lion urinals. "I'm sorry. I overheard you. It's hard not to in here."

She gestured at the magnificence of the place with a proud smile.

"May I ask who you are?" Freya said. It was a blunt question that some might have taken out of context and found mildly offensive. But the lady bore the question with grace and the type of manners rarely found in Ben's line of work.

"Janice," she replied. "Janice Trehern. I'm what they call a lay member of the chapter."

"A lay member?" Ben said, hoping she might indulge him with a bit more insight into what that actually meant, and whether or not she could help them.

"I help out here," she said, waving off Ben's clear lack of under-standing. "You're looking for the dean. Is that right?"

"That's correct," Freya said. "And she held her warrant card open for the lady to inspect.

"Oh, I see," Janice said. Ordinarily, women of Janice's age gasped when they were presented with the police logo. But if the lady in front of them was at all shocked, she did a good job of hiding it. "Well, then you'd better follow me."

Without waiting, Janice stepped around them and marched down the central aisle. Freya followed close behind, leaving Ben to bring up the rear, breathing in a strange concoction of Janice's floral yet urinal scent and Freya's expensive yet masculine perfume. A few tourists stood to one side, one of them pointing high into the eaves.

"He's busy this morning," Janice said, hissing over her shoulder to be heard without disturbing any of the visitors. She came to a stop outside a door in what Ben assumed was the transept. She gripped the handle, and Ben heard the rumble of deep voices inside. "But I'm sure he'll squeeze you in."

"Wait," Ben said, and Janice froze, staring at him, a little confused. Ben cupped his hand to his ear. "Is that him I can hear?"

Janice cocked her head to one side, then nodded.

"Yes, that's him. He has a lovely voice. You should hear his sermons—"

"We'll wait," Ben said, ignoring Freya's quizzical stare. "We're not in a rush, and well, he obviously has a visitor already."

In his peripheral, Ben saw Freya relax as she realised what he was doing.

"He's right," she said. "If he has a visitor, perhaps their needs are greater than ours. I wouldn't feel comfortable interrupting something important."

"Well, that's lovely of you," Janice said, her face beaming.

"We'll just wait here," Ben added.

"I'm sure he won't be too long," Janice replied. "If you need anything else, I'll just be over by Saint Hugh."

"Saint Hugh?" Ben said, recalling one of the names on the list Jackie had read out.

"That's great. Thanks so much for your help," Freya said, offering Janice a kind smile, before turning her back and leaning on the wall outside the office.

"What can you hear?" Ben asked, and she winced, irritated as she tried to listen in to the conversation inside.

Feeling quite conspicuous, Ben leaned on the wall on the other side of the door frame, focusing on the two rumbling voices inside. He stared at Freya as he listened, tuning out the growing hum of visitors from various parts of the huge building.

"I really do appreciate you taking the time to talk to me," the first voice said. "To tell the truth, I didn't think you'd give me the time of day."

"It's an absolute pleasure," the second voice said, which was far deeper with age. It was the type of voice Ben imagined would fill the entire cathedral, capturing everyone's attention. "Did I tell you, my wife's a fan?"

"Oh really? Well, I'll have to send you a copy of this one. I could even mention you in the acknowledgements."

"No, no. Honestly," the older of the men said, then continued with some reservation in his tone. "I'm all for helping out where I can, but there are a few individuals that might frown at seeing my name published in the back of a murder mystery, however innocent it might be."

"Well, then that begs the question of why *they* might be seeing your name there in the first place," the younger man said, and Ben imagined the two men sharing a casual smile at some stuffy, old has-been secretly reading a murder mystery. Freya caught Ben's attention with a glance and a shake of her head. "It's not like you told me the best place to bury a body here, is it?"

Freya's eyebrows flicked up as a dog's ears might at the sound of somebody approaching the front door.

"No, you're right," the older man said. "Anyway, you probably know the answer to that one better than I do anyway. How many is it now?"

"Murders?" the younger man said. "Thirty-something. I lose track if I'm honest. I suppose I should make an effort. You know? In case anybody comes looking for a few more details."

"That's incredible," the older man said. "I don't know where you find the time, and what's more, I don't know how you plan them all so well."

"Years of experience," the younger man said, and Ben pictured an accompanying wink. A scrape of chairs followed, along with more pleasantries as the two men likely shook hands.

"If you need anything else, I'll be only too happy to help," the rumbled voice groaned, the sound of a mature man pushing himself from his seat.

"Access to the crypt?" the younger man said, and the two men shared a laugh before the door opened, and both Ben and Freya stepped away from the wall. "I'll send you a copy in the post. For your wife, of course."

"She'd be over the moon, Mr Banner. Thank you," the older man said, as the door opened fully. He smiled at Freya and Ben, and gave a wave of his hand as if to say, 'I'll be with you in a moment.'

Kevin Banner shook the older man's hand once more, then turned, and apologised when he saw Ben and Freya, as is both the way of the English and the guilty alike. He turned to sidestep past Freya with a polite, "He's all yours."

"Actually, Mr Banner, it's you we came to see," Ben said, and the pair of them discreetly showed their warrant cards. "Can we have a word?"

"A word? With me?"

A gentle vibration began in Ben's pocket and he reached for his phone. It was Chapman's desk phone.

"Perhaps you'd like to use my office?" Harold Swain said. His voice boomed in the transept, reminding Ben of when his mum used to watch *Songs of Praise*, with the show's presenter Harry Secombe. "It's quite private, you know?"

He stared down at his phone again.

"Can I take this in there?" Ben asked, and the dean nodded.

"May I ask what this is about?" Banner asked.

Ben stepped inside the office, finding the room to resemble the type of back office he'd found in dozens of warehouse searches in his time on the force. The room lacked the grandeur of its surroundings but clearly served a purpose. Freya followed Banner back into the room and closed the door behind them, thanking Harold Swain and gesturing that they would only be a few minutes.

Ben hit the button to answer the call.

"What on earth is this about?" Banner asked, and any polite tones he had used previously had all but gone from his voice.

"Chapman?" Ben said. "Everything okay?"

She spoke clearly and slowly, relaying an urgent message with professionalism. It was like Ben had been hit by a bat. He stared at Banner, the man they had tracked to the cathedral with every intention of bringing him in.

"Thanks for letting me know," Ben said, and ended the call, letting the phone drop to his side.

"Well?" Banner said, his voice rising with clear irritation. He held his hands out, expecting an answer. "How did you even know I would be here?"

"I'm afraid we've got some bad news for you, Mr Banner," Freya said.

"Bad news?" he said. "What bad news?"

"It's your wife," Ben said, cutting Freya off and receiving a hostile glare in return.

Banner stared at him, his head cocked to one side. "My wife?"

"I'm afraid there's been an accident," Ben said, and he turned his attention to Freya. "She's hurt."

Banner looked shocked. "What? Where is she? I want to see her."

"You can," Ben said. "But we have a few questions we'd like to ask you first."

"Questions? What questions? And how the hell did you find me here?"

"Perhaps we can explain in a little more depth, Mr Banner," Freya said, "at the station."

CHAPTER TWENTY-SEVEN

Despite their efforts not to cause a scene, all eyes in the cathedral were on them as Freya led Kevin Banner through the nave towards the exit. Ben walked behind them, a menacing reminder that should Banner run, he wouldn't get far.

"Are you going to tell me what happened to my wife?" Banner said, for the third time. "Is she okay?"

"There was an explosion at your mother-in-law's house this afternoon. She's alive, Mr Banner," Ben said. "That's all we know."

Freya stepped out into the warm evening air, noting the liveried car that was waiting nearby. Had Banner tried to run, he wouldn't get far. The space was enclosed on all sides by what appeared to be ancient buildings, some of them medieval. At one end was a huge, stone gateway with its ornate arch, and at the other end, the road that led out to the busy city.

"What's this?" Banner said, seeing the car parked nearby with two uniforms standing at its side. "What the bloody hell is going on here?"

"Like we said, we need to ask you a few questions, Mr Banner," Freya said. "At the station."

"I want to see my wife. If she's hurt–"

"We can argue about this all day if you want," Freya said.

"My wife—"

"Is in good hands, and very likely unable to receive visitors," Freya finished for him.

"I don't understand. You said you..." He paused. His eyes narrowed and his mouth hung open as his mind fathomed Freya's expression. "You were looking for me. You must have been."

His tone was almost accusing, and as he said the words, it was clear he was beginning to develop a story.

"Nobody knew I was here," he said. "You said the explosion was this afternoon."

"I think we should discuss this at the station," Freya said, and she waved the uniforms over.

"I'm not going to the bloody police station. I want to see my wife."

"Well, the quicker you answer our questions, the quicker you can go and see her. You can either go voluntarily, or we can arrest you. But I'm sure you don't want to cause a scene," Freya said, then turned to the approaching uniforms. "Take him back to the station, will you? We'll meet you there."

The uniforms waited patiently for Banner to move, but he stayed put.

"So, I'm not under arrest?" he said.

"Not yet, but you can be, if you want to be," Ben said. "We thought we'd give you the opportunity to volunteer some information."

"Information? What information? I don't know what bloody happened. I haven't been home for days. How the hell would I know what's happened? I didn't even know she was going to her mother's house."

"That's the other thing that concerns me, Mr Banner," Freya said. "You haven't once asked how your mother-in-law is, or if she was hurt."

"So?" he said, much softer than before.

Freya waited, watching his face work through a charade of expressions.

"How is she, then?" he asked quietly.

"Dead, Mr Banner. Your mother-in-law is dead," Freya said. "I'm sure you understand why we need to speak to you, now."

"Dead?"

"I'm afraid so."

"Myra? Myra Dicks? You're sure you have the right person?"

"We're positive."

"I don't understand," he began, then paused again, his eyes widening. "And you think I had something to do with it?"

"I think we need to ask you a few questions, Mr Banner. That's all," Freya said, and he turned his face away, processing the information.

"And I can see my wife afterwards?"

"That all depends on what you tell us, Mr Banner," Ben said. "The question is whether or not you come to the station voluntarily, or..." He gestured at the uniforms, and Banner rolled his eyes.

"Not much of a choice, is it?" Banner said.

Freya gave the uniforms the nod and they stepped in to usher Banner away.

"This isn't right. Surely you should let me see my wife," Banner called back, with each of the uniforms holding one of his elbows. But his argument grew stronger, forcing the uniforms to coax him along with a little more effort. "This isn't right. I want to see my wife."

He continued to call out all the way to the car.

"He didn't seem very upset to hear about his mother-in-law," Ben said.

"Tell me what Chapman told you," Freya replied, as they both watched the car pull away with Banner's face at the rear window.

"Only that Gold accompanied Claire Banner to Myra Dicks' house. There was some kind of explosion. Gas, she thinks. Uniform have the scene closed off."

"And Jackie?" Freya asked. "Is she okay?"

"It was Jackie who called it in. From what I can gather, the blast blew the front door off its hinges and was probably what protected Claire Banner from the flames."

"So, she's alive?"

"Alive but heavily concussed," Ben replied. "Jackie's at the hospital with her now. Chapman is lining up CSI and the fire service to investigate the cause of the blast."

"So Myra Dicks is strangled to death then a gas leak destroys her house."

"We don't know if it was gas yet."

"Oh, come on. What else could it have been? Whoever did this wanted her dead, Ben," Freya said. "Get Gillespie and Cruz on the scene. Maybe the neighbours saw somebody come and go? I'll call a briefing for this afternoon. Talk to Michaela. See if she can get the forensic results on fast track."

"Me? What makes you think she'll hurry them up for me?"

"Because she has a soft spot for you, Ben," Freya explained. "Despite your previous attempts."

"A soft spot? I think I well and truly blew my chances with her, Freya."

"I'm not asking you to marry her, Ben. I'm asking you to do your bloody job and get some results. So, don't forget to sprinkle her with some of that rugged charm you're famous for."

"Rugged charm?" Ben said, and his face screwed up in astonishment. "What do you think I am?"

But Freya ignored him, deep in thought. "Hopefully, we can get some answers from her. I'd settle for anything right now."

"DCI Granger will need to go public with this. Even he can't brush an explosion under the carpet."

Freya considered the facts, nodding her agreement. "If I can give Granger the CSI results, along with a plan of action, that should keep him happy. Nillson and Anderson should have something for us by then, too."

"Lots of moving parts," Ben said contemplatively.

"We have one dead body, Ben, and if you count Claire Banner, one attempted murder. We need to make some progress before this escalates."

"Kevin Banner?"

Freya nodded. "How far is the hospital from here?"

"Five minutes on foot."

"Let's go and see Gold. I want to make sure she's okay. We should arrange for her family to visit. She'll want them to know she's okay."

"I'll ask Chapman to make the arrangements," Ben said. "What about Banner?"

"Let's leave him to stew for a while. Give him some time to gain some perspective, perhaps. I find an hour or so in a cell is good for that sort of thing."

"I'll bear that in mind," Ben said. "The next time I try to understand you."

Freya ignored him and seemed to be voicing her thoughts more than engaging with him.

"All we need is his movements for the past few days. I'd be keen to understand why his van was seen in the area."

"We don't know that it was *his* van. There must be loads of blue vans out there."

"If there's one thing we can be certain of it's that coincidences are rare. That said, I think we should give him the opportunity to give his version of events. I'd be keen to know how much detail he provides, and how easily. If, later on, we discover he withheld information, or if he got a little creative in his storytelling, then we'll have even more reason to bring him in on a more formal appointment, something CPS can't argue about."

"And if he doesn't have much to say?" Ben asked.

"Let's cross that bridge when we come to it. Right now, we have a team member who was involved in an explosion," Freya said. "Besides, I want to see Claire Banner. Something tells me she hasn't been completely honest with us."

CHAPTER TWENTY-EIGHT

The accident and emergency department at Lincoln Hospital was exactly as Freya had expected it to be on a weekday evening – filled with tired and restless children, tired and frustrated parents, and a handful of lone adults with no sign of injury or discomfort at all. They waited their turn and then approached the counter, where a middle-aged lady continued to type into a computer without so much as a gesture for them to wait. Eventually, she signalled she was ready to hear what they had to say by shifting her dull grey eyes at Freya and raising her eyebrows expectantly.

"We're here to see Jackie Gold," Freya began. "She was admitted earlier this afternoon."

"And you are?" the lady replied, turning her attention back to the computer and presumably typing in Jackie's name.

"Colleagues," Freya said, feeling Ben's burning stare. No doubt he would have just flashed his warrant card, but Freya rather enjoyed testing the Public Health Service to see what kind of response the general public received.

"I'm afraid you'll have to wait. Close family only, and she's already had her son and mother go through," the lady said, then looked past

Freya to a man with no apparent injuries who had joined the queue behind them. "Next."

"Charlie, you mean?"

The lady held her hand up to the gent behind them and sneered at Freya. "Excuse me?"

"Charlie. Jackie's son. He's here, is he?"

"I didn't get the boy's name. Now if you'll excuse me—"

"You see, she was in a bit of an accident," Freya said, and the lady behind the counter sighed audibly.

"Well, she's in the right place then, isn't she?" she said. "Now, if you'll just take a seat—"

"Well, I say accident. What I really mean to say is that she was involved in an explosion."

"An explosion?" she replied under her breath. She raised a hand to her temple and rubbed it in a small circle. "I've heard it all now."

"You have another patient. Claire Banner," Freya said. "They were both involved. My understanding is that she came off slightly worse. Quite a bit worse, as it happens."

A few keystrokes later and the lady nodded, and gave Freya an irritated expression.

"Sorry, who did you say you were?"

"Oh, my apologies," Freya replied, fishing her warrant card from her pocket. "Detective Inspector Bloom. This is Detective Sergeant Savage. We'd just like a few words with the victims."

The lady shook her head in astonishment.

"Why didn't you just say who you were?"

"I didn't realise that flashing my badge unlocks a premium level of service," Freya replied.

The lady stared at her, then at Ben, who smirked and rolled his eyes.

"Through the doors all the way to the end. You'll find another reception. They'll point you in the right direction."

"Ever so kind," Freya said, mustering every ounce of sarcasm she could. Then she leaned in closer and lowered her voice. "I hope if ever I end up in here one day, I'm conscious enough to flash my badge."

The lady stared at her but only managed a second or two before her face reddened and she called to the man behind them, "Next."

"You really are a piece of work," Ben said, as they shoved their way through a set of double doors.

"Not really, Ben. If there's one thing I can't stand, it's rudeness. It's one of the lowest traits of society, in my opinion."

"You don't know how long she's been at that desk. She could be at the end of a twelve-hour shift for all we know."

"And that's an excuse to treat people like that, is it?"

"Treat people like what?"

"Like they don't deserve to be spoken to with any courtesy, Ben. It's downright rude. There's absolutely no need for it."

"Wow," Ben replied, as they marched along the corridor.

"What?"

He shook his head in disbelief.

"I'm going to record you one day so you can hear how you talk to people."

"I'm not rude, Ben, and neither am I discourteous. Blunt, opinionated, and too clever for my own good, yes. But never am I rude."

"Oh no," he replied. "God forbid you'd ever be discourteous. Short maybe. Blunt, often. Patronising, sarcastic, and forthright yes. But, no, never discourteous."

Freya stopped walking and grabbed onto his arm so the two were face to face.

"Is there a problem?" she said. "I was kind of hoping that you and I had reached some sort of agreement."

He shook his head and glanced down for her to remove her hand from his arm.

"Is this because I turned you down?" she hissed.

"Turned me down?" he cried out in amazement. "Freya, you dragged me to Paris, damn near tore my clothes off, and then tossed me away at the first sign of a promotion. I'd hardly call it turning me down. More like chewing me up and spitting me out. So, forgive me if I take longer than a single day to come to terms with it. But you know what? It's okay. I can handle it. I'm not going to let being chewed up and spat out get in the way of our jobs. So no, this is not about us. It's not about me whatsoever. It's about you and the way you bloody treat people."

"If you have a problem with the way I talk to people, why have you never mentioned it before?"

"Because normally, I can laugh it off. We all have our little foibles, Freya. But that..." he said, jabbing his index finger at the double doors they had just passed through. "That was outrageous. You purposefully led that woman down the garden path, gathering all the ammo you needed to bring her down a peg or two at the end. It was uncalled for. You could have just flashed your warrant card and we'd have been let straight through. But no, you had to push her buttons, didn't you?"

"I didn't like her tone. And I don't bloody well enjoy being ignored."

"Well, imagine how the rest of us feel, Freya, when you're on your high horse."

"Is that how you feel?"

"It doesn't matter how I *feel*. My *feelings* aren't relevant. This is work. It's my job. It's not play school."

"And the others? Do they feel the same way?"

He sighed and put his hands on his hips. "I don't know, Freya. I don't bitch about you to anybody. There aren't any little gatherings in the gents or writing on the walls about you. You can just be a..."

"A what, Ben?" she said.

Suddenly, Freya was acutely aware they were being watched, and from Ben's changing expression, so was he. Slowly, they both turned their heads towards the end of the corridor, where they found a young boy, wide-eyed.

"Mum says everyone can hear you," he said.

"Charlie?" Ben said. "Is that you?"

The boy nodded.

"Blimey, look at you."

"Mum said to tell you she's in here," he replied and glanced to his side then back at them.

"Tell your mum we're just coming," Freya said. "We'll be there in a second."

He nodded and disappeared from view, leaving them with two

options – continue the argument, or leave it where it was. Freya guessed Ben would want to leave it, but he'd started something now.

"You were saying?" she said, quietly this time.

"Leave it," he replied.

"No, if I recall, you were about to insult me. You could at least have the decency to finish with a noun."

"Bitch," he said without faltering. "Sometimes you can be a complete bitch."

Freya prided herself on her ability to let insults wash off her, like Teflon. But somehow, when Ben spoke that word, that single syllable, it hurt. It hurt far more than Freya was ready for.

"I'm sorry..." he began.

"No. No, don't apologise. I deserve it. I've been unkind. Selfish, even. You don't deserve to be treated like that."

"Freya–"

"What I did wasn't fair," she said before he could try to convince her not to take it to heart. She checked the corridor to make sure nobody was within earshot. "I hoped we could be something. Honestly, I really hoped we could, and I thought we were there."

"It's not about that–"

"It is about that, Ben. And even if it's not, you deserve an answer. The truth is, since I arrived in Lincolnshire, you've shown me nothing but kindness. I can't tell you how many nights I've dreamed you were by my side, fantasised about it even. But the fact is that no matter how we dress it up, we either work together or we be together. We can't do both."

"I know," he said.

"You don't get it," Freya said. "Even if we tried to keep it under wraps–"

"I said, I know," Ben said, and Freya stopped talking. "I've known it all along. And you know what? At one point, I would have gladly thrown away my career to be with you."

"No–"

"I would," he said, silencing her. "But at the end of the day, I have to ask myself what's more important. Being *with* you, or being around you, as a friend."

"And?" she said softly.

"I didn't mean all those things I said."

"Yes, you did."

He waited a moment then smiled that boyish grin.

"You're right. I did. You *can* be a bitch," he said, as he took a slow step to start them moving again. "Shall we?"

She walked beside him, each of them walking slowly, contemplating what was said.

"So we're okay?" Freya asked quietly.

"Yeah, we're fine. I mean, I *was* disappointed, but you're right," he replied, as they rounded the corner and were faced with a series of curtained-off beds. He leaned in and whispered into her ear, "Besides, the way I see it, I've got the best of both worlds. I've sampled the goods, as it were."

"Sampled the *what*?" she cried. But Ben ignored her and stepped into the open cubicle to stand beside Jackie's bed, ruffling Charlie's hair.

"How's the patient?" he said to Jackie, whose left hand had been bandaged. He glanced back at Freya and winked.

"Oh, I'll be fine," Jackie replied, looking suspiciously between Freya and Ben. "It's just a few fragments of glass. They've got most of them out."

"She was lucky," Jackie's mother added, with far more of a Scottish accent than Jackie. "It could have been far worse."

"Mum, leave it."

"I'm just saying. You told me this FLO thing was safer. Said you'd be making tea and talking, just talking."

"Mum?" Jackie hissed, accompanied by a stern glare. She turned to Ben and Freya. "You didn't have to come."

"Of course we had to come," Ben said and took Charlie by his shoulders. "That's what friends do, isn't it? We look out for each other."

'Well...'' Jackie began, but Ben dropped to a crouch beside Charlie.

"Your mum's a hero. Did you know that?"

"I'm not a hero—"

"She's a hero, Charlie. You should be proud of her, like we are," he said, looking Freya in the eye. "We're proud to be her friends."

"Wow," Jackie said with a laugh, and she turned to her boy. "Charlie, this is what it sounds like when somebody wants something from you."

Charlie didn't quite understand, but Freya did, and she had to hand it to Jackie for handling it well.

"We did come to see you, Jackie," she said.

"And?"

"And I'd like you to talk to Claire for us."

"For you?"

"Okay then *with* us. I'm afraid she won't open up to me alone. I seem to lack empathy," Freya said, then added, "apparently, anyway."

CHAPTER TWENTY-NINE

"How are you feeling?" Anna asked as she pushed through the door to the fire escape stairwell into the ground floor corridor.

Jenny followed, carrying a blue file. "I'm alright. I just feel a bit set back. Do you know what I mean?"

"It's knocked your confidence?"

"I just need to get back on the bike," Jenny explained.

"What actually happened? Did he hit you?"

"No, nothing like that," Jenny said. "I heard the sirens and I figured uniform were close by. So, I ran into the alleyway and smashed straight into him. He must have been running at full pelt. Knocked me flying."

"And I suppose he must have heard the sirens too and legged it back to his house, hoping we'd be running around the streets looking for him?"

"I suppose so. To be honest, the next minute or so was a blur. Until you came, that is."

"Well, if whatever happens, we can charge him for assaulting a police officer."

"No," Jenny said when they came to interview room one. She dropped her voice to a whisper. "I don't want to push forward with that."

"But, Jenny–"

"I don't want it on my record," she said. "I don't want people knowing."

"It's nothing to be embarrassed about."

"I know. I just..." she said, clearly having some difficulty finding the words. "I just want to forget about it."

Anna studied her, noting the way she couldn't meet her eye to eye.

"Alright," she said. "If that's what you want."

"It is."

"We'd better hope he talks then," Anna said, as the door at the far end of the corridor opened up and Sergeant Priest leaned through.

"All yours, Anna," he called out in his heavy Yorkshire accent. "Room one. He's ready and waiting."

"Legal rep?"

"Didn't want it," Priest said.

"Alright, thank you," Anna said, and with one hand on the door handle, she turned to Jenny. "Ready to get back on the horse?"

Jenny nodded.

"Yep. Let's do this."

They pushed through into the room, finding Adam Frost seated in one of the chairs and a uniform waiting patiently behind the door.

"Thanks," Anna said to him. "You can leave now."

The uniform nodded a thanks and left the room, closing the door behind him, while Anna and Jenny prepared for the interview. Jenny began by setting up the recording while Anna flicked through the files.

Neither said a word and the silence, as Anna had hoped, seemed to heighten Frost's anxiety.

"This is a bit much, isn't it?" he said, to which Anna said nothing. She made a point of reordering the paperwork in her file, while Frost fidgeted opposite her. "I declined the offer of legal support."

Again, Anna said nothing, at least until Jenny hit the button to initiate the recording and a loud buzzer commenced for a few seconds.

Anna announced the date and time and then listed those present. Finally, she took a deep breath and stared at Frost.

"Now then, Mr Frost. Do you understand why you're here?"

"Assaulting a police officer, you said. But I didn't mean to."

"You didn't mean to assault a police officer?" Anna asked.

"No. It was an accident."

"And how did that accident happen?"

"She was in my way."

"In your way? So what, you shoved her?"

"No. Nothing like that. I was..." he said, then gave up trying to hide the truth. "I was running."

"Ah, I see. And why was it you were running, Mr Frost? You aren't exactly dressed for a morning jog, and you left your back door not just unlocked but wide open. Surely that's a little careless? Not to mention the sausages you were cooking on the grill."

He stared at her and Anna could see the cogs in his mind whirring, so she decided to fill the gap.

"Perhaps it was because you saw us at your front door and you heard us knock?" she said. "Do you agree?"

He sighed and nodded.

"For the recording, please?"

"Yes," he said aloud.

"Okay, then," Anna continued. "So perhaps you could tell us why it was you ran when you saw it was us at your door? As I understand it, the last time we spoke, you told us that your car had been stolen, which would make you the victim of a crime. Victims do not run, Mr Frost. At least, not in my experience."

He said nothing.

"Anything to say?" Anna asked, but he just stared at her, as if he wanted to say something but was also afraid of something.

"Okay then, perhaps we can move on," she said. "Can you please tell me about your relationship with Myra Dicks?"

"With who?"

"Myra Dicks," she repeated.

The name seemed to catch him off guard and he gave her a quizzical look.

"She's the woman from the heritage board, isn't she?"

"The Heritage Advisory Board," Anna said. "Yes, she is. So, you do know her?"

"I know of her. Of course I do. I dare say every archaeologist in Britain knows who she is," he said. "I'm sorry, what does she have to do with this? Was it her who called you lot? Is that what this is about? Bloody woman is a thorn in my side, I can tell you. Whatever she's said about me–"

"She hasn't said a word about you, Mr Frost," Anna said, and stopped his rant.

"She hasn't?"

Anna shook her head.

"She couldn't, even if we asked her."

"I'm sorry. I don't understand."

"She's dead, Mr Frost," Anna explained. "We found her body on Sunday."

He sat wide-eyed with his mouth ajar.

"Dead, you say?"

"Murdered, to be precise."

That was when it struck him. The realisation that he wasn't there purely for assaulting a police officer.

"Well, I didn't bloody do it," he said, his voice rising in pitch. "If that's what you think, you can think again–"

"Your car was discovered parked close to hers in the Stepping Out car park in Dunston, just off Dunston Fen Lane," Anna replied.

"My car? I told you, it was stolen."

"And by coincidence, the thief abandoned it close to where a woman's body was found, a woman who, as we have since discovered, you have had several professional disagreements with."

"Disagreements?" he muttered. "Yes. Yes, I have..." His voice seemed to fade away. "I'm sorry, how did she die?"

"We probably don't need to go into those details, Mr Frost. Not yet anyway," Anna said. "What we could do is discuss why you were in Dunston last Sunday at the same time Myra Dicks was."

"I didn't know she was there."

"So you *were* there?" Anna said, and he puffed his cheeks out, deliberating whether or not to give up the truth, or at least provide another version of it.

"I was there," he said and averted his eyes with the guilt of lying to them.

"When we spoke to you earlier this week, you told us you were at home all day."

"I lied," he said and held his hands up in defeat. "Alright? I lied to you. I said I was home, but I was there."

"Why did you lie?" Anna asked. "Were you hiding something from us?"

He said nothing again and bit down on his bottom lip. Anna slid the first of her documents across the table.

"Do you recognise this?" she asked. "You should do. I found it on your kitchen table. For the benefit of the recording, I am presenting Mr Frost with exhibit NKMR-071, a proposal for an archaeological excavation in Dunston, just three hundred metres from where Myra Dicks was found. Do you recognise it, Mr Frost?"

"Of course, I do. I wrote it."

"And do you see the red stamp mark?" she asked. "The one that says *Not Approved?*"

"I see it."

"Can you please read the signature of the individual who rejected your proposal?"

"Myra Dicks," he sighed. "But that doesn't mean anything."

Anna slid three more documents across the table.

"And these?" she said. "Do you recognise these?"

He rolled his eyes and stared at the timer on the recording as it clicked by.

"For the benefit of the recording, I am presenting Mr Frost with exhibits NKMR-072, NKMR-073, and NKMR-074. All of which are proposals for archaeological excavations, and all of which have been declined by the same individual who declined the Dunston proposal, NKMR-071. Myra Dicks. Now, Mr Frost, can you now see why I find it extremely difficult to understand why you were in the same vicinity as Myra Dicks."

"I don't know why she was there," he snapped. "How should I know? I don't bloody know her. I've never met the woman."

"But you know why you were there?"

"Of course," he said. "I was digging, alright? I didn't agree with the decision that she made. I was hoping to find something that would convince them that the site was of historical significance."

"Tell me what happened," Anna said, and she sat back in her chair, waiting for him to answer.

"Look, I'm in trouble," he started.

"Who with?"

"Financial trouble," he explained. "I've been working on a project for nearly a year now. It was supposed to solve all my issues. I had a production company lined up–"

"I hear they pulled out," Anna said.

"How did you know that?"

"Research," she said. "Carry on."

"She ruined it. She ruined me if truth be told. She rejected all four of my digs. Of course they pulled out. Without the right permissions, there would be nothing to film. I had to find something to get my proposals approved."

"So you went alone to Dunston, did you?"

He nodded.

"Listen, if this gets out, I'll never work again. I'll tell you what you need to know. But can we just keep this private?"

"If we were to visit all four of these locations, tell me what we'd find," Anna said, not committing to keeping anything under wraps.

"Trenches. Not many, but enough," he replied.

"Enough for what?"

"Enough for me to get the proposals approved. Whet their appetites, as it were," he said. "Look, I was at Dunston, and yes, I was digging. I saw the police car arrive and figured you lot were onto me."

"It's not a crime, as far as I'm concerned. It's a civil case," Anna said. "As long as you had the permission of the land owner. You did have permission, didn't you?"

He nodded.

"Edward Rose. He was disappointed with the rejection as well."

"So you saw the police car, then what?"

He shrugged. "I ran, of course. I ran along the riverbank back to my car."

"But you left your car there. Why?" Anna asked.

"There were people there. I don't know. Some kind of argument."

"Where? At the car park?"

"Near it, yeah. Some bloke and a woman," he said. "I didn't want them to see me. So I figured I'd go back later."

"Where did you go?"

"I ran to Wasps Nest then into Nocton. Ended up catching a bus home."

"You did all that just so you wouldn't be seen?"

"You don't know what it's like. If anyone finds out I was digging there, nobody would ever let me dig again. I wouldn't even get a job sweeping the floor at a museum. I could lose everything."

"And did you go back for your car?"

He nodded.

"I went back the next day, but there were still vans and cars there. I just thought they were onto me. To be honest, I was surprised it took you so long to find me."

"And so you reported your car stolen to throw us off the track?"

"I didn't know it was a bloody murder, did I?"

"I see," Anna said, still undecided if he was telling the truth or not.

He leaned across the table to Jenny.

"Look, love. I'm sorry if I hurt you. Honestly, I just panicked. I'd never hurt anyone."

"It's okay, Mr Frost," she replied.

"Will you press charges?" he asked. "I said I'm sorry. I'll do whatever I can to make it up."

"We'll have to confer with the rest of our team," Anna said.

"Does that mean I can go? And will all this stay private?"

"I think that given the seriousness of the crime, and the weight of the evidence against you, if I were to let you go, I'd be out of a job by nine a.m. tomorrow morning, Mr Frost."

"I've got to stay here?" he said.

"You lied to us about your car and your whereabouts," Anna said. "I'm afraid I'm going to need some serious convincing that there's any truth whatsoever in what you've told us today."

CHAPTER THIRTY

A perpetual series of beeps of various tones and pitches was the chorus of the ward in which Claire Banner was staying. Aside from a lady who displayed no signs of injury or illness, save for a relentless snore every half minute or so, Claire was alone.

"I remember you," Claire said, although she didn't smile.

"Shh, just relax," Jackie said, as she came to sit in the visitor's chair. "How are you feeling?"

"Like a bear with a sore head," Claire replied, searching the side table for something, then wincing at the pain of moving her eyes. She licked her lips dryly and took a deep breath.

"Would you like some water?" Jackie asked, and she rose without waiting for a response, poured a glass from the jug, and placed it to Claire's lips. She took a few sips then, after another lick of parched lips, she took a greedy mouthful, seeming to delight in the sensation. "Not too fast. You'll bring it up again."

Claire said nothing. She sat upright in bed with her eyes closed.

"The nurse said you have a severe concussion," Jackie started. "You might be in for another day or so. Can I bring you anything?"

"Is that standard for a police officer?" Claire said. "I'll have to let my husband know. He always makes you lot out to be a bunch of–"

"It's not standard," Jackie said, interrupting her. "But then again, neither is being blown across your mother's front lawn by a gas explosion."

"Is that what it was? And here's me thinking I'd just had a good night down the pub."

"It's nice to see you haven't lost your sense of humour. You'll need that," Jackie told her. "Claire, do you remember much of what happened?"

"At Mum's house, you mean?"

"All of it. The past few weeks," Jackie said. "Can you give me a better picture of what happened between Kevin and your mum?"

"Ah," Claire replied knowingly. "I see."

"We just want to eliminate him, Claire. But it's getting quite difficult when there's so much stacked against him. I can't imagine what you're going through–"

"No. No, you can't."

"I'm sorry to ask, Claire."

"It's okay," Claire said after a few moments. "I'm sorry, I've got a splitting headache."

"Now that I *can* imagine," Jackie said, and Claire opened her eyes long enough for her to see her accompanying smile. "Claire, you told us that Kevin and your mother didn't get on."

"I told you that, did I?" she said. "Is that why you've come to see me?"

"No, of course not. Well, not entirely. I came to make sure you were okay. It's just that…"

"Your boss wants some answers?" Claire said. "I may have a concussion, but I do still have my common sense, thankfully. Why couldn't she come down and talk to me?"

"Who?" Jackie asked.

"Your boss, that's who. The one with the ego the size of Europe."

"I did, actually," Freya said, and she stepped into the ward, her heeled boots clicking loudly on the tiled floor. "If you must know, I thought you might want a little privacy."

"I'm sorry," Claire said. "I didn't mean–"

She winced and held her temple, clearly in a lot of pain.

"To be overheard. Yes, I know," Freya said. "But don't worry. If one can't handle a few home truths then perhaps one should reconsider how they earn a living."

"You haven't found Kevin, then?" Claire said, keeping her eyes closed.

"Oh, we've found him. He's at the station now helping us with our enquiries."

"And Kevin agreed to that?" Claire said.

"He took some persuading. But yes, he agreed," Freya said, and she perched on the edge of Claire's bed. "May I ask you a personal question?"

"I suppose you might as well," Claire replied. "I'm not exactly going to run away anytime soon, am I?"

"Do you think your husband could be involved in this?"

From where she was standing, Freya caught the surprised look on Jackie's face. It was a direct question and one that could have waited.

"Why do you ask?" asked Claire.

"We'll be interviewing him later this afternoon," Freya explained. "So if there's something you think we should know, something that might help us get to the bottom of all this, then now is the time to tell us."

"What do you want me to say? Do you want me to tell you he did it?"

"No, I want to know what your thoughts are. You've already told us they didn't see eye to eye. I wonder if you could give us a little more detail?"

"I really could do with some rest—"

"Then we shall be as quick as we can," Freya replied, leaving Claire little alternative.

Lying there in the dim cubicle with three of the curtain sides drawn and her eyes closed, Claire appeared to be tiny, her fragility only belied by the bitterness in her voice.

"I'm afraid it all sounds a little like one of my husband's novels," Claire said. "You know? Infidelity, greed, lies, and betrayal."

"I'm not following," Freya said, and Claire sighed heavily.

"My mother was not the innocent, mature lady you might think she was. I mean, yes, she was intelligent. She had three PhDs, you know? But she was far from innocent, and she could manipulate the world to play the tune she wanted to hear, when she wanted to hear it. If she wanted to be alone, then she would. If she wanted some company, then she would get it. Male company, that is."

"She had a boyfriend?" Jackie said.

"That's one way of putting it."

"He was married?" Freya said, and Claire smiled her confirmation.

"It was a man she worked with—"

"Jeffery Steel," Freya said, saving her the effort.

"Yes. Have you met him?"

"Briefly. We went to the university on Monday. Ho took the news rather badly, I'm afraid. I suppose it makes sense now. But I don't see what this has to do with your husband."

"Oh," Claire said in the midst of a long exhale, "Well, in all his wisdom, after years of keeping their affair secret, Kevin decided to expose her."

"Expose her?" Jackie said. "How?"

"He called Jeffery's wife. Told her everything," Claire said. "You can imagine the consequences, I hope."

"Why did he do that, Claire? I mean, it's none of his business what your mother does, is it?"

"Oh, why do they do anything?" Claire said, clearly tired of the topic, as if it had been going on for years. "She complains about him and he complains about her, and I'm stuck in the middle trying to hold it all together."

"Sounds tiring," Jackie said. "I never knew my mother-in-law."

"Oh, you're married, are you?"

"Was," Jackie said. "Long story."

"They always are," Claire agreed. "So, Kevin told Jeffrey's wife, Veronica, and I'm guessing you want to know what I did with that information?"

"It might help us narrow down the narrative," Jackie said.

"Well, me being me, I told my mum."

"Oh, really?"

"Of course. I tell her everything. I tried not to, of course, but she has this way..." Claire said, then corrected herself. "Sorry, she *had* this way of getting information from me, you know? It's a mother thing."

"It is a mother thing. Mine does it too. I can swear to myself that she won't find out about something and ten minutes after seeing her, I'm blabbing everything."

'It's nice to know it isn't just me," Claire said. "So, anyway, I told her and she hit the roof. Standard reaction FYI. Followed by a torrent of reasons why I should never have married him."

"Well, that's one bullet I dodged," Jackie said.

"She really had a way with words, my mother," Claire said. "I don't know how, but she could spurt out a five-minute tirade of abuse using every verb, adjective, and adverb in the book. Some of them would even impress Kevin."

"But I still don't understand why he did it," Jackie said. "Why then? I mean, he knew about the affair, didn't he?"

"Relationship," Claire said. "My mother always referred to it as a relationship. We weren't allowed to mention the A-word."

"But it wasn't a real relationship, was it?"

"As far as she was concerned, yes, it was. They went on holiday together, ate out together, and obviously worked together, so weekly lunches, you know? The usual tricks."

"But all of this had to be worked around Jefferey Steel's wife, Veronica?"

"Oh, yes. I mean, Veronica got the meat on the bone, that's for sure. If Veronica needed him, then Mum would be cast to one side. But if that's what made her happy, then so be it. You've heard of happy wife, happy life, right?"

"I've heard of it. Never quite experienced it myself."

"Well, in my experience, the same can be said for mothers when they get to a certain age."

"Right, I see," Jackie said, grinning at the thought of her own rather difficult mother, and the lengths Jackie had to go to keep her smiling. "Claire?"

"Yes?" she said.

Jackie waited a moment, deciding whether or not to push for a response. But that was why she was there.

"You still didn't tell us *why* Kevin called Veronica," Jackie said. "What triggered him to do that?"

"Ah," Claire said, again. "You really want to know, do you?"

"We have to, I'm afraid."

"Mother and Jeffery used to go to lunch. Not every day. He kept her on a tight leash if you know what I mean? But once a week, they'd do lunch somewhere. And it just so happens that last week, they lunched in The Cosy Club."

"I've heard of that. It's supposed to be lovely."

"I wouldn't know," Claire said. "I haven't been. But Kevin has. And whether or not it's fortuitous or not, I don't know, but he decided to lunch there on the very same day that mother and Jeffery did."

"Oh, that's awkward," Jackie said.

"Indeed," Claire said. "Except he wasn't alone."

"No, surely not?"

"It seems that my mother's infidelity has, over the years, rubbed off on him," Claire said, and she opened her eyes fully this time to reveal a picture of hurt, loss, and bitter resentment. "She sent me the photos of them, of course. And I imagine she took great pleasure in doing so."

The moment Claire learned of her husband's disloyalty played out in Jackie's mind. She felt rather than imagined the stab of betrayal, and it took a moment for her to gather her thoughts, by which time Claire had closed her eyes once more, hiding those windows into her pain but leaving behind a tell-tale tear that tracked across her skin.

"Why would she want to hurt you, though?" Jackie said softly.

"She didn't," Claire said as if she had been waiting for her to ask. "The truth is that the photo is all the evidence she needed to drive Kevin and me apart. She's never liked him."

"She'd rather see you alone?"

"Of course. Independent, alone, and free," Claire said flatly. "Just like she was."

"Claire?" Freya said, quietly. "One more question, then we'll leave you alone, I promise."

"Go on."

"You told us that Kevin went on a research trip for his book last Saturday. Is that true?"

"Oh, it's true, alright," she replied. "Slightly premature, but it's true. I'm afraid our discussion around the mystery woman might have got a little heated."

"You kicked him out?"

"No, he left. He told me things would all work out," she replied. "He told me that when he got back, things would be better and that I'd understand."

CHAPTER THIRTY-ONE

It was midday by the time Gillespie and Cruz found the address in Woodhall Spa that Chapman had provided them. Cruz prepared his warrant card, notepad, and pen, then checked his reflection in the passenger sun visor mirror.

"Are you wearing aftershave?" Gillespie asked. "And have you polished your shoes?"

"Yep and yep," he replied. "First impressions count, Jim."

Gillespie gave a little muted laugh.

"Just let me do the talking, eh?" Gillespie said. "You just focus on impressing him with your shiny shoes. You never know, when your perfume hits him, he might even fall at our feet and beg for mercy."

"Very droll, Jim," Cruz said. "Very droll indeed."

The house was large, fine, well-maintained, and the type that Cruz considered to be out of reach of anybody with less than six figures in their bank account, and more in line with seven figures.

"Would you just look at this place?" Gillespie said when he saw Cruz gazing up at the property in awe. "Imagine the cleaning. It'd be like the Humber Bridge. By the time you've cleaned it all, you'd have to start over."

"Is that why you don't clean your place?"

"Hey, I clean. When I've got time, anyway," Gillespie said. "Besides, I'd like to think that if ever I can afford a place like this, I'd have somebody do all that for me. Along with the cooking, the laundry, the garden, and maybe a little massage to relieve my aching bones."

"Oh, I see," Cruz said. "So, you have a certain demographic in mind for this role, do you?"

"I do, as it happens," he said with a wink. "A man can have goals, can't he? Without goals, Gabby, we're just ambling through life."

"So your goal is to have a house like this with somebody, I dread to think who, doing all your dirty work and giving you massages?"

"Aye," Gillespie said. "That sounds about right."

"That, Jim, is what you call a dream," Cruz said, as he pushed open his door and climbed out.

Gillespie followed suit and joined him on the footpath.

"So what are your goals then?" he asked. "Don't tell me, you'd like to grow tall enough to reach the top kitchen cupboard?"

"Hilarious," Cruz replied, as they made their way up the garden footpath.

"Is that where Hermione keeps the sweeties, Gabby? So you don't scoff them all while you're watching CBeebies?"

"You're not funny, Jim."

"Who changes the light bulbs in your house?"

"Just leave it, eh?" Cruz said, reaching up to push the doorbell.

"Hang on, do you need a leg up there?" Gillespie said. "Can you manage it?"

Cruz ignored him, instead choosing to occupy his mind with the property. The front door was central to the house with large bay windows on either side and an open porch with glazed green tiles on the inside. Two pairs of wellington boots stood to one side, along with a small trug bearing a pair of secateurs and some cut flowers.

The doorbell rang inside the house, a classic doorbell sound that seemed befitting to the property, where a modern, digital substitute just wouldn't suffice. A few moments later, the door was opened by a mature lady wearing a headscarf and a light blouse partially covered by denim coveralls.

"Hello?" she said, searching both of their faces for some kind of early indicator as to the reason for their visit.

Gillespie held up his warrant card and Cruz followed suit.

"Mrs Steel?" he said. "Lincolnshire Police. We were wondering if we could have a quick word."

"A word?" she replied, clearly hoping for a little more information. "With me?"

"With your husband, actually. Jeffery? Is he home?"

"I'm afraid not. Is he in some kind of trouble?"

"Oh no," Gillespie said. "We were just hoping he'd help us with our enquiries."

"I could call him. Although, I did try him a while back and he didn't answer."

"Aye, that would be grand, Mrs Steel. Do you think we could come in and wait?"

"Well, I was just going to pick some vegetables for my dinner—"

"We won't take much of your time, Mrs Steel. It's quite important."

"Oh, I see," she replied, and she glanced inside as if searching for a reason to deter them. "I'm afraid the place is rather a mess."

"We're not here to judge you on the tidiness of your house, Mrs Steel," Cruz added.

"Well, then I suppose you'd better come in," the mature lady replied, and she peered out through the porch, presumably to see if any of the neighbours were watching. "Go through to the parlour," she said. "Should I fetch something to drink? Some tea maybe?"

"Some tea would be cracking, thank you," Gillespie replied, and he pointed to the first door off of the large, tiled hallway. "In here?"

"Yes, dear. Make yourselves comfortable. I'll just be a moment. I've not long made a pot."

"Take your time," Cruz said politely, following Gillespie into the room. Two large Chesterfield sofas were positioned on either side of a large and rather ornate fireplace.

"I bet you she brings biscuits," Gillespie said, as Cruz studied a few framed photographs that had been neatly arranged on a sideboard.

"Is that all you think about?" Cruz replied. "When was the last time you actually ate a vegetable?"

"A what? A vegetable?"

"Yeah," Cruz said, working his way around the room. "Or a fruit?"

"Had both last night actually," Gillespie replied. "I had peas and carrots with my chicken."

Cruz turned to see if he was being genuine and found him with a sincere expression on his face.

"You had meat and two veg for dinner last night? Did you cook it yourself?"

Gillespie gave a laugh.

"Me? No, Gabby. I'm not much of a cook if I'm honest. I had the woman down the road do it for me."

"The woman down the road?"

"Aye. Mrs Chang."

"She runs the Chinese takeaway," Cruz said. "Why would she cook you chicken and veg? Have they diversified?"

"What? No, she did me chicken chow mein and vegetable fried rice."

Cruz stared at him, utterly bewildered. The man seemed to genuinely believe that was a healthy dinner.

"I've got some leftover, too, so I'll probably have it tonight. You know? Chicken ding ding."

"Chicken ding ding?"

"Aye. You put the chicken in the microwave and after a minute or two, it goes ding ding."

"You know, after working with you for all this time, I'm still unsure when you're trying to be funny and when you're genuinely mentally challenged," Cruz said.

"Right, then," a small voice said, and the door was nudged open. Mrs Steel came in with a tray with a teapot, a small bowl containing a pile of sugar cubes, and a little jug of milk; all of which were matching. She set the tray down on the coffee table that stood between the two sofas and then waited for Gillespie and Cruz to select where they would sit.

Cruz opted for the sofa with its back to the window and Gillespie sat beside him, leaving Mrs Steel with the view of the front garden and the sun in her eyes.

"Shall I be mother?" Mrs Steel said, almost playfully, but when she collected up the teapot, Cruz noticed a slight shaking of her hands as she began to pour. Gillespie noticed it too and glanced sideways at Cruz with a slight frown. "Sugar?"

"Aye, two for me, thank you," Gillespie said, and Cruz simply shook his head, absorbed with the woman's inability to stop her hands from shaking.

"Is there something troubling you, Mrs Steel?" he said finally, and almost at once, the lady put the tea pot down and buried her hands in her dungarees, bowing her head to hide her watering eyes.

"Ah, now that's a good cup of tea," Gillespie said, clearly trying to cheer Mrs Steel up. "You missed your calling there. I'd pay money for that."

"People do," she said quietly. "I run a small catering company. Local stuff, you know?"

"That explains it," he replied. "It's a fine brew."

She smiled off the compliment, her mind elsewhere.

"Mrs Steel?" Cruz said quietly. "Mrs Steel, is there something on your mind?"

"It's him, isn't it?" she burst out. "It's my husband, isn't it?"

"I'm sorry?"

"Something's happened, hasn't it? I know it has or else you wouldn't be here. Something has happened to him."

"Mrs Steel–"

"He did it, didn't he?" she cried, and her voice took on that which Cruz had heard a hundred or more times. That nasal sound of loss and regret. "That woman who died in Dunston. It was him, wasn't it?"

"Mrs Steel we do have a suspect in mind, that much is true," Gillespie began, and the woman cried out again, doubling over and hiding her face from view. "But it's not your husband. As far as we know, your husband has nothing to do with it."

"He doesn't?" she said, seeming slightly confused. She searched Cruz's expression for a hint they were hiding the truth and Cruz gave a slight smile to reassure her.

"Mrs Steel, is there something you want to tell us?" he asked. "When did you see your husband last?"

Veronica Steel buried her face again, but this time not from fear. She turned away but that intrusive light from the front window revealed the cold grimace of shame.

"Veronica?" he said, using her first name to try to connect with her. "We're not here to judge, remember?"

The older woman's shoulder sagged and she gave off a sigh like a steam engine coming to a standstill.

"Is he in any trouble?" Gillespie asked softly.

"No. Well, not as far as I know, anyway. But then, what do I know?" She paused as if she had said too much. "I'm sorry. I'm not myself."

"Veronica if there's something we should know—"

"He's gone," she snapped, and she stared up at them both in turn, as if her defiance would counter the shame. "Twenty-eight years we've been married. Twenty-eight bloody years of him doing what the hell he likes."

"He left you?" Gillespie said, hiding his surprise beneath a blanket of professional calm.

"Oh no," Veronica continued. "I wouldn't let him get away with leaving me. Not now, not after all I've been through. I've done enough for him, and, well, he left on my terms."

"On your terms?" Cruz said. "I'm sorry. Can you explain?"

She leaned forward, her red eyes moist and callous with venom.

"I finally did it," she said. "I finally kicked him out."

"You kicked your husband out? When was this?"

"Saturday. The morning, to be precise. I told him to pack his bags and get out."

"And did he offer any argument?" Gillespie asked.

"Yes, of course he did. He always has an argument, that man. That's how we've managed to last twenty-eight bloody years. Anybody else would have managed to get rid of him far sooner. But I'm too soft, you see. Easily manipulated, so they say. My family, that is."

"May I ask why?" Gillespie said. "If it's not too intrusive."

"Because of her," she replied. "Myra. The woman you found. The whole village is talking about it. Well, good bloody riddance. I think deep down I always knew. But you sort of put it to one side, don't you? You hope it's not true."

"Your husband was having an affair with Myra Dicks?" Gillespie said, and just verbalising it in such a blunt manner clearly drove the blade a little further. Veronica squeezed her eyes closed, then nodded slowly.

"And how did you find out about them having an affair?" Cruz asked.

"How? Because she's a spiteful cow is how," she said, and she pulled a tissue from the sleeve of her blouse to wipe her eyes. "I'm sorry, I shouldn't speak ill of the dead, but it's true. It obviously wasn't just me she had upset. Oh no. Her son-in-law called me. Kevin something. A famous author or something, although I'd never heard of him. Anyway, he called me to say he'd seen the pair of them together."

"Why?" Gillespie asked. "Why would he do that?"

"Because maybe there's some good left in this world?" she replied. "Maybe he'd had enough of her too? Poor sod has her as a mother-in-law. God knows what he has to put up with."

"Kevin Banner?" Cruz said. "Is that who you're talking about? Just to be clear."

"That's him. He called me out of the blue. Said there's something I should know, and then he told me. Just like that. He told me everything."

"Everything?"

"How they'd been seeing each other for years," she replied. "I feel like such a fool. That's the worst part. It's not the deceit or the lies, it's the believing. The hoping. The trusting."

"And you had it out with Jeffery that day?"

"As soon as he walked through that door," she said proudly. "If I had waited, perhaps I wouldn't have. So I had to do it. I had to get it out. He pleaded, of course. He said he'd finish it, and he said he was sorry, and all the things you expect them to say. You know? More lies."

"I imagine that must have been a dreadful conversation to have, Veronica," Cruz said.

"I gave him an ultimatum," she replied. "I said you leave her and you can stay in the spare room, but you'll never share my bed again. Not as long as there's breath in my body. I told him not to come back until it was over."

"And what did he say to that?" Gillespie asked.

"He said he would. Leave her, that is. He said he'd do it. I heard him leave. Heard the door close, you know? I heard the sound of his car starting. And I just sat here. Just like this."

Gillespie glanced across at Cruz, who was scribbling down the key facts in his pad. Eventually, Veronica looked up.

"And then it was over," she said. "And I haven't left the house since."

"You haven't been anywhere?" Cruz asked, losing his empathetic tone in favour of something far more direct. "You're sure of that?"

"Of course," Veronica replied after a moment. She held his stare as if her life counted on it, not daring to pull away. "I've been waiting for him to walk through that door ever since."

CHAPTER THIRTY-TWO

"What are we doing here?" Ben asked.

"I just want to have a look around," Freya replied.

They stared up through the windscreen at the ruined house.

"It's boarded up," Ben said. "Are we calling in support to get that front door open?"

"No, I'm sure you'll manage," she replied. "Did the blast really do all that?"

"I'd say the fire was responsible for the blown windows and the blackened fascia. The front door as well, of course. But other than that, the rest of it looks like neglect."

"What are you saying?"

"I'm saying that if I owned a house like this and couldn't afford to get it fixed, I'd probably blow it up. Or pay someone to, at least."

"Let's not go down that road unless we have to," Freya said. "No. I think we have enough suspects on our hands not to venture down the arson route. But it does make you wonder. She seemed so respectable. And it's not like she was incapable of cutting the grass. She was fit enough."

"I guess some people just don't value aesthetics like you or I."

"It's more than aesthetics, Ben. The place is a dump. Look at it. Now, look at the other houses. They're all immaculate."

"Didn't you live in a camper van less than a year ago?"

"I lived in a camper van for a week, Ben, and it was at least clean. I'm not judging her on the quality of her house—"

"But you *are* judging her," Ben said.

"I'm judging her values," she replied. "I just think that one should represent one's self in the best possible light."

Ben laughed at the comment and reached for the door handle.

"Come on," he said, not wanting to listen to any more hypocrisy. He shoved open the door and waited for her to comment across the bonnet. And she did, less than ten seconds later.

"If you have something to say, Ben..."

"I've said everything I have to say, Freya," he replied. "If you have an opinion on the way Myra Dicks lived her life, then that's your business. Is your opinion going to help us solve her murder? Probably not."

"I'm being a cow, aren't I?'

"Yes, Freya, but it's okay, I won't judge you," he said, holding the garden gate open for her.

"Sorry," she muttered as he passed him. "You'll have to let me know if I do it again."

"Is that permission to call you out on your flaws?"

"Not all of them," she said. "Just when I'm being a cow. I have far too many for you to keep track of them all."

She marched directly into the property and trudged through the long grass toward the side of the house.

Ben followed, taking large strides in her wake, smiling to himself as he went. He checked along the street to make sure there were no twitching curtains. It was the type of street where two random people walking down the side of a house raised eyebrows and set tongues wagging.

At the rear of the property, Freya began checking beneath flower pots and lifting random items, presumably looking for a key. Given the number of random items on the patio, it was a formidable task. Any minute now, Freya was bound to make a comment on how untidy it was.

"Have you trod in something?" she asked, pulling a disgusted face.

"Me? No, I bloody haven't," Ben replied, checking the soles of his shoes just in case. "It's probably you."

"I certainly haven't," she replied, sniffing the air with apparent distaste. She moved to the corner of the patio where an old, galvanised bin sat beside the fence. Cautiously, she raised the lid, then slammed it back down and moved away, covering her mouth and her nose. "Oh, for God's sake."

"Doggy doo?" Ben said.

"A bin full of it," she said. "It's not even in little bags. Who does that? It's right outside her bloody kitchen window."

Laughing to himself, Ben held his breath, strolled over to the bin, and using the sole of his shoe, tipped it up to peer underneath.

"There's your key," he said, eyeing the single brass key on the floor.

"What the hell is it doing under there?"

"Safest place for it," he said, reaching down and grabbing the key. "My brother does something similar with the keys to the tractor shed."

"What? He keeps under a bin full of excrement?"

"No, he keeps them in his kitchen," he joked, tossing her the key and smiling at her reaction to holding it. "You've got to be severely disturbed to go in there unless you're dying of hunger."

Freya used a tissue to hold the key and unlocked the back door.

"Sometimes I wonder if I'll ever get used to living up here," she muttered under her breath.

"You've got that wrong," Ben replied. "You see, the rest of us are all wondering if we'll ever get used to you coming here. I mean, we keep trying to convince you to leave. But do you take the hint? No."

"It'll take more than hiding a key beneath a bin full of..." she began, but couldn't bring herself to describe the contents of the bin.

"Doggy doo?" Ben said.

She shook her head and entered the house, which opened into what used to be the kitchen. The smell of singed wood and melted plastic hung in the air, overpowering even the odour from the bin on the patio.

"What exactly are we looking for?" Ben asked. "You do remember we have Banner at the station, don't you?"

"Of course, I remember, Ben. It was my idea to bring him in," she replied. "And it's not like the clock is ticking. Not yet, anyway."

She stepped through the kitchen into the charred hallway. Black smoke had stained every inch of the walls that hadn't been burned and the carpet was laden with water from the fire service. She stepped through into the lounge. It was a nice size, Ben thought. It would have been a lovely family home.

"Just so you know," Freya said. "I won't make any comments on the state of the décor or the vast quantities of tat on the shelves."

"You mean photo frames and ornaments?"

"Yes, that's what I said. Toot."

"Wow. You do realise not everybody can fit all their belongings into two suitcases and a box, don't you?"

"Why do I need a box?" she replied. "Two suitcases is plenty."

"For your clothes, maybe. But you'd need something to hold your wine collection," he joked.

"So I'm an alcoholic now, am I? As well as a cow?"

Ben gave his response some thought, rubbing his chin thoughtfully.

"Just, don't answer that," she said, then moved back to the hallway. "Come on. We're leaving."

"We're leaving? We only just got here. I was going to pop the kettle on."

"There's nothing here, and if there was it's very likely a pile of ashes. We'll just have to do this the hard way."

She was at the back door by the time Ben reached the hallway.

"We haven't looked upstairs," he called to her.

"Be my guest," she replied, and she stopped to see if he would dare to try. The stairs were bare wood and, in places, it was clear they might have once been a golden oak. But now they were charred and as uninviting as Freya in a bad mood.

"Banner it is, then," he said, giving the stairs a final look. Freya had already left, so he followed, closing the door behind him. He considered pocketing the key but thought better of it. Again, using the sole of his shoe, he tilted the bin back and tossed the key beneath it.

A few moments later, he found Freya at the front of the house, peering over the fence into the neighbouring property. The grass was immaculate, the flower beds looked as if Monty Don had popped round and worked his magic, and the house could have been built the week before, it was so clean.

"I bet they don't have a bin full of doggy doo in the back garden," he said.

"No, I bet they don't, and I doubt very much the owner will be too happy about having Myra's bin so close to the fence. Surely they can smell it?"

They waded through the long grass back towards the car and Freya hit the fob to unlock the doors.

"You know," she said. "I'm beginning to think Myra Dicks was just a nasty old woman."

Ben opened his mouth to say something but was distracted by a noise from behind him. A whistle, tuneful, unlike the monotone nursery rhyme that Cruz irritated the first floor with. He turned to find the postman strolling along in his shorts and trainers, digging through his bag as he walked.

"I'll take that," Ben said, as the postman approached.

The man pulled his earphones from his ears.

"You what, mate?"

"I said, I'll take the post," Ben said, and he nodded at the boarded-up house, then flashed him his warrant card. "I'll see to it the owner gets it."

"Fine by me," the postman said, and he slapped a bundle of envelopes into Ben's hand.

From the car, Freya had watched his every move. She waited for him to pop the post into her glovebox and pull on his seatbelt.

"Well?" she said.

"Well, what?"

"Aren't you going to say anything?"

"About what?"

"About the similarities between Myra Dicks and myself. Surely you have some kind of witty comment to get off your chest?"

"Oh, that?" he said, with a laugh. "I have to admit, there are some similarities."

"I knew it," she replied.

"But I'm pleased to say, your standards are higher," he said. "Besides, most of the people that want you dead are in prison already."

"Lucky me," she said. "Lucky me indeed."

CHAPTER THIRTY-THREE

The incident room was buzzing when Ben and Freya emerged from the fire escape stairwell and made their way along the corridor. It always intrigued Freya that the team were so free and easy-going in her absence, yet so reserved in her presence. It was only natural, she presumed, and allowed them the opportunity to bond.

There was laughter from the girls and, as usual, it was both Gillespie and Cruz who were the loudest. Freya and Ben peered through the windows in the doors to watch the episode, both of them smiling at the scene.

Gillespie was sitting with his feet up on a spare chair, leaning on his desk like he was in his local pub, supping a pint. Chapman was typing away, paying attention but driven by diligence. Nillson and Anderson were sitting close to each other, each of them with their laptops open and a spread of paperwork before them.

Cruz, however, was standing, re-enacting the moment when he had discovered the flattened patch of grass and nettles in the dyke.

"I knew straight away, of course," he began.

"You knew what?" Nillson asked.

"That the killer had been there," Cruz said. "I could just tell. It all made sense."

"At this point," Gillespie added, "I think it's worth noting that our hero, young DC Cruz here, was having a wee sit down."

"Yeah, well, my laces had become untied," Cruz said defensively, and he was about to continue his tale when Gillespie began to get into the swing of his side of the story, which, to Freya, was far more realistic.

"In fact," he began. "Let me tell you how I think it played out. I left you to carry on searching the area, while I went and spoke to the farmer."

"You mean, you were too lazy to do the search–"

"I prioritised the interview," Gillespie said. "Allocation of resources. That's how you make budgets work."

"No–"

"And then you had a sit down to tie your laces, but being the clumsy oaf you are, you fell into the dyke."

The team all looked to Cruz for a sign it was true. He dragged his foot back and forth on the carpet.

"The grass was already flattened. Somebody had been there."

"And any evidence the killer, or whoever, might have left behind is now tainted with your filthy DNA and bootprints."

Cruz sighed, and his shoulders slumped in defeat.

"It's alright, Gabby. At least you found it," Anderson said.

"Yep," Gillespie agreed. "And you broke a record too. You should be proud."

"What record?" Cruz said as he took his seat.

"Clumsiest officer in the East Midlands."

"Alright, that's enough," Freya said, barging through the doors. If her voice didn't silence the team, the squealing hinges would. The doors slammed closed behind her and Ben and Freya took her spot at the front of the room, while Ben sat at his desk. "We're getting there," she said, as she slipped her bag onto the back of her chair. "What we need to focus on here is creating the narrative. We need to piece the story together, but with a couple of twists to add in. You should all know that we have Kevin Banner in custody, and as I understand it, we have Adam Frost, too."

"Already interviewed, boss," Nillson said.

"Excellent, hold that thought, will you?" Freya said. "Gillespie and Cruz, please tell me you've interviewed Jeffery Steel, Myra's lover."

"Ah, well," Gillespie began.

"Are you about to let me down?"

"He wasn't there," Gillespie said sheepishly.

"Oh, really? You mean you went to his house and couldn't find him so you thought you'd just leave it, and hope nobody would know?"

"Not entirely, boss," he said.

"Or perhaps you thought I'd send somebody else to pick him up? Somebody capable?"

"I think that's a wee bit unfair," Gillespie said. "We spoke to his wife."

"Veronica Steel?" Freya said.

"Aye, boss."

"And what did you learn?"

"Well, for a starters, she and Jeffery–"

"Had an argument. Yes, I know all that," Freya said. "Is there any new information?"

"Apparently, Myra sent–"

"Myra sent Claire some photos of Kevin and another woman at a restaurant. Kevin then retaliated by telling Veronica about the affair. Yes, we know all that. I was hoping that two of my resources spent the morning gathering some kind if new information," Freya said.

"She runs a small catering business," Cruz added, to which nobody reacted.

"And she hasn't seen him since Saturday," Gillespie said. "That's something."

"And what about her?" Ben said. "Given that she's the jilted wife of Myra's lover, I think it's wise to acknowledge she had a motive as strong, if not stronger, than Kevin or her husband."

"She hasn't left the house," Gillespie said. "Said she's been waiting in for him to come home."

"Yeah, right," Nillson said. "That's what Frost said when we first met him. Turns out he was actually at the crime scene."

"Oh really?" Freya said, turning her attention to the female duo. "Am I to presume he told you all you wanted to hear?"

"Kind of," Nillson replied. "It turns out that Myra Dicks rejected a few of his proposals to excavate local areas of interest. The result was that the documentary series he had planned, fell through, and Frost found himself in financial difficulty. So much so that he was desperate to convince the Heritage Advisory Board to give him the go-ahead."

"How desperate?" Freya asked.

"Desperate enough to dig on his own, without permission, risking his entire career."

"I'm sensing a piece of information coming that will make all of this relevant."

"You'd be right," Nillson said. "The last proposal that was rejected was for a spot beside the River Witham, about three hundred metres from where Myra Dicks was found."

"Are you telling me he just happened to be there digging when Myra decided to walk her dog there?"

"He claims to have seen the police car arrive and thought uniform were there for him."

"Why would uniform arrest him for digging a trench?" Cruz asked. "If he dug without permission, surely that's a civil case between him and the board, or the National Trust maybe?"

"Very good, Cruz," Freya said. "Nillson?"

"That's what he said, boss. According to him, he saw the police car and ran along the river back to his car."

"But he didn't take his car?" Freya said.

"No, and this is where it gets interesting. He said, when he arrived back at the Stepping Out car park, he saw a man and woman arguing. He didn't want to be seen there, for obvious reasons, so he hot-footed it through Wasps Nest into Nocton, where he caught the bus into Lincoln."

"That's a rather well-thought-out tale," Freya said. "And if I might add, very convenient. Where is he now?"

"In custody. We've got until tomorrow morning with him."

"Right let's make the most of that time. Good work, both of you. It's becoming ever more evident that not only was Myra Dicks having an affair with a married man, but she was simply not a nice person. However, murder is murder."

"Ah, there's nothing wrong with a wee affair," Gillespie said. "I've dated plenty of married women. It happens all the time."

"There's a lot wrong with that, Gillespie," Freya said without looking at him. "But it's not our place to judge."

"Right, but you just judged–"

"I gave an opinion based on my experience of being married to a man who was cheating on me; of being the victim."

"Right. So, you judged him, then. You judged him based on your experience, and I judged him based on my own experience. Any married women I knew were trapped in an unhealthy relationship, or one that was fine in every respect except one."

"And you provided that interim service did you?" Nillson said. "You were supplementing the marriage with your... What exactly?"

"My taste, refinement, and sexual prowess," he said, smoothing his long hair back over his ear. "If you think about it, I probably saved a marriage or two. Hubby goes out to work, provides for the kids, and keeps the roof over their heads. While he's out, I go in and..."

"And what?" Anderson asked, visibly horrified at the idea of Gillespie working his charm with anybody other than the bathroom mirror.

"Make them feel special," he said. "To put it politely. Show them a good time, you know? A steak dinner, a few glasses of wine, a wee walk along the beach at night. By the time I drop them off at home, they're relaxed, satiated, and satisfied."

"Oh, God. I think I'm actually going to be sick," Nillson said, to which Gillespie took offence.

"Don't you knock it, Anna. Not until you've tried it." He offered her a wink as if to punctuate his offer.

"Right or wrong," Freya said loudly, as a school teacher might get the attention of unruly kids. "We're about to interview Kevin Banner, after which we're going to have to either arrest him or let him go. What else do we have on him?"

"Of all the places Myra and Jeffery could have gone for lunch, they went to the same place that Kevin was having lunch, and we already know how they don't get on."

"I imagine Sunday roasts were a barrel of laughs with those two at each other's throats," Gillespie said.

"Oh, they didn't argue," Gold said. "Not according to Claire, anyway. In fact, to the outside world, Myra was lovely to Kevin. She'd make small talk, show interest in his books, and even help out where she could."

"I'm sensing a but coming," Freya said.

"As soon as she left, she'd phone Claire to complain about how horrid he was to her. She used to complain about all the little things he did to make her feel uncomfortable and unwelcome."

"And I suppose Kevin was a saint, was he?" Freya asked.

"No. But I get the feeling she made Claire feel like she was trapped in between a never-ending argument, and that Kevin was to blame, while Myra was, on the outside at least, blameless."

"That's toxic behaviour," Anderson said, jabbing a finger in the air. "My ex-boyfriend's mum was like that. It's toxic, and let me tell you something, it's enough to drive you insane. It's something to do with the mother-in-law not wanting to relinquish control of her child."

"Child? She's thirty-something," Gillespie added.

"It doesn't matter. To a mother, a child will always be a child," Anderson said.

"Yeah, it's just that some don't like to let go of the apron strings," Chapman said. "It sounds to me like Kevin Banner had his hands full with her. But I don't get why it mattered if they were at the same restaurant and he saw Myra with Jeffery Steel. He already knew about the affair, didn't he?"

"Oh, he knew about her affair with Jeffery," said Gold, "but Myra didn't know about *his* affair. What if Myra had somehow seen he had a lunch date and had convinced Jeffery to go there so she could check up on him?"

"That is definitely the type of thing my ex's mum would have done," Anderson said. "Ruthless, they are."

"Naturally, Myra would have seen it as an opportunity to pull her daughter away from Kevin a little more. The whole toxic behaviour thing. She took photos of Kevin and the woman and sent them to Claire."

"Oh, for God's sake," Nillson said. "It's like a bloody soap opera."

"So, when Kevin said he was on a research trip—" said Gold.

"Claire had actually kicked him out," Freya finished for her. "Kevin comes home, Claire goes bananas. They argue. She kicks him out. Am I right?"

"Spot on," Gold said.

"Sadly, this news does absolutely nothing for us," Freya said. "Other than strengthen Kevin Banner's motive."

"I agree," Ben said. "If the mother-in-law was interfering with his marriage, it's reasonable to assume he'd go and have it out with her. All he'd need to know is where to find her."

"But how would he know she would be there at that time?" Freya said. "That's what we're missing here."

All eyes fell on Freya to make the call. They had two suspects downstairs in the cells, and the evidence against Kevin Banner was too strong to ignore.

"Nillson and Anderson," Freya said, after taking a moment to think.

"Boss?" Nillson said.

"I want you to interview Kevin Banner. Apologise for the delay, thank him for his patience, then get what you need. Who was he meeting in the restaurant? What was he doing when Myra was killed? And when was the last time he saw Myra?" Freya said. "The evidence against him is too damning to ignore. His story better be bloody good."

She collected her bag from her desk and scooped a few files into her arms.

"Right. Anything else?"

Nobody said a thing.

"Good. I want a briefing first thing tomorrow morning. Ben, can you give Michaela a nudge? Her reports might give us enough to actually make a decision," she said, as she yanked open the doors, then turned to face the team. "With any luck, by this time tomorrow, the only thing we'll have to worry about will be our futures."

CHAPTER THIRTY-FOUR

DS Anna Nillson checked her watch. It was five forty-three in the afternoon. She shoved open the door at the end of the ground floor corridor and found Sergeant Priest, the custody sergeant who, in his own words, was the longest-serving member of the station, due to the fact that he had never wanted to move further up the chain than the position he held. He was filling in a form on the custody desk and peered over his thick-rimmed glasses at the interruption.

"Ah, the delightful, Anna," he said, his gruff Yorkshire accent seeming to emanate from the walls of the room. His ageing face creased into a genuine smile. "Kevin Banner?"

"Freya wants me to interview him," she said.

"Room two is ready for you."

"And our guest?" she said.

"He's comfortable," Priest replied. "Though I dare say he'll be keen to learn some news of his wife. He's been here all day, and he's getting quite impatient."

"Well, let's hope he's ready to talk then," Anna replied. "Thanks."

She closed the door and found Anderson waiting patiently behind her, staring at her phone.

"Don't let Granger see you on that," Anna said. It was a friendly warning, that she hoped Jenny would pick up on and put her phone away.

"I was just checking the news," Jenny said, looking up from her phone, but not putting it away. "The local rag is all over the explosion."

Anna gave the comment some thought as they walked towards interview room two. She placed her hand on the door handle.

"I have a feeling this will be over before the media are demanding a statement. I just hope they wait until after Harper's funeral."

She opened the door and stepped inside, holding the door for Jenny who followed her in and closed the door behind her. Kevin Banner was sitting at the table with his fingers interlocked and his head bowed. He looked up when he heard them, eyes wide.

She'd read many of Banner's books, and of course, knew what he looked like from his picture on the dust jackets. But in the flesh, he looked as human as the rest of the world and as guilty as sin.

Anna dropped her files onto the table, then took the seat nearest the door, while Jenny prepared the recording.

"I was getting ready to leave," he said, making no attempt to move.

"The door's open," Anna replied. "You're not under arrest yet."

"And how far would I get?"

"To the door," Anna replied confidently.

"Should I have some kind of legal representation?" Banner said, watching Jenny work.

"You can call your lawyer if you want, or we can provide you with a duty solicitor. But, right now, we're just establishing who was where at the time of death. Of course, if you feel you'd like legal representation, I'm in no place to stop you."

"Am I being accused of anything?" he said.

"No, not at the minute. We'd just like you to answer a few questions," Anna said, adopting a friendly approach. "We're in the process of eliminating close family members–"

"I'm aware of the process," he said, cutting her off. "I write about it every bloody day."

"Right," Anna said, and the recording device sounded a long three-second beep to announce it was active. She stated the date and time, and the names of the present individuals, then set her pen down atop her files and stared across the table at Banner. "Perhaps you can start by telling us where you were on Sunday at around midday."

"Sunday?" he said, sounding a little surprised. Then he searched the corner of the room, recalling the facts. "I haven't been home since Saturday. I've been to all sorts of places. Skegness, Bardney, Alford–"

"Specifically, Sunday lunchtime, Mr Banner," Anna said, and this time it was her doing the cutting off.

"Woodhall Spa," he said, slowly, holding Anna's eye contact as if his life depended on it.

"And since then?" she said.

He puffed out a long breath through pursed lips.

"I was in Woodhall for most of the day. Left there at about four o'clock, and headed to the campsite."

"Which campsite is that?"

"Coningsby," he said. "You can check if you like. I believe there's a camera on the entrance."

"We will," Anna replied, with a glance at Jenny to make a note. "And what was it you were doing in Woodhall?"

"Research," he said after a moment, and he shrugged as if to say, *'What do you think I was doing?'*

"Research?"

"For the book I'm writing," he explained. "That's why I haven't been home. I'm collating my research."

"Specifically, Woodhall Spa, Mr Banner," Anna said. "What were you researching there?"

"I was talking to an old school friend of mine. Trevor Copeland. He owns a little gun shop there. Not the one on the High Street. He's just out of town. Nice bloke. Always helps me out when I need it."

"Are you purchasing a firearm?"

"No. I was doing research like I said," he explained. "The devil is in the detail, Sergeant Nillson. You can't fake detail, not in a novel, especially when it comes to firearms. People out there. The gun nuts. They pick up on little factual errors."

"Can't you get that information from the internet?"

"Some, maybe," he said. "But nothing beats actually holding the weapon my character is holding, feeling the trigger, the weight, the length. If I want my character to talk about a particular weapon, a Remington eleven hundred, for example, I want to have held one so I can describe the sensation with conviction."

"That's admirable," Anna said and nodded for Jenny to add Trevor Copeland to the list of people to contact. "So, you left Woodhall Spa, and went straight to the campsite at Coningsby, did you?"

"No," he replied. "I stopped at the little Co-op in Tattershall. Picked up a few bits, you know?"

"I don't understand why you stayed at a campsite when you could have just returned to your home."

He sighed and leaned back in his chair as if he was bored of having to explain how he works.

"It's a mindset thing," he began, and he leaned on the table, interlinking his fingers. "When I start a book, I'll go out in the van, and spend a few days on the road. I'll think of nothing but my book. I don't think of my wife, my daughter, my house, money, nothing. Only my book. If I was to pop home each night, I'd talk to my wife, wouldn't I? She'd tell me all about her day, she'd ask me about mine. I'd most likely spot a few bits around the house that need doing—"

"Such as?"

"The guttering needs cleaning. The lawn needs mowing. You know? That kind of thing. But when I'm out on the road, all I think about is my book."

"And that makes a difference to the story?"

"It makes a big difference," he said.

"And that's why you were at the cathedral, is it?" Anna asked.

"I was talking to the dean. He was kind enough to grant me some of his valuable time. He's a nice man, as it happens."

"Your latest book is set there, is it?"

"No spoilers," he said with a creepy smile, and he tapped his nose conspiratorially.

Anna said nothing while she waited for him to answer the question. His smile faded.

"Yes, that's where a part of my book is set. But I don't want that known," he said, waving an index finger at them. Only you, me, and the dean know about that, and I'd like it kept that way, please."

"I can assure you, Mr Banner, we won't be adding that to our press release."

"Press release?" he said, with concern in his voice.

"A woman has been murdered. Your mother-in-law to be precise. And another has been injured. Your wife, Mr Banner. The public will want to be kept abreast of the facts."

"But you won't mention my name, will you?"

"Will you give us reason to mention your name?" Anna asked. "I mean, the way I see it, the more you help us, the more likely we are to help you."

He stared at her, and for the first time, Anna could see he accepted there was a greater reason for him being there.

"What do you want to know?" he said dryly.

"At around the time your mother-in-law was killed, a blue van like yours was seen in the area."

"There are hundreds of blue vans–"

"Not in Dunston, there isn't. Specifically, Dunston Fen Lane," Anna explained. "It's a dead-end road. Very little traffic. So when a blue van is seen nearby, the locals tend to notice."

He nodded and bit down on his lower lip, flicking his gaze from Anna to Jenny and back again.

"So you see, Mr Banner, we won't mention your name in our press statement, but we will need to mention the blue van that was seen," Jenny said, adding her two pennies' worth to support Anna.

"You can't do that. Everyone will think it was mine."

"Why's that?" Anna said, and she cocked her head waiting for him to answer. "Because yours is the only blue van like that in the area? While we're on the subject, we're probably going to want to have a look at the van. Can you tell me where it's parked?"

"Westgate," he said. "But I don't see why you want to look at my van?"

"We're giving you the opportunity to eliminate yourself from our enquiries, Mr Banner," Anna said. "Can you be a little more specific?"

"In the NCP car park. You'll know which one is mine."

"By the colour?" Anna asked.

"No. Mine will be the one with the bloody parking ticket, "he replied. "It ran out an hour ago. I don't suppose I'll get any help with that, will I?"

"Can we have the keys?" Anna said, and slowly, he retrieved them from his pocket and slid them across the table. "We'll have it collected and we'll be in touch when we're done."

"Is that it?" he asked. "May I go now?"

"That depends, Mr Banner. You see, this is a voluntary interview—"

"Hardly," he mumbled.

"Which means that any information you give us now which helps us in our enquiries will work in your favour," Anna continued. "And any information you withhold will work against you. So by all means, you're welcome to go and see your wife. But I'd give serious thought to what else you might know that could help us eliminate you from the investigation."

He buried his face in his hands, then checked his watch.

"Do you want to see your wife, Mr Banner?" Jenny asked, and he nodded, swallowing hard.

"You didn't tell me exactly how she died. Myra, I mean."

"You didn't ask."

"I'm asking now."

"She was strangled," Anna said. "Ring any bells?"

He didn't respond to Anna's question, instead choosing his own line of questioning.

"Was it quick?" he asked. "Did she suffer?"

Anna watched him, trying to read his body language for any indication of his concern being disingenuous.

"We don't think so," Anna said.

"And Claire. Does she know?"

"One of our colleagues was escorting her to Myra's house when the explosion happened."

"Were they hurt?" He asked. "Your colleague. Were they hurt?"

"No. Not really. As for your wife, she took the full force of the front door hitting her on the back of the head. It could have been a lot worse, Mr Banner."

"Did she say anything?" he asked. "Claire? Did she say anything about me and Myra?"

"Only that you'd had an argument," Anna replied, to which he gave a little stab of laughter. "Is something funny?"

"Yeah. Yeah, it is. The argument she told you about lasted about fifteen years. We've never got on, Myra and me. Believe me, I've tried to get on with her."

"That's pretty much what Claire said," Anna said quietly, sensing a revelation coming. "Was this fifteen-year argument bad enough that you might want to hurt her, Mr Banner?"

He buried his face again. His hands were immaculate. His nails had been trimmed, and despite him spending his months at his laptop creating some of the best mysteries Anna had ever read, his hands had a strength to them. In fact, his arms were well-toned. Not thickset like a body builder, but muscular still, and with his broad shoulders, Anna considered him to be quite a powerful man.

"Mr Banner?" Anna said again. She glanced across at Jenny, who clearly suspected the same revelation. He was going to talk. His mind was likely battling with what to say and what not to say. Just enough. That was the usual starting point for suspects in Banner's position. Until the barriers broke and they just had to get it all off their chest. "Is there something you want to tell us?"

He raised his head wearily, and sighed, laying his hands flat on the table before him.

"There's something you need to know," he said, nodding. "But I want this off the record."

He flicked his eyes at the recording, then raised an eyebrow expectantly. Anna gave Jenny the nod, and she hit the pause button.

"You've got one minute," Anna said.

"Alright," he replied, and he took a deep breath. "My wife told you about what Myra did, I'm guessing?"

"She mentioned an incident, yes," Anna said.

"About the restaurant? When I bumped into her and loverboy having a cosy lunch in The Cosy Club? Am I right?"

"That's about right."

"So I suppose you know Myra sent photos of me and another woman to my wife?"

Anna nodded.

"The woman I met. She wasn't a lover. I mean, I'm not having an affair."

"That's of no significance to me, Mr Banner."

"But it is, don't you see? I'm not a bad man. I'm not like that."

"So who was she?"

He squeezed his eyes closed, fighting the urge to hold his tongue, but then relented.

"It was a TV Producer. A famous one, too. She wants to get my series on the screen. Netflix or Amazon Prime, most likely. It's the chance of a bloody lifetime."

"So why didn't you say that? Why didn't you just tell your wife the truth? I'm sure she would have been happy for you."

"Because I signed an NDA. A non-disclosure agreement."

"I know what an NDA is, believe me," Anna said.

"And besides, why should I have to break the terms of a contract that could change our lives forever just for that miserable old witch?"

"I presume you're talking about your mother-in-law?"

"Of course I am. I love my wife. I'd never do anything to hurt her. And I certainly wouldn't kill her bloody mother."

Anna gave his comments some serious thought, studying his expression for any telltale signs of deceit. Then she nodded for Jenny to start the recording again.

"Mr Banner, I've read your books; many of them, at least. Would you agree, you are extremely familiar with police procedure?"

He shrugged. "Of course. It's what I do."

"So you'll understand our concerns," Anna said. "Your mother-in-law, with whom you argued for the past fifteen years, has been found strangled to death beneath a tree, exactly as the killer does in your book, *Dance With Death*. Your van is spotted at the scene of the crime, just as the killer's vehicle is seen in your story, and you can provide no evidence that you were not in Dunston at the time of the murder."

"You can't honestly think—"

"Kevin Banner, I'm arresting you on suspicion of murder. You do not have to say anything. But, it may harm your defence if you do not mention when questioned something which you later rely on in court. Anything you do say may be given in evidence."

"This is ridiculous. That was just a book."

"Damn realistic, though, wasn't it?" Anna said.

"I need to see my wife."

"You're aware of what happens next, I presume?" Anna said.

He stared at her, his jovial nature replaced by bitter scorn.

"You lock me in a cell, and then do everything you can to convince Crown Prosecution to support a charge," he said, and Anna nodded approvingly. "And given that, until one minute ago, I was here voluntarily, you have twenty-four hours to do so."

"Very good, Mr Banner," Anna replied, and she matched his pose, interlocking her fingers opposite him. "But for the first time in my career, I really hope I'm wrong about this."

CHAPTER THIRTY-FIVE

Copeland, Taylor and Sons was a small independent gun shop on the edge of Woodhall Spa. Being out of the main town afforded the owners a large frontage with plenty of parking space, and according to a sign, even a small indoor .22 firing range to the rear. When Nillson and Anderson arrived, there was only one car in the little car park. The driver's door was open and the engine was running. She met Anderson at the back of their car, and together, they made their way to the shop, where they were met almost immediately by a man wearing jeans, a check shirt, and a flat cap.

"Sorry, you'll have to come back tomorrow," he said, turning his back on them to lock the doors behind them.

"It'll just take a minute," Nillson explained.

"Any other time, duck, and I'd oblige," he said, testing the door with a shove. He turned to face them and pocketed the keys. "But I'm running late."

Nillson fished her warrant card from her pocket and presented it at arm's length.

"It'll just take a few minutes," she said, to which he seemed to groan inwardly. "Inside, please."

"If this is about that young lad, I'll tell you what I told your colleague. I don't sell knives to kids—"

"This is not about a knife crime, Mr Copeland," Nillson said and left it there until he had unlocked the door. He went about disengaging the alarm in the back office, while Nillson and Anderson looked around. For the most part, the walls were covered in a large array of air rifles and a smaller area bore single-shot firearms. A variety of scopes, bipods, and other accessories filled in the spaces, and hunting and firearms magazines filled a turnstile rack set to one side, along with a few publications on country life.

"Now then," he said, as he emerged from the back room. He stood behind the glass-topped counter as if they were customers. It was as if he was striving to retain the power in the dynamic.

Nillson continued to look around, spying at least two CCTV cameras located in the corners of the main shop, and one more behind the counter. She was sure there would be one more outside too.

The counter on which he leaned held an array of knives, from multitools to folding pen knives, and fixed blades in leather sheaths.

"All above board, I can assure you," he grumbled.

"I'm sure," Nillson said, reaching into her pocket. She produced the folded warrant, opened it, and laid it on the glass counter, saying nothing. The warrant spoke for itself. She watched his eyes dart down and read the fine print, then she stepped away to continue perusing the wares.

"Are you going to tell me what you're looking for?" he asked.

Nillson ran her finger along the wooden stock of a rifle, noting the exquisite craftsmanship and detail.

"Are you able to tell me your opening hours?" she began, as Anderson stepped into view from where she had been flicking through a rack of camouflage hunting jackets.

"There's a sign on the door," he replied. "You'll notice we closed thirty minutes ago."

"I saw the sign," Nillson said. "It says you're closed on Sundays."

"That's right. We are."

"And you were closed last Sunday. Is that right?"

"Last Sunday?" he said, feigning deep thought. "That was a Sunday, wasn't it?"

Nillson stared at him. His poor humour not only reminded her of Gillespie but seemed to be an attempt at distraction.

"Of course, we were closed," he said, finally. "We're closed every Sunday. If we opened, I wouldn't get any work done."

"Work?" Nillson said.

"Repairs and such. I'm in the workshop mostly," he said, then jabbed a thumb behind him. "That's out the back."

"Did you have any visitors?" Nillson asked. "Do people come and collect their belongs on a Sunday?"

"We're closed on Sundays," Copeland said, pulling a face as if she was intellectually challenged. "I'm not sure how much I can dumb it down for you."

"So you were working in the workshop last Sunday and you had no visitors," Nillson said. "That's fine. I just wanted to establish the facts."

"That's good we got there in the end, didn't we?"

"If I could just see the footage from the CCTV," Nillson said.

"From my what?"

"Your security cameras," she explained. "I imagine an establishment such as this will have to conform to regulations regarding the safeguarding of data."

"Sorry?"

"You must have systems in place to maintain security footage for a prescribed period of time," Nillson said.

"A prescribed period of time?"

"Listen, Mr Copeland. I'm not sure how much I can dumb this down for you. But I'll do my best," Nillson said. "Now, get me the video footage from last Sunday."

He stared at her questioningly, as if he might argue that the cameras weren't working, but thought better of it.

"I'll be a moment."

"Take all the time you need, Mr Copeland," she said, following him into the backroom with lazy steps. "We're not going anywhere."

She found him seated at a computer in a tiny room that smelled of gun oil. A warm draught from another open door licked at her ankles, and she peered inside spying a bench with a vice, a neat array of hand tools, and various gun spares.

"Neat workshop," she said, genuinely impressed.

"Here," he said, ignoring her comment. He sat back in the seat to allow her a view of the screen over his shoulder.

"May I?" she said, very aware of becoming too close to him in such a confined space.

Reluctantly, he moved, offering some advice on how to navigate the system as he did.

"It's okay," she said. "It's not the first time I've used a security system."

It took a few moments for her to get her bearings with the particular system, noting the timestamp in the bottom right-hand corner. The screen was split into four boxes. The first two showed the inside of the shop, which were the two Nillson had spotted. The bottom left-hand box displayed behind the counter and another showed the car park with a focus on the front door. She scrolled the footage back to midday on the previous Sunday, then hit play, adjusting the speed to 4X. The internal cameras had caught Copeland coming in and out of the back office for one reason or another. His movements were almost comical being played so fast, reminding Nillson of an old Chaplin movie. Twelve-thirty passed, then one o'clock, one-thirty, and two o'clock.

Anderson poked her head into the back office, signing with a slight shake of her head that she had found nothing untoward.

Nillson hit stop on the video footage.

"See?" Copeland said.

She said nothing. Instead, she pulled her phone from her pocket, found Ben's number in her contacts and hit the button to call him. In her peripheral, Copeland leaned on a shelving rack where a kettle and a few dirty mugs were stored along with a jar of cheap coffee.

"Anna?" Ben said, answering on the second ring. "How are you getting on?"

"Nothing," she replied. "I've checked the security footage. Nobody came or went between twelve and two p.m."

"How about the search?" Ben asked.

"I'm going need some help with that," Nillson said. "This place is so full of junk, it'll take a week just to find the floor."

"Oy," Copeland said.

"Is that him?"

"It is, yes," Nillson said, idly hitting play again to watch the rest of the day.

A black shape flashed by on the scrolling footage and Nillson hit the space bar to stop the playback.

"Hold on," she said, more to herself than to Ben. She hit the left cursor a few times, taking the footage back frame by frame, until, on the quadrant showing the front door, a black shape moved into view. The image wasn't clear enough to identify who it was, but the few frames revealed him stooping at the door, then peering through the glass and knocking. "I've got something."

"Banner?" Ben asked.

Using the cursors, she scrolled the footage forward frame by frame. The quadrants displaying the inside of the shop showed Copeland coming from the back office, unlocking the door, and letting somebody in.

"Who's that?" Nillson asked, turning to Copeland. He leaned in for a better view of the screen, as she adjusted the replay speed to half speed.

The two men in the video shook hands. The visitor handed Copeland something, and then they moved into the back offices out of the camera's range.

"I said, who was that?"

"Just a mate," he replied. "I told you. I don't have customers on a Sunday."

"His name?" Nillson said, then spoke to Ben "Are you hearing all this?"

"I am," he said quietly.

"My mate, Kev. Known him donkey's years, I have."

"Kevin Banner?"

"Yeah. So? He's just a mate. Look, is this going to take long? I'm supposed to be meeting somebody. It's quiz night tonight."

"What did he give you?"

"What?"

"He handed you something when he came into the shop. What was it, Mr Copeland?"

"Nothing. He..."

Nillson dragged the footage back to the exchange and paused it on the frame.

"What was that?" she said.

"I don't know. Just the paper, I think. You know? The junk they leave every month. Local stuff. He probably just picked it up from the doorstep."

"How well do you know Kevin Banner?"

"We go back years, Kev and me," Copeland said. "He comes in from time to time for a tea. Usually wants to pick my brains about guns. For his books, you know?"

"Is this it?" Anderson said, emerging from the shop front holding a folded newspaper. "Is this what he gave you? I found it beside the till."

"Yeah, that's it."

She unfolded the newspaper and an A4 envelope fell out onto the grubby floor.

Copeland closed his eyes in defeat. Nillson had seen that expression too many times to know it was not one of innocence. She leaned down and picked it up.

"You okay, Anna?" Ben said.

"Yeah, are you with the boss?"

"Freya? No. I'm getting ready to go out."

"Oh? With anyone we know?"

"With a friend," he replied before she could press for the icy details. "Come on, what's the update?"

"Looks like we found something. It's an envelope. We've checked the CCTV. Kevin Banner came here at two-thirty on Sunday, and asked Mr Copeland to hide it."

"I didn't know..." Copeland began, and Anna placed her hand over the mouthpiece and addressed him directly.

"Mr Copeland. I'm afraid your old buddy Kevin Banner has landed you in the middle of a murder investigation. So unless you start talking, you'll find yourself at the station with a far bigger problem than being late for a bloody quiz night. Aiding and abetting a criminal, for example."

He stared at the envelope for a few moments, then sighed.

"Look, I didn't know what it was," he said. "Kev asked me to look after it. That's all."

"Look after it? Why?"

Copeland shrugged.

"I don't know. Honestly, I don't know," he said. "He just said it was important, and that I'd be doing him a favour."

"Who is it addressed to?" Ben asked.

"Have a guess."

"Not Kevin Banner?"

"Nope."

"Myra Dicks?"

"Correct."

"Has it been opened?"

"Yes," she replied. "It's torn."

"What's inside?" he asked.

"Hang on," Anna said, edging the phone between her shoulder and her cheek. She pulled a latex glove from her pocket and fished inside for the contents, pulling the little pile of A4 paperwork out just enough for her to read the title.

"I've seen this document before, Ben," she said. "It's a copy of Adam Frost's rejected proposal."

A few seconds passed, during which time Anna imagined Ben undergoing a confused facial expression, just as she and Jenny were.

"Now why would Kevin Banner be hiding that in his friend's gun shop?"

"Hang on, Ben," she said, examining the paperwork in the light of the computer monitor. "The proposal itself is a photocopy, but there's something written on it."

"What does it say?"

"JS. Sunday. One p.m.," Anna replied. "It wasn't written on the original. I'm positive."

"JS? Jeffery Steel?" Ben said. "So he *was* there, after all."

"You know what it means, though?" Anna said, staring Copeland in the eye. "It means that Kevin Banner knew exactly when and where to find Myra."

"So they both had the opportunity," Ben said.

"Looks like it," she replied.

"Okay, bring it to the briefing in the morning. Let's see what Freya wants to do."

"Ben," she said before he hung up.

"Anna?"

She licked her lips, aware that both Jenny and Copeland were watching her and she was thankful the call was not on loudspeaker.

"He's in custody."

"You arrested him?"

"The evidence is stacked against him," she explained. "I had to check his alibi before he had a chance to warn his friend at the gun shop."

"You did the right thing," Ben said. "But I get a feeling you don't want it to be him. Am I right?"

She bit her lip, understanding exactly how unprofessional it sounded.

"Well, you know what they say," he told her with a heavy breath. "Never meet your heroes. I'll see you in the morning."

CHAPTER THIRTY-SIX

At his desk, Ben set his coffee down and fired up his laptop. On a good day, the laptop the force had provided him would be powered up and whirring away in just under five minutes. The little cursor would then spin round and round for at least five more minutes before it was usable. Typically, Ben would hit the keys in frustration, wondering why on earth everybody else's laptop seemed to work just fine yet his was like an old man starting his day. But following the conversation with Will, he used the time to reflect on the changes he had seen over the years. '*Change is the only constant,*' Will had said.

There was a time when the large room had bore an unofficial division, with DI Standing's team at the far end, and DI Foster's team, now Freya's team, closest to the doors. Now the room was home to a single team, leaving the far end of the room, in near darkness; a void of memories, none of which Ben truly cared for.

Somewhere, in the distance, somebody whistled. It was a tuneless effort, repetitive, and almost like a nursery rhyme. But before Ben could figure out who was producing the sound at six-fifteen in the morning, the doors opened, squealing as if they were in agony.

The insufferable doors were the only thing that hadn't changed. In fact, not only was the squeak the only constant, but it seemed to be getting worse.

"Morning, Ben," said a cheerful Cruz, as he tossed his little backpack onto his desk. "You're in early."

"Yes," Ben said, though he struggled to find anything to follow up with. The truth was, that the early arrival of Cruz had jarred him. This was his time. Time for him to sort his thoughts into some kind of order. "Just getting a head start. You?"

"Yeah, same," Cruz replied. He was the youngest member of the team, not just in age, but in the mind as well. Naive, emotional, and gullible, were the three words Ben thought of most when he considered him. But today, his shirt was a gleaming white, brand new if Ben wasn't mistaken. His trousers were pressed and clean. His shoes had been polished, too, and even the tell-tale untied laces were neatly knotted. "I'm going to make a coffee. Can I get you something?"

"I'm good," Ben replied, gesturing at his mug, and offering a weak smile.

"You alright, Ben?" Cruz asked, running a hand through his hair, which was normally an unkempt mess but this morning appeared to have been styled. "You look like you've got the weight—"

"Of the world. Yes, I know," he finished for him. "I'm just waiting for my laptop."

"Oh," Cruz said. "You want to get that seen to. Have you contacted support?"

Ben had to stop himself from giving a Freya-like retort, facetious, and aggressive. Instead, he swallowed and selected a more forgiving statement.

"Oh, you know what they're like. They'll just tell me to turn it off and on again, and I'll have to wait another fifteen minutes for it to boot up."

"Yeah," Cruz said, edging towards the door, clearly in need of a coffee. They squealed open, and Ben stared at his laptop in defeat.

"Cruz?" he said without turning to face him.

"Yeah?"

"Are you happy here?" Ben asked, though had he given it more thought he was sure he could have constructed the question better.

"Happy?"

"Do you enjoy coming to work? Do you like the team?"

"Well, yeah," Cruz said, and he let the doors slam shut as he stepped into Ben's line of view. "It's good, isn't it? Like a little family."

"A family?" Ben repeated, considering the word, and began to agree. "There's been a lot of change, don't you think? Over the past couple of years, I mean. What with David Foster dying and Steve Standing's transfer."

"I think there'll aways be change, Ben," Cruz said, in a rare moment of wisdom. "But if you're asking if I prefer it now to back then, then I'd say, yeah. Is everything okay, Ben?"

"Everything's fine, mate," Ben assured him. "So, you're happier working for Freya than you were working for Steve?"

Cruz stared up at the empty end of the room. The desks and chairs that he, Standing, Gillespie, Nillson and the other members of the team used to sit at were all stacked up. The space had become a kind of informal furniture storage area. A place where nobody ventured.

"Can I say something, Ben?"

"Sure."

"Steve Standing was a right bastard. I mean, don't get me wrong, DI Bloom has her moments, and there has been days when I've gone home and wondered what the bloody hell I'm doing with my life. But usually, it's Hermione, my girlfriend, who reminds me of the changes. Always having to go door to door sometimes feels like I'm the runt of the litter. I never get the good jobs. But she reminds me that with Steve Standing, I never even got to do that. I'd be stuck here writing up his reports. It's easy to dwell on the negatives, but she always finds the positive in things. And from what DI Bloom was saying to me the other day—"

"The other day?"

"Yeah, you know? At the crime scene in Dunston. She was saying there's a real chance for me to accelerate my career. To take the next step. Steve would never have given me that chance."

"I see," Ben said, suddenly understanding why Cruz was dressed like he was going for a job interview. "She's right. There will be opportunities. But do me a favour, Cruz, will you?"

The younger of the two shrugged, and a worried expression washed over his face.

"Yeah, of course."

"Don't get your hopes up, mate. I mean, it can take years to move up the ladder. Look at me. I was all lined up for DI before Freya came along. But you know what? You'll take that step one day. And it might come when you least expect it."

"Is this your way of letting me down?" Cruz asked, and for a moment, the positive Cruz faded to reveal the Cruz that Ben was used to – a sensitive, impressionable young man with a heart of gold.

"No, Cruz. I'm just saying, that things don't always turn out the way we want them to," Ben said, remembering the threat of change from his conversation with Will. "But if you work hard, you'll get there one day."

"It's like my mum says. You can be blown about at the mercy of the wind," Cruz said, in a sudden pang of maturity. He made his way back to the doors and they squealed open, but somehow the squeal was dulled by the promise of some nugget of wisdom from the team's youngest member.

"Or?" Ben asked, not looking at him, but imagining him in the doorway, with his shirt untucked, creased trousers, and shoelaces untied. That was the Cruz that Ben knew and loved.

"Or you can be the wind," Cruz finished. He let the doors slam shut, and his tuneless whistle faded down the corridor, leaving Ben more than a little perplexed.

CHAPTER THIRTY-SEVEN

From the station car park, Freya took the fire escape stairs to the first floor, as she normally did, ascending to the percussive echoes of her heels on the concrete steps, leaving behind a cloud of her new perfume. In the corridor, however, she made every effort to walk with stealth, having seen both Ben and Will Granger's car in the car park.

Somebody was whistling from further along the corridor. It was tuneless, and repetitive, reminding Freya of the music to a children's TV show her ex-husband's son used to watch when he was a toddler. From inside Granger's office, she heard files rustling, and then the sound of somebody straightening a stack of papers with the click of a stapler to finish.

Then, before she could slip into the incident room, the whistling stopped and Cruz appeared in the corridor ahead.

"Morning, boss," he called as she neared the incident room. He looked different somehow, even from a distance. He appeared smarter, or at least cleaner. "Beautiful morning, isn't it? Can I get you a coffee?"

The sound of shuffling papers ceased almost immediately, and she winced at her failure to arrive unnoticed by Granger, who came to stand in his office doorway with a mug of coffee in his hand.

"Morning, Freya," he said.

"Yes, please," she told, Cruz, then turned to Granger, summoning a smile as close to pleasant as she could. "Morning, guv."

"How is the Dicks investigation going?"

"I sent you the reports yesterday."

"And I read them," he replied. "Thank you."

"We're making progress," she added, sensing he wanted to hear the informal details that were typically omitted from formal reports. "We have Kevin Banner in for questioning."

"And?" he said, waiting for her to embellish the comment.

"Nillson and Anderson interviewed him yesterday. I'll speak to you when I have all the facts."

"What about Gold? How's she?"

"A few minor cuts in her hands. Other than that, she's fine. She'll be back this afternoon," Freya said, then before Granger could get another question in, she took control of the conversation. "Claire Banner is stable. Severe concussion. With any luck, she'll be released tomorrow. We're building a picture, guv."

"What about the explosion?" Granger asked, and he stared at her over the rim of his coffee mug. "Coincidence?"

"We're pressing Michaela for some early results. My thoughts are that the incidents are related. A blast like that can destroy forensic evidence, so the results will be limited. But you never know. We might get lucky."

He nodded, saying nothing, and over his shoulder, Cruz emerged from the kitchenette doorway carrying two mugs. Granger glanced back, then eyed Freya.

"The funeral is this week," he said. "It would be nice if the team weren't too busy to attend."

"Guv," she replied, by way of confirmation, and he slipped back into his office.

"Here you go, boss," Cruz said, handing Freya a mug. He shoved open the incident room door, and the hinges squealed as if their sole purpose was to irritate Freya. He held the door open and Freya followed him inside, setting the mug down on her desk and then hanging her bag on the back of her chair.

She felt Ben's stare while she prepared herself for what was promising to be another tumultuous day.

"Good morning, Ben," she said. "Have you heard from Michaela?"

"I've arranged for her to come in to give a briefing of her findings at both crime scenes and the house."

"She's coming in?"

"It was her idea," he said, without looking up. He was tapping a button on his laptop repeatedly, clearly growing frustrated with its lack of response. "She said there's so much information to present, it would be easier to show rather than sending a report."

"Oh," Freya replied. "Well, that's good news. If there's one thing we're short of, it's information."

"My thoughts exactly," he replied.

"Are you going to be okay with her being here?" Freya asked, highlighting Ben's failed attempt at taking the investigator on a date a few months ago.

He smiled at the memory and pulled a sheepish expression.

"I'm sure I can suffer an hour of embarrassment for the sake of some leads."

"Speaking of information. Cruz?" Freya said, and the young detective looked up from his laptop, his face a picture of puzzlement. "What are you working on?"

"Eh?"

"You're in early, which is commendable, but what are you working on?"

"I, erm..."

Freya sensed the answer was not one she was going to appreciate.

"I'm just doing today's crossword, boss. You know? To get my mind going." He added a little side-to-side movement with his head to indicate energy.

"The crossword?" she replied flatly.

"I've finished going through the reports," he said defensively. "I always do the crossword with my morning coffee."

"*You* do the crossword?" Freya repeated, unable to hide the surprise in her tone. Ben smirked and returned to hitting the button on his laptop. "Wonders will never cease."

"Is that alright, boss? Can I carry on?"

"It's your time, Cruz," she said, checking her watch. "And if sharpens your mind, then I'm in favour."

He sat straight in his seat, cleared his throat and returned to his laptop, just as the doors to the incident room burst open and Gillespie entered, coming to a stop at the doors.

"Well, well, well," he said. "Having a wee party without me, are you?"

"It's hardly a party, Jim," Cruz said.

"Ah, I see you're doing a wordsearch," he replied, obviously hoping to incite some trouble for Cruz.

"It's a crossword, actually."

"Ah, right. Crosswords on company time, eh? Will you be attempting the dot-to-dot when you're done?"

"You're hilarious," Cruz groaned.

"Morning, boss," Gillespie said, ignoring Cruz's comment. He laid his jacket over the back of his seat and nodded a greeting to Ben. "Did I miss anything?"

"Only a cup of bad coffee and a to-do list as large as your ego, Gillespie," Freya told him.

"Bad coffee, eh?"

"I suggest you make yourself one. We're in for a tough day."

"Aye, boss. You don't have to tell me twice," Gillespie said, stretching, and then making his way to the doors. He looked around the room, noting three full mugs on the desk. "Looks like a cheap round."

He turned to open the doors just as they opened and in walked Anderson and Chapman who house shared and travelled together.

"Morning, all," Chapman said to nobody in particular. She made her way to her seat, opening her laptop so it could boot whilst she hung her coat and set herself up for the day. Anderson acted similarly but was paying a little more attention to the mood in the room.

"Did we interrupt something?" she asked.

"No, nothing at all," Gillespie said, catching the squealing door as it closed.

"Gillespie was just asking if anybody wants coffee," Freya said.

"Oh, that would be lovely," Chapman said, as she settled into her seat. "Thanks, Jim."

Gillespie's mouth hung open, with a defeated smile emerging through the three days of growth on his face.

"Jenny?" he said, mustering as much enthusiasm as he could.

"Thanks, Jim," Anderson added. "Black, no sugar."

"Aye, no bother," he said turning to leave. "Absolutely no bother at all."

It was then that Gold appeared in the doorway, ducking beneath his arm with a soft, "Morning all."

"Jim's on coffee duty," Cruz told her, smiling at the glare Gillespie sent his way.

"Ooh, coffee. Yes, please, Jim," she said, sliding off her light jacket to reveal a bandaged hand.

"How's the hand?" Freya asked her, as the doors closed and Gillespie made his way to the little kitchenette.

"Ah, I'm fine," Gold replied. "Just a few scratches. They managed to get the glass out."

"And do you think this is an ideal place for it to heal?"

"With all due respect, ma'am, I can't sit at home doing nothing all day. Besides, I'm getting to know Claire Banner quite well. I think I should go back and see her."

Freya considered the HR ramifications of allowing an injured member of staff to work, weighing them against the loss of a valuable team member.

"If you're in pain, I want to know. If your cuts open up, you're going home. Understood?"

Gold nodded, and smiled as a child might try to please her mother. "Ma'am."

"Good. Thank you," Freya said, looking around the room. "We're just waiting for Nillson."

"Shall I call her?" Chapman asked.

"Yes. See how long she'll be," she said. "I must say, it's a pleasure to see so many faces so early in the morning."

She stared at them all in turn, then checked her watch. It was only seven-thirty. Cruz lowered his face behind his laptop screen, Chapman busied herself with the call to Nillson, and both Gold and Anderson were discussing one of the printed reports.

Only Ben was looking her way, a wry smile on his face. There was no need to ask him if he'd arranged for them all to come in early, and there was no need to ask him why. But he gave her an answer anyway. Because that was how Ben operated. No games.

"DS Nillson is five minutes away," Chapman announced without looking up. Freya turned her attention back to Ben.

"We have an opportunity to make a difference," Ben explained, sipping at his coffee. "You have your team. Just tell us what you want us to do."

CHAPTER THIRTY-EIGHT

Nillson entered the room in a squeal of door hinges. She greeted nobody until she had opened her laptop, pulled her notepad from her bag, and silenced her phone. It was only then that she looked up, just in time to find Gillespie backing through the double doors carrying a tray of coffees.

"Is there one for me?" she asked him, and Freya grinned at Gillespie's downtrodden expression.

"Eh?" was all he could say.

"It's not a difficult question, Jim," she said. "Is there a coffee there for me or should I make one for myself?"

"I'm sure he wouldn't mind popping back and making one more, would you, Gillespie?" Freya said.

"Eh?"

"A coffee," Freya replied.

"I've just made–"

"So I imagine the kettle will still be hot."

"Ah, for crying out loud," he grumbled. "What's the point of having Cruz reporting into me if I have to make the coffees? What's he doing?"

"Crossword," Cruz said, matter-of-factly. "It's a little game where you have to fill in all the white squares after working out the clues."

Gillespie pulled out his seat, reached for his coffee, and was about to sit down when Freya spoke.

"Gillespie?" she said, and he paused in a kind of squat, hovering above the chair.

"Aye, boss?"

"Coffee? Nillson?" she said and gestured at Nillson who stared at him expectantly.

He sighed, then stood slowly. "Aye. Coffee," he mumbled, then jabbed a finger at Ben on his way to the doors. "You. This is your doing."

"Don't blame me," Ben said with a laugh.

"Come in early, you said. The boss'll thank me for it, you said. You'll get into her good books," Gillespie snarled as he yanked open the doors again. "Bloody good books. Turns out, I'm the bloody tea boy. If this is her good books, I'd hate to be in her bad books."

"You're about to find out what that's like," Freya snapped. "Now stop wasting everybody's time and make the damn coffee."

He sulked off, letting the doors slam behind him, and Freya took a deep breath as she gathered her thoughts.

"Thank you," she told everyone. "Before we start, it's worth mentioning that there will be changes coming. It's inevitable. I've spoken to some of you already, but for the rest of you, the death of Detective Superintendent Harper will have a profound effect on the team. It's times like this that I'm reminded of how close this team is, and how well we work together. If we do our job well, then we can deal with whatever changes come. If we argue," she said, with a curt glance at the doors Gillespie had just walked through, "then we won't do our jobs effectively. I don't think I need to embellish that point any more, do I?"

"We get it," Nillson said, speaking for the room. "It's why we're here."

Freya walked slowly to the desk on which Gillespie had left the coffees, and passed them across to Chapman and Anderson.

"We've got a lot to get through, and not much information to go on, so who wants to go first?"

"I'll go," Nillson said, checking with Anderson that they were ready "We interviewed Banner like you asked."

"Okay, is he a keeper or are we letting him go?"

"He's a keeper for now," Nillson said, checking her watch. "For the next few hours at least. We placed him under arrest."

"What do we have on him?" Freya asked. "Aside from what we've already established."

"His alibi is pretty loose. He says he was in Woodhall Spa researching his book, which included a visit to the gun shop on the way out of town."

"That sounds ominous," Freya remarked.

"The owner is an old school friend of his," Nillson explained. "A Trevor Copeland. We checked the CCTV and saw Banner arriving at two-thirty."

"That gives him time, doesn't it?" Freya asked, looking for a response from Ben. He nodded.

"Plenty of time," he said.

"He also gave Copeland an envelope to look after," Nillson added. "Although I think he didn't want anybody to know he'd done it. He hid the envelope inside a newspaper so that all we saw on the security footage was a man handing his friend a newspaper he found on the doorstep."

"So he was expecting somebody to check the cameras?" Cruz said. "Bit weird, isn't it?"

"What was in the envelope?" Freya asked. "Don't tell me. It was a confession?"

"Quite the opposite. It was a rejected proposal for an archaeological excavation in Dunston."

Freya digested the information and then sat back on the edge of her desk.

"Who created the proposal?"

"Adam Frost," Nillson replied.

"And who rejected it? Myra?"

"Bingo," Nillson said. "It was a photocopy of the original though."

"How do you know?"

"Because I found the original in Frost's house. There was only one major difference."

"Go on."

"The copy Banner left in the gun shop had some handwriting on it like somebody had made a note so they don't forget. It said, 'JS, one p.m., Sunday.'"

"JS, one p.m., Sunday?"

"Jeffery Steel," Ben said.

"And do you know what else?" Nillson said. "The excavation in question is three hundred yards from where Myra was found."

"The one he was digging when he saw the police cars?" Freya said. "So why was Myra there?"

"Well, seeing as we can't ask her, why don't we ask Jeffery Steel?" Ben said.

"Do we know where he is?" Freya asked, turning to Gillespie for an answer.

"The man is missing," he said. "He's not at home, I've called the university, I called his mobile phone. He's up and vanished like a fart in the wind."

"Please don't be vulgar," Freya said. "If you can't find him, just say so and I'll give you more resources."

"I can't find him, boss."

"Okay, take Cruz and find him."

"Eh? I thought you said I could have more resources?"

"You have. Cruz."

"I had him already."

"Ah, but you didn't have a warrant for Jeffrey Steel's arrest, did you?"

"How is that supposed to help me find him?" Gillespie asked.

"Well, I was hoping you'd be a little more motivated to make an arrest, especially given that our futures are all at stake here."

"Ah," he said. "I see."

"Exactly. Arresting murderers always goes down well with the top brass."

"I'll find him."

"I thought you might," Freya said. "Where are we now? Ben, give us a rundown, please?"

Ben sat forward in his seat, flicked his notepad back a page, and then cleared his throat.

"We have Adam Frost in custody on suspicion of murder. We can place him at the scene, we have a motive of sorts, and there's no doubt he would be capable of strangling Myra Dicks. What we can't prove yet is his knowledge of Myra's whereabouts."

"Okay, so we can't charge him even if we wanted to."

"We'd need a stronger case for CPS to back the charge," Ben explained.

"How long can we hold him for?"

"Lunchtime today, unless we get an extension," Chapman advised.

"Next?" Freya said, turning her attention back to Ben.

"We also have Kevin Banner in custody awaiting a charge," he replied. "We can place him near the scene of the crime with eye witnesses, a.k.a. the farmer and Adam Frost. He definitely has a motive, and the key difference between him and Frost is that, with the document Nillson found at the gun shop, we know that he knew Myra would be in Dunston at that time."

"Still not enough for CPS to back the charge," Freya said. "There are too many unknowns for a defence team to introduce doubt. How long do we have with him?"

"About eight hours," Chapman said, looking up from her screen.

"Right. We have some work to do on him then."

"The only other person with a motive is Veronica Steel," Ben said. "According to Gillespie and Cruz, she was at home all day, waiting for her cheating husband to come home. We could do with firming that up."

"Realistically, could Veronica Steel have strangled Myra Dicks to death?" Nillson asked. "I mean, they make it look easy in the films, but it's a big ask."

"Gillespie?" Freya said. "You've met her. What do you think?"

"I think she'd struggle opening a bottle of wine," he replied. "There's no way she could have overpowered Myra Dicks."

"And lastly?" Freya said to Ben.

"Jeffery Steel. No known motive, but he was closest to her, and we know Myra had agreed to meet him there."

"Yeah, but did Myra arrange to meet him, or did Jeffery Steel arrange to meet her?" Nillson asked with a wry smile. "That could make all the difference in a premeditated murder investigation."

"True," Freya agreed.

"And the obvious one," Ben continued. "Nobody can find him."

"Well, we know he's around. We saw him on Monday." Freya said. "Okay, let's leave it there. I think it's about time we called Michaela in."

"She's downstairs. I'll send her a text," Ben replied.

"Right, washroom break," Freya announced, clapping her hands. "We're nearly done."

"One thing," Gillespie said, and those who had moved froze in anticipation.

"Go on," she said.

"Are we allowed to make things awkward for Ben when Michaela comes in?" he asked.

"Oh, come on," Ben said.

Freya smiled.

"Are you suggesting that you use Ben's failed attempts to date Michaela to your advantage and to embarrass one of your colleagues?" Freya asked.

"I am, boss, aye."

"Well, then knock yourself out, Gillespie," she said, smiling at Ben from across the room. "I'll buy a beer for whoever makes him blush the most. How does that sound?"

CHAPTER THIRTY-NINE

Curious, Freya stared at the doors along with every other member of the team. Chapman peered over her glasses, her fingers still hovering above the keyboard. Gold was checking her reflection in a small compact mirror she kept in her handbag. Nillson and Anderson were both leaning over Anderson's laptop. Gillespie, however, stood beside his desk with his hands in his pockets. Freya watched his eyes widen with approval as the doors squealed open behind her. A wry smile emerged through his stubble and Freya turned to find a familiar face in the doorway.

"I hope you don't mind," Michaela said. "Ben said it might be a good idea to present my findings in person."

"It's not standard procedure," Freya said, eyeing the pretty blonde. She wore a dark blue trouser suit – tasteful, professional, yet light enough for the heat of summer. Without her white suit, hood, and mask, the ten years or so difference between her and Freya was more than evident.

"But given the volume of information..." Michaela added.

"I thought it best if Michaela afforded us the opportunity to ask questions," Ben said. "Rather than have us pick out pieces of information from a sterile report."

Freya checked her watch.

"Okay," she said, with a wave of her hand. "The floor is yours, Doctor Fell. Enlighten us with your findings."

"I'm not sure how enlightening it will be, Freya," Michaela said, moving over to the whiteboard and dropping her bag on the carpet. "Right, so first things first. Myra Dicks."

She waited for the team to resettle, and only once they were all seated and paying attention did she continue.

"I'll start from the top," she began. "When we examined her in situ, we found very few belongings. Merely an identification card for the university, a mobile phone, and her car keys. No fingerprints other than Myra's were found on the devices. However, when we had exhausted all forensic methods, we passed the mobile phone to the tech team who managed to unlock it."

"It took them three days?" Freya asked.

"That's fast. These things take time, Freya. However, I think the wait was worth it. The last caller has been identified as Claire Banner, her daughter. But the last message she received was from a Jeffery Steel."

"Her colleague and lover," Freya added.

"Is he in the frame?"

"Somewhat," Freya replied. "He's missing and therefore we're looking for him. What did the message say?"

"'Okay, see you there,'" Michaela replied, and Freya watched a confused expression sweep across the room like a Mexican wave.

"I'm guessing Myra sent him a message before that, something along the lines of, 'Meet me at X at one o'clock,'" Freya said.

"'I need to see you,'" Michaela stated. "'Can you get out on Sunday? The Dunston site. One p.m.'"

"The Dunston site?"

"She was going to the dig site where Frost was digging," Nillson said, slamming her hand on the desk. "I knew it wasn't a coincidence."

"May I?" Michaela said, and Nillson quelled her excitement.

"Go on," Nillson said.

"Once the pathologist had finished with the victim's body, we ran a few routine checks. Fingerprints, DNA swabs, the usual," she explained. "And I'm pleased to say we have a partial fingerprint on Myra's eyelid."

"Any matches?"

"None," she replied. "Which means that whoever they belong to is not listed in the Central Police Database."

"We have two suspects in custody," Freya said.

"Yes, a Kevin Banner and an Adam Frost," Michaela said, her tone professional but curt. "Ben sent me them yesterday evening. No match, I'm afraid."

Freya looked across the room at Ben, who, despite acting without being asked, appeared unperturbed. If anything, he appeared to be mulling over the same questions she was.

"Regarding the location DC Cruz identified as flattened," Michaela said, referring to her notes, "which was approximately one thousand metres from the crime scene, we found no forensic evidence."

"Ah, crap," Cruz said, then, unlike Nillson, immediately apologised.

"We may have found footprints in the dry soil at the bottom of the dyke, but they appeared to have been disturbed. So, all we can really tell you, which is more Ben's bag than mine, is that whoever lay in that dyke was covered in stinging nettle rashes. In fact, Pat, my assistant, was badly stung on the legs and arms."

Cruz made a subtle attempt to pull his cuffs over his hands and his face had turned a rosy red.

"Then we have the victim's vehicle, which again was free of any fresh third-party finger prints. Hair samples were discovered, mostly canine, as you can imagine. Even if we matched the human hairs to an individual, it wouldn't help your investigation as we have no bench-mark before the time of death. We have them in our storage facility. If we need to use them at a later date, we can always retrieve them to help build a case."

"Thank you, Michaela," Freya said. "I'm keen to learn more about the house. I think it's an area that, so far, we have failed to connect to the murder, despite the obvious connotations."

"The house," Michaela said, flicking through her notes. "Well, it's an interesting scene, that's for sure. The fingerprints and hair samples found around the house on doorframes and handles match those found in her car, which, until we need them, have been stored. They most likely belong to her family and friends, and of course, the dog. It's worth mentioning that the hairs we found in the car and the house all belong to the dog we discovered at the scene of the crime. And trust me when I say we had millions of samples to work with."

"I'm sensing a but," Freya said.

"Then your instincts are accurate," Michaela replied. "I worked with the fire service to determine the cause of the blast, which as I think we all guessed was a domestic gas leak. However, the ignition source was the kitchen light fitting. The live feed had been disconnected and left in such a way that when the switch was turned on, an arc formed from the cable to the fitting."

"A spark?" Gillespie said, leaning back in his chair. "The house was rigged?"

"And the next words that come from your mouth, Michaela, I hope are that you discovered fingerprints on the light fitting," Freya said.

"I'm afraid not," she said. "Wiped clean. The same as the oven hob."

"But?" Freya said, and Michaela moved to perch beside her on the edge of the desk, allowing her to address the team without having to turn and engage with Freya.

"Whoever did it turned the power off at the breaker."

"They didn't wipe the breaker down?" Ben said, and Michaela stared at him solemnly.

"Sadly, no match on either Adam Frost or Kevin Banner."

"But if we can match the fingerprints to the ones found on Myra's eyelids—"

"No match," Michaela said, cutting him off. "That was the first thing I checked."

"So we have two individuals involved, and neither one of them are Frost or Banner?" Nillson said. "That doesn't make sense. We've got stacks against them both already."

Michaela held her hands up apologetically.

"All I can do is tell what you the data says," she said. "It's your jobs to get down and dirty with the suspects."

"Down and dirty, eh?" Gillespie said, and he glanced back at Ben with a wink, clearly expecting to incite some laughter from the team. But from where Freya was sitting, they were far too engaged with the investigation to break their trains of thought.

Michaela was the only one to react, and even then it was just a disgusted eye roll.

"Right," Freya said, shoving herself off the desk and clapping her hands to get their attention. "We have a few hours left before Frost is released, and a few hours more before Banner follows him."

"Aye, and then we have a few hours more to find someone else who doesn't fit the bill," Gillespie said, his Glaswegian accent adding weight to his dejection.

"Gillespie, you and Cruz find Jeffery Steel. Do you need uniformed support?"

"No, boss. I'm working on a wee idea."

"Good. Do what you have to do. If you need a search warrant, talk to DCI Granger when he gives you the arrest warrant."

"Aye, boss," he said, looking less than confident.

"Nillson and Anderson, I want you both to do some more digging on Frost."

"No pun intended, eh?" Gillespie said, and again, he was the only one not with his head in the game. Nobody laughed.

"Oh, come on," he said. "That was ripe for the picking, that was."

"You said Myra rejected more of Frost's proposals," Freya said, still addressing Nillson.

"That's right. At least three from what I can find."

"I need to know if she went to the others," Freya said, turning to Michaela. "How far back do the messages on Myra's phone go?"

Still perched on the edge of the desk, Michaela cocked her head in thought.

"I can check," she replied.

"Use the phone, Freya told her. "Can you find out if there are any other similar messages in the last three months? I have a theory that Myra was trying to catch Adam Frost in the act of digging on sites for which she had rejected proposals to excavate."

"Why would she visit them?" Ben asked. "What's her reason behind trying to catch him?"

"Because that's who she was," Michaela said, then stopped. "Sorry. I was just thinking out loud."

"No, don't apologise," Freya said. "You're right. Myra Dicks was vindictive. We know that from what she did to Kevin Banner. If she could expose Adam Frost for digging the sites, he'd never work again."

"What would she get from that?" Gillespie said.

"Satisfaction," Freya replied. "Trust me. I know how vindictive cows like her operate. I understand them more than most of you."

"Should I go and see Claire, ma'am?" Gold said, her quiet voice somehow penetrating the hum of activity.

"Yes. Stay with her. If we're forced to release her husband later today, he'll go straight to her."

"No problem," Gold replied.

"And us?" Ben asked.

Freya collected her files from her desk and then slung her bag over her shoulder.

"We're going to use your skills to our advantage," Freya said with a smirk. "We're going to follow up on one of Cruz's observations. We're going to see the farmer. Once you're finished seeing Michaela out, I suggest you get your wellies on," she said, as she opened the door, and gave Michaela a polite nod of thanks. "I'll see you at the car."

CHAPTER FORTY

Any debris from the blast that had been strewn across the street had been collected into a pile at the front of Myra Dicks' house. The gaping holes where the front door and windows should have been had all been crudely blocked with plywood, like the eyes and mouth of a cartoon building, with heavy scorch marks resembling eye liner above the windows and a bushy moustache above the front door.

The tattered remnants of the police cordon fluttered in the warm summer breeze, and a few rogue pieces of glass on the footpath glistened in the afternoon sun.

Gillespie pulled his car to a stop outside the house and yanked the handbrake up.

"What a hole," he said.

"Imagine it?" Cruz said in wonder. "If she'd survived the attack in the field, then come home and put the kettle on."

"It's a wonder the daughter survived," Gillespie said thoughtfully. "Jackie too. She was standing at the front gate."

"Bloody lucky," Cruz muttered quietly as if he was imagining the blast.

A curtain twitched in the neighbouring house then fell back into position, the movement catching Gillespie'e eye.

"Don't look now. We're being watched," Gillespie said.

Immediately, Cruz looked up, searching the nearby houses.

"I said, don't look now," Gillespie said. "For crying out loud. Now he knows we've seen him."

"Who?"

"The neighbour. He was peering through the wee window there."

"Does it matter? What are we doing here anyway? Is this your big idea?"

"I just want to have a wee looky-loo."

"That's not even a word," Cruz mumbled, as Gillespie ventured onto the property and down the side of the house to the back garden.

For some reason, he imagined a woman such as Myra Dicks would have had a neat back garden, with pruned bushes and a well-kept lawn. But the truth was, that the rear garden was worse than his own.

In one corner of a weedy old patio was a stack of old newspapers that, by the looks of things, had been rained on so much, they had eventually morphed into a single papier-mache block. Beside the stack of papers were several old brooms and mops, each one beyond the point of ever being useful. And beside them, an old galvanised bin.

Cruz pulled a face, sniffing the air, and then he checked the soles of his shoes.

"Is that you?" he said.

"Bloody cheek," Gillespie replied, and he quickly checked the soles of his own shoes. They were clean.

He searched the ground for the offending mess, but whichever way he turned, he found old junk, ruined by time and the weather. There were old trainers on a low wall, a grow bag with several dying strawberry plants looking sorry for themselves, and even an old armchair. It was as if the rear garden had been used as a storage space for anything and everything Myra no longer wanted, and to make matters worse, the entire area had been covered in shattered glass from the blast.

"Crikey," Cruz said. "It's worse than your place."

"Oy!" Gillespie said, checking the back door and finding it was locked.

He spied a small table and chair in the far corner of the patio. The table was covered in old plant pots, none of which had anything in them but soil, or compost, or whatever it was, and he found the air to be cleaner.

He brushed the glass from one of the seats and took the weight off his feet with a sigh.

"It's funny, isn't it?" he began, gesturing for a daunted-looking Cruz to take the other seat, and even brushing the glass clear for him. "Somebody gets killed, and we have nothing to go on. Literally nothing."

"Right?" Cruz said.

"But then we find one little clue. One wee titbit of information and everything changes. Suddenly we have several people in the frame, and it's down to us to work out who did it. I mean, it's a process of elimination, right?"

"That's what we do, Jim. That's literally our jobs," Cruz said, taking the other seat.

"Aye, I know. But it's the approach that concerns me. Take Myra Dicks for example. Her body was found in a field. So, it makes sense that we investigate the field. But do you know what I think?"

"I'm sure you're going to tell me," Cruz said, sounding bored.

"I think the answer lies here."

"In the house?" Cruz said.

"Aye, in the house. You know, CSI took fingerprints from all over this place."

"Again, Jim, that's literally their jobs. We've just had Michaela explain what she found. Are you feeling okay?"

"Imagine it, though. You pay a visit to an old friend, or a lover maybe? Unwittingly, you leave a few fingerprints behind. But then a few days or weeks later, they die. Mysteriously too. What happens next? The police find your fingerprints in the house and you have to explain it."

"You are not making any sense at all, Jim. I think you've finally lost the plot."

"You're not listening, Gabby. How would you feel? I mean, how could you even sleep at night, knowing the police might suspect you of murder, but you can't tell them the truth, because you weren't supposed to be in the house in the first place."

"I guess you'd have to weigh up the consequences," Cruz said. "But if it were me, I wouldn't want to be suspected of murder if I didn't do it."

"Right," Gillespie said. "Exactly."

"I think I'm going to call Ben," Cruz said reaching into his pocket for his phone. "I don't think you're quite right in the head."

"Ah, but I am," Gillespie said. "It's a question of doing the right thing, isn't it? A question of morals, if you like. Take this house. CSI found a set of prints inside that we know do not match any of our suspects."

"Right?"

"So, therefore, whoever rigged the house is yet to provide us with a fingerprint sample," Gillespie said, glaring at him to just shut up for a moment. "And if you'd been inside the house, you'd be a little worried right now, wouldn't you? You'd put aside the consequences and confess that you had been in the house, for whatever reason it was, just to get yourself eliminated from the murder."

"Well, yeah," Cruz said. "Unless, of course, it was you who actually murdered her, in which case you'd keep quiet."

"Ah, yes," Gillespie agreed. "In which case, one of the people whose prints we do *not* have is most likely the murderer. All we have to do is match the fingerprints."

Cruz shook his head and peered into Gillespie's eyes as if he was searching for signs of life.

"It's like you're reciting the *Detective Work For Dummies* book, Jim. Have you had too much coffee?"

"No, Gabby. I'm just airing my thoughts," he said, and he pushed himself up with a groan. "Well, I suppose we'd better try and get inside the house."

Cruz followed at a distance, as Gillespie made his way to the back door wearing a bemused expression.

"I think we should come back," Cruz said, as Gillespie tried to force the door handle.

"Let me do the thinking, Gabby, eh?" he replied.

But the door didn't budge, so Gillespie peered through the filthy glass. "I'd break a window if they weren't all boarded up."

"Excuse me," a voice said, and Gillespie grinned inwardly. A man's head popped above the fence. He was a mature man; Gillespie gauged him to be in his sixties, with a mess of hair and heavy, dark bags beneath his eyes. "Excuse me, I couldn't help overhearing you."

"Oh, hello," Gillespie said, fishing his warrant card from his pocket. "Nothing to worry about, sir. We're with Lincolnshire Police."

"I know. Well, I kind of gathered that from what you said."

"You must be Vince Hodges," Gillespie said. "I think you introduced yourself to our colleague, young lass, nice eyes."

"I remember her. Is she okay?"

"Ah, she's doing great. A few cuts, that's all."

"And Claire?" he asked. "Is she okay?"

"As far as I know, she's got a severe concussion," Gillespie said. "I was wondering, I don't suppose you have a key for this place, do you? We need to get inside for a few moments."

"I don't, I'm afraid. I'm afraid Myra and I never really—"

"Saw eye to eye?" Gillespie said. "I'm hearing a lot of that."

"But there's a key," Hodges said, and he pulled himself up further to point down at the bin. "That's where she keeps it."

"The bin?" Gillespie said, and he budged Cruz forward to have a look.

"Why me?" Cruz complained.

"Just, get on with it, brains," Gillespie replied, and he grinned politely at Hodges. "Youngsters these days. Don't know they're born, do they?"

"Oh, for God's sake," Cruz said, and he slammed the lid back down. "It's full of bloody dog poo."

"Yeah, she keeps that there to annoy me," Hodges said. "She knows I sit here to get the morning sun. I've even had to plant a load of lavender just to mask the smell."

"She sounds like a right piece of work," Gillespie said.

"Try underneath the bin," Hodges said, so Cruz pushed the bin back with his foot, keeping his hand well and truly over his mouth and nose.

"Nothing," he said, and he let the bin fall back into place, before moving away as fast as he could.

"Oh? It was there yesterday."

"Oh really?" Gillespie said. "Have you been here?"

"No, no, nothing like that," he said. "I heard some of your colleagues. Posh woman with a local lad."

"Ah, that'll be the boss. Did you talk to them?"

"No, I didn't dare," Hodges said. "Although, between you and me, I reckon she and Myra would have got on like a house on fire."

Gillespie laughed, happy to be bonding with the man on the other side of the fence.

"They definitely put it back," Hodges said. "I mean, I heard them leave. The bloke did it. Used his shoe like he just did."

"And has anybody been back since?"

"No," Hodges replied, a little too fast. "Not that I know of anyway."

Gillespie crouched at the lock. It was a Chubb lock, which ordinarily should have fortuned him a narrow slice of daylight when he peered through it. But he saw nothing.

"The key is in the lock," he muttered quietly, then stood up straight. "On the inside."

"Don't be daft," Cruz said. "How could Ben have left the key in the lock and then locked the door?"

Gillespie stared at him, hoping for the love of God that he was feigning ignorance. But Cruz's expression was serious, biting his lip as he tried to work it out.

Even Hodges was astonished at the remark.

"Stand back," Gillespie said.

"You're not going to break the door down, are you?" Cruz said.

"Aye, I am."

"Why? Can't we just have the boards removed?"

"No time for that, Gabby," Gillespie said, as he took a step back and prepared to lunge at the door.

But just as he was about to begin, they heard a metallic click. Gillespie peered up at Hodges, who shrugged. Cruz scratched his head and stared at the door with suspicion.

Then the handle depressed and the door opened to reveal the one man they had been looking for.

"Ah," Gillespie said. "Mr Steel?"

"Can I help?"

"Aye, that you can," Gillespie replied. "That you can."

CHAPTER FORTY-ONE

Returning to the scene of a crime always invoked an eerie sense of loss for Freya. It was never her loss, but even so, there was rarely a crime scene she visited that hadn't devastated families, ruined lives, and altered the course of history.

She pulled up outside the farmer's house and turned the engine off, letting the silence fill the space for a moment of clarity.

But that moment of clarity eluded her once more, as an incoming call flashed up on the dashboard screen.

"Your favourite detective," Ben said, reading Gillespie's name.

Freya took a deep breath and then hit the button to answer the call.

"Gillespie, give me some good news," she said.

"As of five minutes ago, boss, Jeffery Steel is en route to the station. He'll be there in under half an hour."

"Oh, well, that is music to my ears. Well done, Gillespie."

"Thanks. It was obvious when you think about it. He hasn't been home. He hasn't used a credit card to book a hotel. Where else was he going to go?"

"Not Myra's house."

"Exactly. Came to the back door like he owned the place."

"Well, I never," Freya said. "Ben and I were there."

"Aye, I know. I found his bag upstairs. It's not too badly damaged up there and the windows are still intact. Stinks to high heaven, mind," Gillespie said. "Do you want us to interview him?"

Ben smiled and turned to peer out of the window, leaving Freya to make that decision.

"You can interview him," she said. "You found him, after all."

"Ah, boss. You're all heart, you are."

"But I want to be there," she said. "Give me an hour."

"I'll have it all ready to rock," he finished and ended the call.

"That's a turn-up for the books," Ben said.

"What are you thinking?" Ben asked.

"Other than who the two fingerprints belong to?" she replied. "Mostly if we've been led down the garden path with Banner and Frost, and what the consequences of that lost time will be."

"Consequences to the investigation?" Ben said. "Or consequences of the top brass learning of it?"

"Both, if you must know. But I must remind you," she said, as she shoved open the heavy car door, "you should never ask a lady what she's thinking. When she has something to say, you can rest assured that she'll say it."

She waited at the front of the car for him to follow.

"You will let me know when we meet one, won't you?" he said, smiling. "A lady, that is."

"You've been spending too much time with Gillespie," Freya said, and she reached up and rapped on the front door three times, before fishing her warrant card from her pocket. "I'd like you to lead this. You have a far greater understanding of farming practices than I do."

The door was opened by a heavy-set man, wearing a well-worn John Deere cap and a green Barbour gilet. He glanced up at Freya's Range Rover and then appraised them both before even uttering a word.

"Mr Rose?" Freya said, and she flashed him her warrant card. "DI Bloom. This is DS Savage."

"Right?" he said, leaning against the door frame.

"We wondered if we might have a word with you."

"Now?"

"Yes now," she replied. "It's concerning the activity on your property over the last few days."

"The dead woman, you mean?"

"Yes," Freya said, expecting him to step aside to let them in.

"Alright then."

"Perhaps it's best if we speak inside," Ben said.

"It's a nice day. What do you want to be holed up inside for?"

"Okay," Freya agreed. "Let's go for a walk, shall we?"

She stepped down from the step, and onto the drive, hearing the two men's footsteps behind her.

"It's about the statement you provided one of our colleagues," Ben explained.

"Ah, Scottish bloke. Looks like he needs a good bath."

"That's him," Ben replied. "It's just that you told him you were out baling on Sunday. That's when you saw the blue van. Is that right?"

"Yep," he said.

Freya stayed in front, leading them down the lane, away from the crime scene and towards the Stepping Out car park.

"When did you harvest?" Ben asked. "Sorry, I should explain. My dad—"

"You're a Savage," he said, and Freya turned to find the broader of the men stopped with his hands on his hips. "You must be the first Savage who hasn't carried on the family business."

"How did you know?" Ben asked, to which Rose merely shrugged.

"You have your dad's nose."

"That's what I tell him," Freya said.

"What are you? His mother?"

Freya opened her mouth to speak but no words came out, and Ben did his best to conceal his grin but failed.

"It's just that we harvested on Saturday," Ben explained.

"Right?"

"And we didn't bale until Monday or Tuesday. The sun was shining, the breeze was warm."

"And when you say *we*," Rose said, "you mean your dad."

"And my brothers, yes."

"So you don't get involved at all?"

Ben ignored the comment. "Mr Rose, you said you were baling on Sunday. I don't know a farmer in a hundred miles of here that would have baled on Sunday. Saturday was the first day the moisture levels were right for harvesting."

"So?"

"What my colleague is trying to say, Mr Rose," said Freya, "and failing at, is that you were out in the fields on Sunday but we know you weren't baling."

"Is that right?"

"We have photos of your fields, Mr Rose, and there isn't a single hay bale in sight."

"Straw bales," Ben corrected her, which she ignored.

"Alright," Rose said. "So I weren't baling. So what?"

Freya began walking again, listening for them to follow. She folded her hands behind her back and imagined she was out for a stroll. There was no denying it; Lincolnshire was breathtaking if you could stop for long enough to appreciate it.

"Mr Rose, do you know an Adam Frost?"

"Frost? Course, I do. Bloody fool, he is."

"How do you know him?"

"He wanted to dig my land. Over there on the other side of the bank." He pointed towards the great riverbank that flanked his fields.

"I understand his proposal was rejected," Ben said.

"Apparently so."

Ben left a pause, which Freya understood to be him mentally phrasing his next question.

"Mr Rose, did you know he was here on Sunday?"

"Did I know?" He laughed. "No, not then anyway. I found his trenches though. Knew it was him, I did."

"And you didn't think to tell us this when my colleague questioned you earlier this week?"

"He didn't ask, did he?" Rose said, arrogant and far too confident.

"Do you understand that withholding information regarding a crime is an offence punishable by prison time?" Ben said, and Freya couldn't help but be impressed by his approach.

"You what?"

"Prison time," Ben said. "A year, maybe?"

"For what, not telling you my business?"

"For withholding information. Look it up. I wouldn't lie."

They all stopped, and Rose studied Ben with a curious stare.

"What is it you want?" he asked.

"What were you doing out here on Sunday, Mr Rose, if you weren't baling *or* meeting Adam Frost?"

Rose paused for a moment as if he was trying to find a sign that Ben was lying. But Freya knew Ben well enough. He could hold his expressions at bay with ease.

"Alright," he said. "I was out here."

"And you weren't baling?" Ben asked.

"And I wasn't baling. Well done, Sherlock."

Ben left a gap for Rose to fill, plunging his hands into his pockets to indicate he could wait all day.

"Adam Frost couldn't get permission to dig my land," he said finally. "But someone else could."

"Somebody else?" Freya said.

"Yep. She reckoned she could get it approved with ease."

"She?"

Rose nodded. He stood as if nothing could touch him on his land, no harm could come his way, and the very sight of such arrogance irritated Freya.

"That's right. Some woman. Myra something," he said finally. "Never met her, myself. Supposed to meet her last Sunday, I was. Never turned up. I suppose you lot scared her off with all your lights and sirens."

"Yes," Freya said, thoughtfully. "Yes, I suppose we did. Can you tell me, was she meeting you alone?"

"Alone? No. One of her colleagues was supposed to be with her," Rose said. "I can't remember his name. Professor something or other."

"Steel?" Ben offered.

"That's it. Professor Steel. He didn't turn up either, come to think of it."

"Now there's a surprise," Freya muttered, giving nothing away. "Well, thank you, Mr Rose. We're sorry to have disturbed you."

"Is that it? You're not going take me in? Withholding information, and all that?"

"Not right now, Mr Rose," Freya told him. "But I can assure you, if we find the information you've given us to be false in any way, we'll be back."

CHAPTER FORTY-TWO

By the time Freya and Ben returned to the station, Gillespie and Cruz had already set up the interview. Jeffery Steel looked uncomfortable in his seat opposite Gillespie, fidgeting with his hands and scratching at the few days of growth that Freya considered to give him a more masculine appearance.

"Shall I leave?" Cruz asked as Freya entered the interview room.

Gillespie nodded.

"For the benefit of the recording, DI Bloom has joined the interview, and DC Cruz is leaving the room."

"Must be serious," Jeffery said, making light of a terrible situation, most likely a result of nerves.

"Cruz?" Freya said before he left the room.

"Boss?"

"Would you mind asking Chapman to chase Michaela up? I presume we've processed Mr Steel's fingerprints."

"Yes, boss. He also volunteered his DNA."

"Oh, good. Very helpful," Freya said.

She took Cruz's seat nearest the wall and made herself comfortable. Then, silently, she gestured for Gillespie to continue. She couldn't recall ever having sat in on one of Gillespie's interviews before and was keen to see how he faired.

"Right, then, Mr Steel. You're a slippery one, aren't you?" he began. "It's hard not to believe you've been evading us for a wee while."

"I haven't been hiding, if that's what you think," he replied.

"Aye, but you haven't been home either, have you?"

"Is that a crime?"

"No, of course not. I would have thought that, being Myra Dicks' lover, you would have had more involvement in our investigation. You know? You could have been a little more forthcoming with information."

"If I'm honest, I'm still learning to deal with the news," he said. "It's like there's a big hole in my life."

"Was that where your wife used to be?" Freya asked, and he stared at her, guilty as sin.

"Shall we start from the top?" Gillespie suggested. "Before we begin, it's worth noting that you are here on a voluntary basis. You're not under arrest. At any time you wish to end this interview, you just say the word."

"I didn't even want to start it."

"Well, we're here now, aren't we? The more information you can provide us, the sooner you can get on with your day. Is that okay, Mr Steel?"

"It's Professor Steel," he said with a healthy dose of indignance. "And yes, it's fine. Let's get it over with."

"Right then," Gillespie started. "Can you tell me your movements last Saturday, please?"

"Saturday?"

"Aye, the day after Friday and the one before Sunday."

He shook his head, like whatever he did the day before Myra was killed had no bearing whatsoever on the outcome.

"I worked," he replied.

"At the university?"

"Of course. I was just doing some catching up. It's a busy time of year."

"And what time did you get home?"

"I don't know. Sometime in the afternoon, I suppose."

"Did you stay in after that?" Gillespie asked, and he tapped his fingers on the table before him to the tune of, '*The animals went in two by two, hurrah*'.

"Must you?" Steel said, and glanced down at Gillespie's fingers.

"Oh, aye, sorry. I don't realise I'm doing it most of the time," he replied. "So? Did you go out again? Or maybe you spent some quality time with your wife?"

"My marriage is none of your business–"

"For the purposes of this investigation, Mr Steel, your marriage is every bit our business as it is yours. In fact, you'd do well to consider us as partners in your marriage. If I ask a question, I expect an answer."

"It sounds to me like you already know my movements and you just want me to repeat them."

"Aye, I do. For the purposes of ascertaining fact over fiction. And there seems to be a hell of a lot of fiction in this investigation," Gillespie said. And he leaned in conspiratorially. "Fiction is something we don't do well with, I'm afraid. We like facts."

"Okay, so I got home and walked into what I can only describe as the verbal rendition of the Somme."

"You had an argument with your wife?"

"She had the argument," he replied. "I was just fending off the attack in no man's land."

"She had you pinned down, did she? Your wife, that is."

"It seems that she discovered my relationship with Myra," he said guiltily. "I can't blame her."

"How do you suppose she found out?" Freya asked.

"Oh, that much is clear. It was Claire. She's never approved of our relationship and had made it clear on numerous occasions that I am not welcome in the Banner family. Suits me," he said.

"Interesting," Gillespie said. "Do you have proof it was Claire?"

"No, I don't have proof. But what I do have is a memory and my senses. It's half the reason Myra and I had to keep things under the radar."

"Not to mention your wife finding out," Freya added.

"Claire Banner has had it in for me since day one. When Myra sent those photos of her husband and the other woman, Claire lost her mind. I'm sure it was her."

"Where did you go?" Freya asked, preventing him from entering into a full-on rant. "You must have gone somewhere."

"Where do you think I went? To Myra's, of course."

"And that's where you stayed, is it?"

"For the night, yes."

"Let's talk about Sunday," Gillespie said. "Tell us what you did."

"I went to work."

"To the university?" Freya asked.

"Yes, to my office. I couldn't think straight. My wife wasn't answering my calls, so I just did what I always do. Bury myself in my work."

"What time did you leave?" Gillespie asked.

"I'm not sure. Lunchtime, I suppose. Maybe later?"

"Did you go back to Myra's house?"

"No, in fact, I went home to grab a few things."

"Oh really?"

"Yes, really."

"Did you talk to your wife, at all?"

"No, Veronica wasn't there if you must know. I half expected her to be waiting for me to come home so we could discuss the matter."

"Does she drive?" Freya said.

"No. She uses public transport. Always has done."

The conversation was going nowhere. Steel was burying himself in a series of half-truths that inevitably he would later change. Freya decided it was time to up the ante.

"The reason we ask for your whereabouts, Mr Steel, is because we have several pieces of evidence to suggest you had arranged to meet Myra in Dunston at one p.m. on Sunday."

"Evidence?"

"A text conversation," she said.

"Is that it?"

"And a handwritten note from Myra on an excavation proposal she had previously rejected."

"That doesn't mean I agreed to it."

"And we have a witness who said you had arranged to be there."

Steel said nothing. He ran his tongue around his lips to moisten them.

"Would you like some water?" Gillespie asked, and he shook his head as if irritated.

"Should I go on?" Freya said, and the layers of Steel's lies began to peel, beginning with his indignance.

It was at that moment that Cruz knocked and entered the room, and slipped a folded piece of notepaper in front of Freya. He excused himself, then left the room, and Gillespie informed the recording of the event while Freya unfolded the piece of paper, and then slid it his way.

"I'm tired of playing games, Mr Steel. We know you were there on Sunday, and we know you had arranged to meet Myra and Edward Rose. All the evidence suggests you were responsible for Myra's death. The only thing I can't fathom is why you did it. But then, I'm not versed in archaeological processes. But that's something a specialist can help us with."

"I didn't kill her," he said softly.

"Mr Steel, your fingerprint was found on her eyelid. The fingerprint you provided has just been through our forensics team. I'm sure in a day or two, we'll also have some DNA evidence to support the facts. We know it was you."

"I didn't kill her," he repeated, his tone sharp and defensive. "I bloody loved her."

"Then how do you explain your fingerprints?" Freya said.

"She was dead already," he snapped, and the bitterness in his tone subsided, giving way to whatever emotions he'd been keeping at bay. "She was dead when I found her."

Gillespie's big, dark eyes rolled around to convey his disbelief to Freya, and while Steel buried his face in his hands, she nodded to indicate she agreed with him.

"You can see how this looks," Gillespie said, and his tone was surprisingly soft.

"Yes, I was supposed to meet her," Steel said, his voice thick and nasal. "I agreed to it for my wife."

"For your wife?"

"I said I'd call it off. I promised her I would. It had gone on long enough. I had to choose between Veronica and Myra."

"And you chose Veronica?" Freya said, and he nodded ever so slightly.

"I left work, went straight there, and found her car in the little car park. I figured she'd gone on ahead of me, so I went looking. That's when I found her. I couldn't believe it. I had practised what I was going to say to her, how I was going to say it. I was prepared to end it. I just didn't get the chance."

"Freya and Gillespie said nothing, instead choosing to wait for him to talk. The guilty always filled in the silence.

"If you're wondering why my fingerprints are on her, it's because I couldn't stand to see her like that. Lying there. She was so still."

"You closed her eyes?" Freya said, and he nodded. "Mr Steel, if I were to request DNA samples to be taken from beneath her dog's claws, can you tell me what they would find?"

He let his head drop back, squeezing his eyes closed as if he could just make everything just go away.

Then, slowly, he pulled up his sleeve to reveal three deep scratches.

"He was defending her," he said quietly. "I'm not proud of it. Jambo was sitting beside her when I found her body. He wouldn't let me near her; snarling and snapping. I tried to run, but he wouldn't let go."

"For clarity, are you saying that you killed Myra's dog? But she was already dead when you discovered her?"

"That's exactly what happened," he said. "I just kind of held him. Tightly, you know? Just so he wouldn't bite me. I didn't even know I'd done it. Not until it was too late, anyway. I'm sorry. I'm so sorry."

"All that remains then, Mr Steel, is to establish why you were meeting her there. Can I tell you what I think?"

He shrugged, lost in thought, but Freya would catch his attention somehow.

"I think that you and Myra were exploiting the efforts of another archaeologist."

He looked up but said nothing, and she smiled at the little win.

"I think Myra rejected Adam Frost's excavation proposals, not to maintain the integrity of our heritage, as some would assume, but for her own gains," Freya said. "Tell me, if we were to visit the locations of the other proposed archaeological digs, what would we find?"

He said nothing but cast his eyes downward.

"I thought as much," Freya said. "Mr Steel, the good news is that you no longer have to squat in Myra's house. In fact, you won't have to worry about keeping a roof over your head for a very long time."

A confused expression washed over his face.

"You're arresting me?"

"The version of events you have provided today proves to me that you were at the scene of the crime. You were in a relationship with Myra Dicks, which you were apparently trying to end. I just think things got a little heated and you reacted emotionally."

"I was the one who called you lot. Why would I do that if I had just bloody killed her?"

"You made the phone call?"

"Yes?" he said, pleading. "I don't care what your evidence tells you, Inspector, but I guarantee you this. Not once, in all the years Myra and I have been seeing each other have we had an argument. Not one word was ever said in anger. Why would I kill the woman I admired? Why aren't you looking at someone who couldn't stand her? There are plenty to choose from."

"All we can do is create a narrative from the evidence presented to us."

"Evidence? Your evidence doesn't mean a bloody thing. You didn't know her like I did. She had a heart. She was caring. Her methods might have upset a few people, like Kevin, for example."

"Kevin Banner?"

"Yes, him. At least I didn't threaten to kill her."

"Did Kevin?"

"Yes, of course he did. He barged into her house on Saturday night. Caused a right scene. Damn near frothing at the mouth, he was."

"Kevin Banner went to Myra's house?"

"Yes, damn it. If you're looking for someone with an motive, why don't you look at him? He's the one who hated her the most, and it's not like he kept his feelings a secret, is it?"

"What exactly did he say, Mr Steel?" Freya asked.

"Oh, I don't know. He was ranting about the trouble Myra had caused with the photos. Said she was trying to destroy his marriage and that he wouldn't let her get away with it."

"So the conversation was heated, would you say?"

"Heated? It was on bloody fire."

"And how did it end?"

"He told her he'd make her pay. One way or another, he would make her pay for what she had done."

CHAPTER FORTY-THREE

Freya held her head in her hands with her elbows resting on her desk. The incident room was empty, and for once, she had time to think. In the short time she had been with the team, she had witnessed plenty of drama in that room. The days when Standing and his team occupied the far end of the room came alive in her mind. She hadn't been able to hold a discussion with her own team without him calling out from up there, interfering and belittling her.

But it had worked out well. Even Gillespie, whose commitment Freya had always questioned, seemed to be an integral part of the team.

It was Gillespie who broke her moment of peace, slowly opening the incident room door. He stood there in the doorway as if he waiting for her to ask him to leave.

"I just spoke to DCI Granger," he said.

"Oh really?"

"He wants us all here later. He said he wants to make an announcement before the funeral."

"Well, our fate is in his hands," she replied. "And sooner or later, we have to face our demons."

"His and DCC Kelly's," Gillespie said. "If it was up to Granger, then I imagine we'd have nothing to worry about."

She smiled at him, briefly, enough to convey peace.

"You did well in there," she said.

"Aye, thanks. We got there in the end, eh?"

"Yes," she said softly. "We did, didn't we?"

"Should I leave?" he asked. "I can give you some space if you want."

"No, stay," she said, then before she had even thought about what she might say, she began to speak. "I feel I owe you an apology."

"No," he replied.

"I haven't told you what for yet."

"For being hard on me, boss? It's okay. I know I can be a clown sometimes."

There was no denying it. She couldn't have articulated it better herself.

"Yes, well... We all have our flaws," she replied. "Me more than anybody."

"Aye," he said, agreeing with her. Then he realised what he'd said. "I didn't mean–"

"It's okay, Gillespie. I know I can be a cow sometimes. I just have high standards, that's all. The truth is that without you, we may be an effective team, but our days would be soulless and quite flat."

"I'm not sure if there's a compliment in there or not."

"There is," she told him. "Have we released Steel?"

"Aye. I've also asked Sergeant Priest to process Banner and release Frost. It was bloody complicated, eh? All that stuff about archaeology and affairs and whatnot."

"Life is complicated," Freya said, then remembered something Granger had said not so long ago. "But sometimes, when things get complex, we must strip things back to basics."

"Oh, aye," Gillespie said. "And the legend of Arthur lives on in spirit."

"It does indeed," she replied. "There's one thing I can't work out, though."

"Oh, aye. What's that then?"

"The fingerprints that Michaela found in Myra's house. If they're not Banner's, Frost's, or Steel's, then who do they belong to? I feel like we're missing something here. And if a defence team get hold of it, they'll crucify us."

"Boss, do you mind if I take Cruz somewhere?"

"Where?"

"It's just an idea I've had."

"You're asking for some autonomy?" she said, and he said nothing in reply. "Go, then. Run with it."

"Thanks, boss," he said, and just as he was backing out of the door, she called out to him.

"You will be back in time for Granger's announcement?"

He held the door from slamming behind him and peered over his shoulder at her.

"Aye, I will," he said. "I wouldn't miss it for the world."

CHAPTER FORTY-FOUR

"Are you actually going to tell me what we're doing here?" Cruz said.

"You'll see," Gillespie replied with a smile. He pulled on the hand-brake and climbed from the car, leaving Cruz to follow.

"I feel like I'm walking into an unwanted surprise birthday party," he said, as Gillespie walked past the gate to Myra Dicks' house. "Hang on, where are you going?"

But Gillespie said nothing. He walked directly into the property next door, strolled along the weed-free footpath, past the flowers that bloomed from the beds and up the front door, which of course had two hanging baskets on either side.

"Right, I'll just keep my mouth shut then, shall I? And follow you about like a puppy?"

"That's fine by me," Gillespie said, as he pushed the doorbell. A gentle tinkling sound ensued from inside. It was digital but designed to emulate a distant yet polite bell.

Gillespie rocked on his feet, patiently waiting for his moment. Eventually, the door opened, and a surprised-looking Mr Hodges stared down at them.

"You again?" he said.

"Mr Hodges," Gillespie replied. "I think it's about time you and I had a wee chat, don't you?"

"A chat? What about?" he asked, and there was a clear nervousness in his tone.

"Oh, you know. A certain neighbour of yours?" Gillespie said, and he sniffed the acrid air from the ruined house next door.

Hodges' breathing became exacerbated and he clung to his front door as if it was a shield.

"Am I in some kind of trouble?" he asked.

"Oh, that all depends."

"On what?"

"What you'd call trouble," Gillespie explained. "I mean, if you work with us, then maybe not so much so. But if you fight us, you know? Then I envisage a very difficult and troubling time ahead."

"I feel like I should have some kind of solicitor?" Hodges said, and he peered tentatively around the room as if the walls were closing in, inch by inch. "Something tells me this isn't a courtesy call."

"If you feel you need a solicitor, then you're welcome to call one. Or, if you prefer, I can arrange a duty solicitor. I'm pretty sure there's one or two at the station, so we wouldn't have to wait."

"At the station?"

"Aye. They're free, too," Gillespie said. "I can get one in if you like?"

"You said you just wanted to ask me a few questions."

"Aye, I do," Gillespie said.

"So?"

"So, what?"

"So, ask me."

"Perhaps we could come inside?" Gillespie said. "We don't want the curtains to twitch, do we?"

Reluctantly, Hodges pushed open the door and they stepped inside.

The interior matched the quality of the exterior. The walls were flat and clean, and the decor was tasteful and clearly expensive. There were vases filled with dried flowers, little infusers giving off a vanilla scent, and a series of artwork in matching frames.

"You must have people falling at your feet to buy this place," Gillespie said, as he walked through to the stylish and contemporary cottage kitchen.

"You'd think, wouldn't you?" Hodges said, and there was a bitterness to his tone.

"Maybe you could begin by telling me about your relationship with Myra Dicks?" Gillespie said, and he leaned on the immaculate kitchen counter like he was an old friend stopping by for a coffee.

"I didn't have a relationship with Myra Dicks," Hodges said, moving around to the far side of the island to regain some kind of control.

"But you were neighbours?"

"Well, yes. Of course. But–"

"And you spoke to her, from time to time?"

"Naturally, we–"

"And when you spoke to her, how would you describe the conversations or the..." Gillespie searched for the right word, making small circular motions with his hand, before settling on, "The mood?"

"The mood?"

"Aye, the mood. Was it friendly? Was it stilted, maybe? Or even fractious?"

Hodges shook his head.

"It was none of those things. We were just neighbours."

"I see," Gillespie said. "You see, I have a report here made a few months back. It seems somebody reported a disturbance of the peace. Can you tell me what that was about, Mr Hodges?"

He thought for a moment, then shrugged casually.

"It was nothing. Just a..." It was Hodges' turn to search for the right word. He settled on, "A misunderstanding."

"A misunderstanding?"

"That's right."

"And what was this misunderstanding all about?" Gillespie asked. "What was it that two neighbours who, as far as I can tell, have lived side by side for more than twenty years, could have been arguing about?"

"Nothing important, as far as I can remember," he said.

"Oh, nothing important," Gillespie replied. "Well, that's okay then.

I mean, if it was important, you'd be sure to tell me, right? This is a murder investigation, after all."

The mention of the word *murder* had the impact Gillespie was looking for. Hodges' eyes darted from Gillespie to Cruz, then settled on a piece of artwork on the wall beside the door. Gillespie followed his stare.

"She borrowed something," Hodges said. "She borrowed something and didn't bring it back. She was always doing it. That's all."

"Ah, right. I see. Classic neighbour from hell, eh? What was it? A lawnmower?"

Hodges gave a mock laugh. A single snort with an accompanying eye roll.

"Something funny, Vince?" Gillespie said. "Can I call you Vince?"

Again, he shrugged, and let out a warm breath that, a few seconds later, polluted the air on Gillespie's side of the table. It was the smell of coffee. Stale coffee. Bad coffee. Cheap coffee. The type of coffee a man might drink, not because he enjoys the rich aroma of a South American bean or the subtle infusions of an African blend, but because he can't sleep. Because he can't function. Because he's at his wit's end, and the effect of the caffeine is all he seeks.

"I thought you might have noticed," he said. "But Myra *never* mowed her lawn."

And that was it. That was the segue Gillespie had been waiting for. That was the root of Hodges' frustrations, the cause of the argument a few months previously, and that was the thread, as DI Bloom would have said, that he needed to pull on.

"Actually, I had noticed. Shall I tell you what else I noticed?"

"The crummy old windows? The overgrown trees?"

"The *For Sale* sign outside your house," Gillespie said.

"So? I'm moving house."

"Although, if I'm honest, I had to look quite hard to read what it said. It's quite faded, isn't it?"

"It's been a hot summer," Hodges said. "I'm sorry, are you here to talk about my *For Sale* sign? Or is there something a little more significant to discuss? I'd like to get on with my day, and as I understand it, I'm not under arrest."

"Well, as it happens, there is something I'd like to know, Vince," Gillespie said. "I'd like to tell you a wee bit about our crime scene investigators, and how they operate. Specifically in a house like Myra's."

"Crime scene?"

"Aye. Crime scene. The scene of a crime," Gillespie said, purposefully embellishing his Glaswegian accent to let the prolonged Rs roll off his tongue.

"If you're talking about next door, it was an accident, wasn't it?"

"I don't know. Was it?" Gillespie said, and he nodded at the empty chair.

Hodges glanced at the back door, then at Cruz, although Gillespie couldn't understand why. Finally, he rested his elbows on the island, adopting a serious yet questioning expression.

"Go on, then," he said.

"You see, in a situation like this," Gillespie began, and casually strolled to the French door that overlooked a beautiful patio, surrounded by pots containing all manner of plants. "The investigators will, first of all, establish the cause of the fire. In this case, the fire started in a light fitting."

"A light fitting?"

"Aye, a light fitting. For some reason, the live wire had been dislodged. Loosened, as it were. The cable had been pulled out too, just enough that when electricity passed through the cable, it would create an arc."

"An arc?" Hodges said.

"Aye, an arc. A spark, in other words. A spark that under the right conditions, i.e. the house being filled with gas would cause a terrific explosion."

"And that's what happened, is it?" Hodges said.

"Aye, it appears to be," Gillespie replied, staring through the rear windows at the little table and chairs that had been set up beside the dividing fence. "Once the investigators have established the cause of the blast, they then seek to use forensics to understand who was responsible. And by which, I mean fingerprints."

"Fingerprints?"

"Aye, fingerprints," Gillespie said.

"And did they find any?"

"No, sadly not," Gillespie said.

"That's a shame."

"Aye, it is. It's a crying shame, in fact. But thankfully the lass that runs the department is a wee bit tenacious. She wouldn't let a wee setback like that stop her. Oh no." He tapped his temple with his index finger. "She's smart too. One of the best, apparently."

"That's good then," Hodges said, sounding less than convinced.

"Aye, it is good. You see, for somebody to dislodge the live wire in a light fitting and pull it out like that, they would have had to turn off the isolating switch. I mean, if they didn't, we'd probably have found them lying on the ground in Myra's kitchen, eh? You'd understand that, wouldn't you, Mr Hodges? Being a retired engineer."

"Right," he said. "Yes, they would have had to turn the electricity off."

"Aye. And if they didn't want to be caught, they'd have had to wipe the wee switch down when they were finished, wouldn't they?"

He shrugged.

"I suppose so."

"Aye, they would," Gillespie said. "But they didn't."

"They didn't?"

Gillespie peered over his shoulder at the man who was now standing with his hands in his pockets.

"Tell me, Mr Hodges, if I were to ask you a personal favour, would you help me?"

"Well, that all depends on what type of favour it was."

"Ah, just a wee one. It would involve you coming down to the station with us."

"What for?"

"I just thought I'd run your fingerprints past our investigator."

"Your investigator?"

"Aye, the smart one I told you about."

"I don't understand."

"Ah, well, you see a few of the others in our team seem to think that you had something to do with the explosion."

"They do, do they?"

"Aye, they do. Not us, of course. But we figured this was the only way we'd prove it wasn't you who rigged the house and then they can stop harping on about you. They'd probably even take your photo down from our persons if interest board. Isn't that right, DC Cruz?"

"Yep. That's right," he replied.

"I'm a person of interest?"

"Aye," Gillespie said. "I mean, you don't get on with her. You had a previous altercation with her. And from what I understand, she's been a neighbour from hell. Am I right, Vince?"

Hodges didn't reply.

"How long has your house been up for sale, Vince?" Gillespie asked.

"My house?"

"For sale, yes," Gillespie replied, nudging him on. "How long?"

Hodges appeared perplexed, worried almost.

"It's okay. I checked," Gillespie said. "Eighteen months."

"Is it that long?" Hodges said innocently.

"Eighteen months to sell your house, Vince? That's a hell of a long time. As I understand it, the market's booming right now. Isn't that right, Cruz?"

"I suppose," Cruz replied, who then fell in with the line of questioning. "Well, that's what I hear anyway. My aunt sold her house in less than a week."

"Booming," Gillespie said, wishing he had never invited Cruz to enter the conversation. "A house like yours should have sold in, what? Three months at the most?"

"So you're an estate agent now, are you?" Hodges said.

"Aye, no. I've too many scruples for that kind of thing," he joked. "But a house like yours, with what? Four bedrooms?"

"Five."

"Two bathrooms?"

"Three, including the ensuite," Hodges replied proudly.

"Nice garden, well presented. A kitchen to die for, too, eh?"

"I've done a lot of work to the place, yes."

"And still, it's taken eighteen months and you still haven't sold it?"

"I've had offers..."

"Ah, he's had offers, Gabby. Did you hear that?"

"I did. Why hasn't it sold then?"

"It's a nice house on a nice street in a beautiful village," Hodges said. "I'm not going to sell to just anybody, you know?"

"Even after eighteen months?" Gillespie asked. "You see. I looked at that house of yours and the *For Sale* sign, and I thought to myself, would I buy this house?"

"You couldn't afford this house," Hodges said with a sneer.

"Aye, maybe. Maybe not. But if I could afford it, and if was looking for a well-presented, five-bedroom house with an ensuite, plus two bathrooms, and a family-sized kitchen diner for my wee bairns to run amok, would I buy it? What would stop me from buying it, I thought?"

Gillespie left a gap long enough for Hodges to add some insight, and long enough for his resolute expression to fade into doubt.

"And then it hit me," Gillespie said.

"What did? What hit you? Because I can assure you, it didn't hit you hard enough."

"You have a motive," Gillespie said. "You're frustrated. Probably out of pocket, too, eh?"

"I can assure you–"

"You seem to assure me a lot, Vince. But, somehow, I'm still left in doubt. You see, when I looked at your house and put myself in the shoes of a potential buyer, the thing that put me off the most is the house next door."

Hodges steeled. His eyes narrowed, and his shoulders seemed to tighten as the swell of his chest grew. A haze of coffee hit Gillespie again, as Hodges' nostrils flared.

"You're right, Myra didn't cut her lawn," Gillespie said. "Nor did she pick up after her dog. And you're right about the windows, too. Her heating bill must have been astronomical."

"Get to the point," Hodges said.

"And as for the bloody great tree out the front of her house, blocking all your daylight, I might add..."

Hodges said nothing, which in Gillespie's mind, was as good as admitting his theory was correct.

"Myra didn't borrow things, did she? She didn't borrow your lawn-mower, did she?"

The information seemed to take a while to sink into Hodges' mind. He sucked at his top lip while he decided how to respond, and Gillespie afforded him all the time he needed. The next words he would say would make or break his argument.

Or so Gillespie thought.

"Are you suggesting I killed Myra?" Hodges said.

The question took Gillespie by surprise.

"Did I ask you if you killed Myra?"

"No. No, you didn't."

"Well, then no, I didn't. But while we're on the topic—"

"No," he said before Gillespie could finish. He shook his head in defiance and opened his mouth as if he might say something. Sensing a shift in his thought process, Gillespie softened his tone. The final part of the conversation would need to be teased from Hodges, like a doctor luring a tapeworm from the depths of a man's insides. "You don't believe me, do you?"

"It's not a question of whether I believe you or not, Vince. That decision is down to the judge and jury."

"The judge—"

"And jury," Gillespie repeated, and it was as if a layer of Hodges' defences had been peeled away by verbalising the reality of his situation.

"I wasn't trying to kill her," he said, suddenly emphatic. But as fast as the outburst had come, it faded to a quiet whisper. "I wasn't trying to kill her."

Gillespie smiled inwardly. He waited a few moments, in case Hodges had anything else to add, and then he broke the silence.

"Vince? If I take your fingerprints, will they match those we found in Myra's house?"

Both of Hodges' hands shot up to his head and he began pulling at his hair. His eyes squeezed tightly shut, and his mouth screamed silently in frustration.

"Vince?"

"I have lost more than seventy thousand pounds on that bloody house," he shouted, tearing a hand away from his head to jab an index finger at Gillespie. "Seventy thousand pounds. I've spent every penny I had to make it nice. So I can sell it. So I can retire in, let's face it, uncertain times."

"I see," Gillespie said.

"No. No, you don't bloody see. I'm not a young man. I don't have another twenty years of work left in me to build up a little pension. That house *is* my pension. That house is everything. Everything I've worked for since I was a bloody boy. It's everything my dad left my mum, everything. Do you understand? It was everything I had. And it's all worth nothing because that lazy bitch couldn't do a few simple things to help me."

"I'm beginning to get an idea—"

"I asked her to cut the tree back a bit so I could get more light in, but no. The tree was her pride and joy. I asked to pick the dog crap up when I had viewings, mow it even, but no, she couldn't do that. I even offered to do it for her, and do you know what she said?"

"No?"

"She's helping the bees. The bloody bees," Hodges said, his rant now in full steam. "Every time I have somebody come to look at the house, it's her place that puts them off. No natural light. Overgrown hedges. The bloody dog squatting in the garden when they pull up. I'm at my wit's end. Even if I sold the house tomorrow, I've had to drop the price so much there'd be nothing left to live on, unless I buy a caravan and freeze my arse off for however long I've got left. If I'm lucky I could afford a pair of fingerless bloody gloves and a woolly hat to complete the picture. She's even moved her bloody bin filled with dog crap beside my fence, so I can't even go out and have a coffee on the patio. Do you see, now, Sergeant? Do you see what she's bloody-well put me through?" he asked, shaking his head as if the very idea was beyond comprehension, and whatever lid had flipped inside of him to release all that pressure had broken the seal on his guilt. A tear formed in his eye, broke free from its constraints, and ran down his cheek into a barrier of whiskers. "I didn't mean to hurt Claire. I would never..."

He choked on his emotions and bit down on his fist.

"It's okay, Vince. It's okay–"

"I just want to be out of here. I just want to sell my house and leave."

"Vince, I just need to be clear," Gillespie said. "Did you create a gas leak in Myra's house with the intention of causing damage?"

He nodded.

"And did you dislodge the wiring in the light fitting?"

Again, Hodges nodded.

"And did you do this because you thought that, if the house was damaged, she'd have to leave or rebuild the house? But what you didn't expect was for Myra to be murdered? That wasn't part of your plan, was it?"

Hodges stared at his hands as if they belonged to somebody else.

"I didn't want to hurt *anybody*," he said softly. "I overheard her talking to someone. She mentioned a key to the back door. She kept it underneath the dirty bin. I don't know why it happened, but as I heard her speaking, the plan just kind of..."

He paused, his thoughts venturing far away to a time in the not-too-distant future.

"Vince?"

"The plan just kind of came together," he whined. "It all made so much sense at the time. I'm so sorry. I'm so, so sorry."

CHAPTER FORTY-FIVE

The last rays of the day's sun tinged the distant clouds with reds and pinks. Ben ended his call and gave the horizon a moment of his time. He enjoyed being at the station in the evenings when a peace fell over rural Lincolnshire like a blanket.

He pulled open the fire escape door and climbed the stairs in search of Freya. On the first floor, faint remnants of her perfume lingered in the air like breadcrumbs for him to follow. Slowly, he pushed open the incident room door, waking the squealing hinge from its slumber, and its cry seemed louder in the near silence.

The room was in darkness, but she was in there sitting in the shadows somewhere. And although he couldn't see her, her mood emanated, glowing like the dying embers of a fire.

"Freya?" he said, and she exhaled somewhere.

He reached for the light switches, feeling amongst the two rows for the single light above his head.

And there she was. The woman he had spent the past nine months or so admiring, fantasising over, and adoring. The woman who bore the airs and graces of high society, but enjoyed nothing more than a blanket, a fire, and a bottle of wine. Those shared moments had been their best. When they became closest. She was the detective who had fought tooth and nail to get where she was, who had endured hardships that no person should have to endure, and who had brought the team together against all odds.

And there she sat, crumpled like the spent wrapper of something sweet. The whiteboard was laying on the floor, the marker having rolled off into the shadows at the far end of the room; the dark end. The end where DI Standing's team had once provided her with the first of her challenges. That seemed like an age now.

Beyond her desk, littering the floor, were files, printouts, and photos.

"Freya?" he said again, and she stared up at him. "What's going on?"

"Leave me alone, Ben," she said. "Please."

Ben could have turned off the light and left the room. He could have gone in search of the team, who, from the cars in the car park, were all still here somewhere.

"If that was me sitting on the floor, you wouldn't leave," he said, and he pulled the chair out from Gabby's desk. "We're going to talk."

"Ben–"

"Get up," he said, but she remained where she was. "I said, get up, Freya. Do you want Granger to come in and find you like this? Or Kelly?"

"I'm not sure I have the capacity to care anymore if I'm honest."

"We charged Banner," he said, which seemed to add insult to whatever injury it was she was nursing.

"I know," she replied. "It was close, though. At the end of the day, we can only charge one of them, and Banner had the MMO and more. Did you know he went to Myra's house? That's where he got the document from, and that's how he knew where she would be."

"Okay then. Did you know Gillespie arrested Hodges, Myra's neighbour?"

"No, what for?"

"The fingerprints on the circuit breaker were his. Who would have thought that giving Gillespie some legroom would pay off?"

"Gillespie is an excellent detective. He just needs reining in every now and then," she replied. "But we have to hand it to him, he's closed off any loose ends. Now it's just a question of fate."

"Freya get up," he said, and he shoved himself off the chair to stand the whiteboard up, working in near darkness to search for markers that had rolled in all directions.

"Just leave it, will you?" she said.

"And have somebody come in and find it? No, Freya. We all have our little tantrums every now and then–"

"A tantrum? Is that what you think this is?"

Ben moved over to the papers she had swiped onto the floor and began pulling them into a pile.

"What is all this?" he asked, holding the top sheet up to the only burning light. "A map?"

"It's the locations of all the excavations Myra Dicks denied Adam Frost from starting," she said, without even looking. "She was letting him do all the hard work and research, then going in and claiming the finds as her own. Her and Steel, of course."

"Is there something we can do?"

"It's a civil matter. As much as I'd like to make Steel pay, all we can really prove is that he withheld information, and even I'm not petty enough to go after that. Besides, I'm not sure I even have the energy."

"You need some time off," he told her, and he jabbed his index finger at the floor. "You've spent your entire career working towards this moment. You've been through hell. Your emotions are high, and that's understandable. I get it. Even if nobody else does, I do."

He dropped the stack of papers onto the desk and stood before her, extending his arm to help her up."

"Come on," he said.

Somewhere further along the corridor, a door slammed closed, and Freya stared at his hand. The hum of voices resonated through the building, and silently, Ben implored her to take his hand.

"Get up, Freya."

"Who is that?" she asked. "It's late."

"Everyone," he said. "Including Granger and Kelly. The announcement, remember?"

She puffed out a breath and as the voices grew loud enough to comprehend, she reached up and he hauled her to her feet. He held onto her for a moment while she caught her balance. But they lingered there, face to face, for a second too long.

"Oh, aye. Are we interrupting something?" Gillespie said, his broad smile seeming to fill the doorway. The team filed in after him taking their respective desks.

"No," Freya said, flatly, and she stepped away from Ben to perch on the edge of her desk. A worried expression washed over her face, and Ben felt obliged to stay close to her instead of retreating to his desk.

Granger and Kelly were the last to enter. They let the doors slam closed and Granger reached for the light switches.

"If you could leave them off, guv," Ben said, hoping the shadows would conceal Freya's red and strained eyes. "It's been a long day."

"As you wish," he said, placing himself under the single fluorescent. It was as if he was on a stage illuminated by an overhead spotlight, and the faces around him appeared to be peering from the surrounding darkness. "First of all, it goes without saying that congratulations are in order. Closing such a complex investigation is a significant achievement in itself, but to have it all wrapped up in four days is beyond comprehension and a testament to every one of you."

"Aye, you could say it's like something from one of Banner's fiction novels, guv, eh?" Gillespie added.

"Quite," Granger said, humouring the Glaswegian's interruption just once. "And might I say, well done to you, Jim. That was fantastic police work."

"Oh, it was nothing, guv. I just had a feeling, that was all."

"Well, it's commendable," Granger said, then returned to address the entire team. "The fact is though, at the beginning of this week, I had no idea what would happen to us all. While we all had certain ideals that we hoped to see come to fruition, nothing was certain. We are, as they say, at the whim and mercy of those above us."

He left a pause for the team to digest his opening, as any good orator might.

"The funeral is tomorrow. It was always my intention to bid our friend farewell as a team. As a result, I have pushed you harder than usual. I want us to begin our next chapter afresh. I didn't want Detective Superintendent Harper's funeral to be tainted with unanswered questions, phone calls, theories, and ideas. I want us to be present, both physically and mentally. For him, if nobody else, because, God knows, he deserves our attention one final time. Again, thank you for all your hard work this week. I realise it's late, so with the Myra Dicks investigation out of the way, I'd like to address the inevitable changes. But before I do, I have a little surprise for you all."

He beamed at them, as a proud father might present the gift they had always wanted.

"I'd like to introduce Deputy Chief Constable Kelly," he said.

All heads turned to the man standing beside Granger. The buttons across his uniformed chest gleamed in the soft light, and the crossed-tip staves on his epaulettes screamed respect.

"Good evening," he said quietly. Briefly, he glanced at everyone in the room. "I don't wish to repeat everything DCI Granger has said thus far, but I feel I should extend my congratulations to you all. Not only have you accomplished a monumental task in a short period of time, but, and I say this with great admiration, you have done so without complaint. This team is a benchmark and you should be proud."

A few murmurs of approval and appreciation coasted through the team, then faded in anticipation of what was to follow.

"I just hope that the collective decision we have made will reflect that positive attitude. It is always difficult to manage teams from afar. I often seek the guidance of senior officers, after all, DCI Granger knows you all far better than I do. But it has to be said, the decisions often lie with me. The death of Detective Superintendent Harper is a terrible loss, not only for the station but for the county. He was a man who gave his life to policing Lincolnshire and played a key part in developing relationships with figures even over my head. He will be missed."

"He will, sir," Granger added, and a few of the team mumbled their agreement.

"However, in such times lies great opportunity. The force is a far different beast from what it was when Dennis Harper first donned a uniform. So when we consider how we must respond, we are forced to simply replace him, this is not simply an exercise in filling offices with warm bodies. We must take this opportunity to rise stronger than ever before. Surely to achieve that is the greatest testament we can give to our friend, Detective Superintendent Harper?"

The pause Kelly left lingered long past its natural duration. It was as if he delighted in the anticipation, feeding off the emotions as each and every one of them faced mankind's greatest fear; the unknown.

"It would then be wise to bring a new leader to the team. A man who has, without a shadow of a doubt, proved himself to not only be up to the task at hand but who will do so with pride," Kelly said. "I would therefore like you to put your hands together for Detective Superintendent Granger."

The clapping was immediate like somebody had flicked a switch. Gillespie thumped his hand on the desk behind him, and Granger, modest as ever, stepped forward to shake Kelly's hand.

"Now..." Kelly said, holding his hand up to silence the team. "That of course leaves a space. Detective Superintendent Granger will have his hands full, so he needs somebody reliable beside him. Somebody time served, experienced, and capable of rising to the challenges we face on a daily basis. This week, you have all shown great promise. In fact, I wouldn't hesitate to say your performance has been exceptional. So for me then to consider who might stand at the helm, I needed to ensure familiarity, trust, and diligence. I need to ensure this team stays together because every one of you is key to continued success, every one of you is a keystone."

He stared now directly at Freya, and the team smiled as they followed his gaze.

"It then gives me great pleasure to announce the second of this evening's promotions. Please join me in congratulating an officer who has shown exceptional capability with an unrivalled desire to grow both personally and professionally." Again, he hesitated, as if reading the room, and held his hand out, as if he was presenting the shadows beyond them.

It was only then that the reality dawned on Ben, and judging by the gasps around him, the rest of the team, as a man stepped forward from the dark end of the room, his face as familiar and unwelcome as the squealing doors.

"Steve Standing?" Gillespie said, voicing his surprise but unable to hide his disappointment.

"Detective Chief Inspector Standing," Kelly corrected him.

"Aye," Gillespie replied.

The room was silent. There was no applause, canned or otherwise. Only a swathe of disappointment as DCI Standing shook Kelly's hand.

Any visible signs of distress were clearly lost on Kelly. Either that or he was just plain ignorant of the tension in the air.

Smiling as if he had delivered them a gift from the heavens, he shook Granger's hand one last time, then turned to the team.

"Get some rest," he said. "I hope to see you all tomorrow, where we'll bid our old friend farewell and show him we're ready for a new chapter."

He paused at the door as the team began to talk amongst themselves, just long enough to turn and offer Freya a knowing glare. And just before he left the room, before he broke that silent connection with her, when he thought nobody else was looking, he winked.

And then he was gone, taking with him the biggest opportunities of their careers.

CHAPTER FORTY-SIX

The sun beamed down on Dennis Harper on the morning of his funeral and the mourners suffered the blazing heat with dignity. The service had gone as planned, and in addition to the heartfelt eulogies from a few of Harper's family members, Will Granger had spoken on behalf of the force. His baritone anecdotes boomed through the chapel so that even those who had been forced to stand outside had heard him with clarity.

The wake was held at the Woodhall Spa Golf Club, Harper's favourite haunt, and the congregation consisted of family, golf club members, and the police force, of which Ben seemed to know nearly everyone, while Freya knew nobody except her close team and a few others.

"Look at him," she said to Ben, as he bit into a prawn vol-au-vent. He followed her gaze across the room to where Standing was entertaining a few men with one of his anecdotes. "Do I sound bitter?"

"Yes," Ben said, still chewing the pastry, and covering his mouth with the back of his hand.

She glared at him, unimpressed.

"I still can't believe it, you know," she said. "That job was mine for the taking."

"Well, we can either moan about it until Granger dies or we can move forward," Ben said. "I know what I'd rather do."

"What's that supposed to mean?"

"It's not supposed to mean anything, Freya. I'm just saying that I can't be bothered to argue. It's not going to do me any good."

"*You* don't have to report into him."

"No, you're right."

"What is it with you?" she said, as he perused the buffet, spying the pile of egg and cress sandwiches.

"I'm hungry," he replied. "Is that okay?"

"Not that. Him. Aren't you even remotely angry?"

"Of course, I am. In fact, I think it's a terrible decision. But do you know what? I can't change it. My options are to transfer, quit, or get on with it. So I'm getting on with it."

"Well, I won't be beaten so easily," she said, as he stepped away to sample the goods on the next table. "I was talking to you," she hissed when she rejoined him.

"Were you?" he replied. "I hadn't noticed."

"Ben? I thought we had each other's backs?"

"We do," he said, again with his mouth full, which was a bit too much for Freya. She couldn't even bring herself to watch him speak.

"You have a funny way of showing it."

He replied, but Freya couldn't understand what he was saying with his mouth filled with quiche.

"What?" he mumbled when she didn't say anything, and she shook her head at him, then chose instead to watch the room.

"And to top it off, the team are off with me," she said, voicing her thoughts.

"I wonder why?" Ben replied, not even trying to hide his flippancy.

"I tried to talk to Cruz earlier but he made his excuses and went to stand beside Gillespie."

"Upstaged by Gillespie?" Ben said, running his tongue around his teeth and finishing with a smacking sound. Then he wiped his mouth with the back of his hand, which he then cleaned on the side of his trousers.

"What?" he said again when Freya gave him a look of disgust.

"I need some fresh air," she said and made towards the door. But Ben remained where he was. "Won't you join me?"

"No," he replied, without even looking her way. "I think I'll stay here and keep the buffet company."

"Why won't you come?"

"Because, Freya, you asked me to tell you when you're being a cow."

"So?"

"So, you're being a spoiled cow," he replied, choosing not to even look her in the eye.

"Oh," she said, glancing at the exit into the car park. "Okay then."

She turned and walked away, stopping at the door to see if he had changed his mind, but he hadn't. He had sidled up to Gold and Chapman and the three of them were already engaged in a conversation with smiles all around.

She found fresh air exactly where she had hoped she would. The air conditioning in her car was a far more comfortable choice than the muggy afternoon outside.

From the doorway to where the wake was being held, a couple fell through into the sun, each of them carrying a glass of something refreshing, and it clearly wasn't their first. The man loosened his tie and then offered his female companion a cigarette. Together they smoked, chatted, and laughed in that animated way that only inebriation could excuse.

Freya found herself tutting to nobody at the distinct lack of refinement. Then a moment later, she cursed herself for being such a snob.

"Christ," she said, and let her head fall back onto the headrest. She checked her phone, but with every one of her colleagues at the event she had just walked away from, there were no messages. Not quite ready to return to the wake, she pulled the folder from where she had stuffed it down the side of the passenger seat. It was the same folder she had used during the investigation. She had initially meant to read through it, hoping to find something they had missed. But the news DCC Kelly had provided had rather dampened her hunger.

She flipped the folder open and flicked through the various photos Chapman had provided. There was the A4 envelope Nillson and Anderson had taken from the gun shop. And then there were the images of Myra's body, held together with a paper clip and bound in a blank piece of paper to avoid somebody viewing the injuries accidentally.

She snapped the folder closed and sat back in her seat with a sigh. Ben was right. She was being a cow. But how could he be so calm after the poor decision to promote Standing? No doubt she would have to submit every report and file associated with the investigation and he'd examine it with a fine-toothed comb, looking for an opportunity to make her life harder.

That was when she remembered the envelopes Ben had taken from Myra's postman and put in Freya's glovebox.

She leaned across to the passenger seat and fetched them, adding them to her already bulging file. By rights, only Claire Banner should have opened Myra's post. But there was something intriguing about the size and the weight of one particular envelope. It was a yellow jiffy package with Myra's name and address written neatly on the front, and the postmark was from Metheringham.

Before she knew it, her pinkie had found its way into the flap of the envelope. She glanced up to make sure nobody was coming, then slid it a little further, feeling the paper give way a little. She could always deny it. Or even better, she could blame DCI Standing somehow.

She had gone past the point of no return, and in a single move, her finger sliced through the entire flap and the contents of the envelope fell into her lap in all its poignant glory.

"Dance With Death," Freya said to herself, and she held the book up in the light.

The cover showed an old oak tree set at the edge of a field, with nothing but farmland around it and a dramatic sky above. She laughed to herself, just once, then popped the cover page to find a message written in the same neat handwriting as was on the envelope.

Myra,
Consider this an olive branch on which we can stand side by side.
Kevin.

She considered the message, and then checked the date it was sent.

"It can't be," she said, checking the date again and working the days back to arrive at the same conclusion. She stared at the book, the olive branch, the alibi, and mouthed a phrase she hoped she would never have to say. "I was wrong."

CHAPTER FORTY-SEVEN

"Where's your girlfriend?" Jackie asked when she spied Ben alone and stepped away from the group she had been talking to.

"Which one?" he said, to which she gave a polite laugh, sipped at her wine, and then moved alongside so they could people-watch together.

"The posh one," she said.

It was rare that he saw Jackie out of work these days. There was a time when they had been close, best friends in a way. But these days, he didn't even know if she was single, if she'd moved house, or if she was even happy.

"Sulking," he said, finally. "And for what it's worth, there's nothing there."

"Oh, come on," she said playfully. "You two are thick as thieves."

"We're good friends. That's all."

"Oh, I see. Friends with benefits?"

"No. No, I see no benefits," he replied. "But we're close enough for me to tell her a few home truths every now and then."

"Hence the sulk?"

"Hence the sulk," he confirmed.

"It's good to see you standing up to her."

"It's easier than laying down," he replied, then added, "and being walked over, before your dirty mind runs wild."

"Oh, come on. You must have..." She nodded to the car park, winking at him.

"What?"

"You and her. You must have... At least once. You know?"

"And here's me thinking my old mate Jackie had come to talk to me to see how I am."

"I just want the gossip, Ben. Come on, the others are killing me. They think you tell me everything."

"They think what?"

"They think we still talk. You know? Like we used to."

"Even if we did talk, I'm hardly likely to tell you if I..." He stopped mid-sentence, and checked to make sure nobody was listening.

"Next time they ask you, tell them to mind their own business."

"Jim reckons that's why she didn't get the job. The DCI role. It had her name all over it."

"Jim said that? Jim Gillespie?"

"Yeah. I mean, it seems pretty obvious when you think about it. They couldn't exactly make her DCI and you DI, knowing you were sleeping together."

"We are *not* sleeping together, Jackie. Will you get that out of your sordid, little mind?"

"Alright, alright," she laughed, taking another sip of her wine.

"How's Charlie, anyway?" Ben asked.

"Oh, you can do better than that, Ben. The whole team think you're sleeping with the DI, Standing makes an unwelcome appearance, we're at Harper's funeral, and all you can think to ask me is if my son is okay?"

Ben shrugged.

"I was just asking. I haven't seen him for ages."

"Yeah, well, perhaps when you stop spending your evenings with the boss, you can pop over to see him. My mum would be glad to see you."

"Oh, your mum. How is she?"

"She still thinks I'm thirteen, Ben. You know how it is."

"No, my dad treated us like thirty-year-olds when we were still at school. I'm not sure which is worse, to be honest," Ben said. "I thought you would be babysitting, anyway. Who's looking after Claire?"

"She was discharged yesterday. She wanted to be alone, which is understandable, given the news of her husband," Jackie said. "So, come on. Steve Standing. What's your opinion?"

"Does it count?"

"To me it does. Do you think he'll make a go of it? Or do you think he'll mess it up through sheer laziness?"

"If you're asking if he's turned a corner and is now a company man, then the answer is no. But he's too shrewd to get caught abusing his power. It's a tough one."

"Jim is running a bet," Jackie said. "I've got fifty quid on Standing being fired within a year."

"Fifty quid?"

"I live in hope," she said, offering him one of those girlish smiles he used to dream about when they were at school.

"Alright then," he said, feeling his phone vibrate in his pocket. He pulled it out and saw Freya's name flash up on the screen.

"Alright, what?" Jackie asked.

He pocketed the phone, ignoring the call. He was actually having a nice time talking to Jackie, and she was right, he should make more of an effort to see her and Charlie.

"I'll put fifty quid in."

"On him making a go of it or being fired?"

"Neither," Ben said. "I'll have fifty quid with you right here right now that Gillespie's little enterprise is discovered, and it's him that gets fired."

She roared with laughter, just like she used to.

"Yeah, you're probably right," she said, as Ben felt a tap on his elbow. He turned to find Nillson standing with a mature lady who wore an immaculate, white blouse and a dark skirt.

"There's somebody I'd like you to meet," Nillson said, presenting the woman like she was some kind of prize.

"Hi," he said, glancing awkwardly between Nillson and the woman. He held out his hand for her to shake. "Ben Savage."

The lady took his hand and shook it gently, the way he would expect a lady of her age to do so.

"Ben, this is Veronica. She runs the catering company," Nillson said, but there was something in the way she looked at him, wide-eyed, that told him there was more to the introduction than a simple polite gesture.

"I'll leave you to it," Jackie said, with a friendly squeeze of his arm.

"Okay," Ben said, suddenly finding himself being the centre of attention on more than one front.

"The vol-au-vents are spectacular," Ben said, and he leaned in with his friendliest smile. "I've had about seven, but don't tell anyone."

"Ben, Veronica is Jeffery Steel's wife," Nillson said.

"Jeffery Steel?" he said, and suddenly realised why Nillson had been so weird when she had introduced them. "Ah, I see."

"She would like a quick word if you don't mind. I couldn't find Freya."

"Right," he said. "A quick word. How can I help, Veronica?"

"It's about Myra," she began nervously. "I was wondering if... Well, I wondered if you'd found anybody."

"I see. Well, suppose it can't do any harm. You're going to find out tomorrow morning anyway, if you read the papers, Veronica. We have charged a man with her murder."

It was as if Ben had slapped her on the forehead. She seems to reel back onto her heels.

"We're releasing a statement later," he said. "It will all be in the papers."

"Oh, I don't read them," she said, turning whiter by the second.

Ben leaned across to a nearby table, made an apology, and took one of the chairs.

"Here," he said to her. "Take a seat. You don't look too well."

"I just knew it," she said. "I knew nothing good would come of it."

Behind her back, Nillson shrugged and pulled a face that suggested she also hadn't a clue what Veronica was talking about.

"Come of what, Veronica?" he said, dropping to a crouch to meet her eye to eye, just as he might have done with Jackie's son Charlie.

"Him and her, of course," she said. "The cow. I know, I shouldn't speak ill of the dead, but carrying on like that. Who do they think they are?"

"I'm sorry, Veronica. I really am sorry you've had to endure all of this."

"How long?" she asked.

"Sorry?"

"How long will he get?"

"Oh," Ben said. "That all depends on the judge, I'm afraid. But given the run around he gave us, and the lies, I wouldn't be surprised if it's upwards of twenty. A guilty plea might earn him a few years back but not many."

"Twenty years?"

"Don't hold me to that," he said.

"I feel like such a fool. That's the worst part, you know? I cared for him. I nursed him when he was sick. I trusted him. *Trusted him.* And look what he's done to me. Well, good bloody riddance to him."

"Sorry, what?" Ben said, more than a little confused by what she was saying. "Veronica, we haven't charged your husband. We've charged Kevin Banner."

She stilled. "Say that again," she said slowly as if she hadn't heard him correctly.

"I said your husband is free. We released him yesterday. We've charged Kevin Banner with Myra's murder. Sorry. Was I not clear?"

"Kevin? What, that sweet young man that helped me? No, he wouldn't have done that. He couldn't have."

"Why, Veronica?" Ben said, hoping the urgent glare he sent Nillson's way was translated as he hoped it would be.

Veronica Steel laughed out loud, rocking back and forth on her heels, either from the joy of hearing her husband hadn't been charged with murder or because of the ludicrousness of Kevin Banner being the murderer.

"Because he stopped me from killing her, love," Veronica said. "He told me where to find her. Must have had a change of heart."

"Sorry, what are you saying?" Ben said.

"I'm saying I was ready to kill the bloody cow, and if it wasn't for him stopping me and driving me home, I bloody well would have."

"Veronica, when was the last time you saw Jeffery?" Ben asked. "I need you to think hard."

She shook her head with uncertainty.

"I haven't seen him for days. Not since I found out about the affair," she said. "That's why I thought you'd locked him up."

"Excuse me," he said, gesturing for Nillson to follow him to the door. He peered out to the car park in search of Freya, but her car was not where she had left it.

"What's up?" Nillson said. "You look like you've seen a ghost."

"We've made a mistake," he replied. "A bloody big one, too."

CHAPTER FORTY-EIGHT

"Pick up," Freya said, as yet another call to Ben was directed to voicemail. She hit redial almost immediately, as she turned into Princes Street in the hope that Ben would answer.

But he didn't answer, and she rolled into the Banner driveway alone.

Claire Banner's car was on the driveway. The property was still and shrouded in perfect silence. She made her way towards the front door, finding it unlocked. Cautiously, she shoved it open and peered inside.

"Claire?" she called out.

She stepped inside and was about to call out again when a noise stopped her in her tracks – a thud, only slight, but alien in the silence. She stepped onto the stairs, drawn by the familiar smell of bath salts. She took another few steps and heard a gentle splash and the sound of running water.

"Claire?" she said. "Claire, it's Freya Bloom."

The running water stopped.

Freya could empathise with her. The woman had been through a traumatic time. She had lost her mother, been injured in a gas explosion, and to top it all, her husband was the cause of nearly everything.

"I'm in the bath," Claire called. "How did you get in?"

"I'm sorry. The door was unlocked."

"I..." Claire began. "I just want to be alone."

"It's okay," Freya said, descending the stairs. "I'm sorry, I was just a little worried about you. That's all."

"Can you just leave?" Claire called out.

"Yes. Sorry," Freya said, as she reached the hallway floor. "Will you call me if you need anything?"

"Just go. Please."

She imagined Claire in the bath with her knees drawn up to her chest, sobbing alone. But there was nothing Freya could do to ease her suffering. In fact, Claire wasn't the only one who needed some time in a hot bath.

She opened the front door, stepped out onto the drive, and inhaled the warm afternoon air.

But instead of walking to her car and driving off, as she probably should have done, she stayed there, unable to quell the fog of doubt that rolled in from all directions.

Something just didn't feel right. She turned and gripped the front door handle, never surer of anything, never more determined, and never so unafraid.

Quietly, she opened the door and pushed it open.

She listened for movement but heard nothing, and slowly climbed the stairs. But this time, she didn't call out. This time, she wouldn't make her presence known.

The bathroom door was closed and the soft carpet under her feet cushioned her steps, until she stood outside, her hand poised above the brass handle.

She heard a splash of water from inside, gentle, as if Claire had raised her hand to wipe away her tears. Another thud, and Freya pictured Claire running her hand along her legs, leaving a trail of bubbles.

And then a whimper of anguish.

A squeak of soapy hands gripping the enamel bath.

And a panicked gasp of air cut short by the splashing of water.

Kicking feet.

The thundering of Freya's heart within her chest beat away that fog of doubt that clouded her mind. She shoved open the door and found Jefferey Steel hunched over the bath. Claire Banner's legs kicked and writhed, searching for purchase, and water splashed across the floor.

And with all the surety of her instinct, Freya lunged at him. She reached for his hands on her throat and pulled him away. They fell together to the floor, and with one arm locked around his neck, they rolled across the room. She splayed her legs to stop the roll and held his arms against the floor in time to see Claire Banner fighting to regain her breath, her head hanging over the side of the bath.

But Steel saw his opportunity and took it. He freed his hand, pulled Freya's arm away and rolled onto her, pinned her with his knees, and then clamped his hand around her throat. He leaned in close to Freya, tears filling his red raw eyes.

"You should have stayed out of it," he whined, then sniffed hard, as if he had no choice but to squeeze harder.

Freya kicked out at thin air, searching for something to hook her legs around, but there was nothing within reach. From her peripheral, she saw Claire fall from the bathtub onto the floor, as naked as the day she was born. She pushed herself up onto all fours, still gasping for breath.

But Steel saw her too, and with his free hand, he grabbed her hair, pulling her closer to where he could control them both.

"It's over," Freya said, her voice box almost entirely closed. "You don't have to do this, Jeffery."

"No. No, I can't," he said, his emotions deforming his features as he agonised over what he was about to do. "I can't go back. I can never go back."

"I know what Myra was doing," Freya hissed, and he squeezed tighter, raising her head a few inches from the floor, then slamming her down.

"You know nothing," he cried.

"I know about the digs," she said. "And the proposals. I know it was all her idea."

"Stop," he said, working his other hand from Claire's hair to her throat so the two women were laying side by side, each with a hand clamped on their throats. But the strength in his grip was fading. "Just stop."

"It was a perfect plan," Freya hissed. "You'd both finally get the recognition you deserve. You'd be credited for discovering Bronze Age settlements. Your names would be in all those books you seem to adore."

"No," he said, and a tear dripped from the end of his nose onto her face, and his grip on her throat loosened.

"Do you honestly think that Myra would have shared the glory, Jeffery?"

Claire kicked into life, struggling against his hold. She managed to pull free and scooted back to the bath, pulling a towel over her. Freya took advantage of the distraction to push herself free.

Jeffery scrambled off her and slumped back against the wall beside the door.

"That's what she did, wasn't it?" Freya said, pulling herself up onto her elbows. "She manipulated you. You were nothing more than a plaything. She didn't care about you. The only person she cared about was Claire."

"She loved me," Steel snapped, and he shook his head as if the reality of the whole affair had just made itself clear.

"No," Claire said sadly. "My mother was incapable of love. Of that kind, anyway. That's why my father left. That's why there's nobody but me."

They sat in a triangle, Freya leaning against the sink, Claire against the bath, and him beside the door. It was like they were three old friends mourning the loss of a fourth.

"I destroyed my marriage," he said finally.

"There's still time to save it," Freya said. "We all need a little wake-up call every now and then. They help us realise what we have, and what's important."

It was rare that Freya shared any type of connection with a suspect, but the way he stared at her, unafraid, as if he was reading her thoughts.

"Go," she said softly. "Go before I change my mind."

"What?" Claire snapped. "You can't let him go—"

"Now," Freya said, a little more sternly.

"What are you doing?" shouted Claire, as she slowly pushed herself to her feet. "You can't let him go. He tried to bloody kill me."

Holding the towel around her, she offered Freya a direct view of the deep scratches across her bare shoulders and arms.

Claire followed Freya's gaze, and like a switch had been flipped, her expression altered. Her body seemed to slump, and she dropped back against the bath, defeated.

"Go," Freya told him again. "Nobody will stop you."

They watched him leave, heard his footsteps retreat to the stairs, and then he was gone.

"Are you mad?" Claire said.

"He won't get far," Freya told him, and she flickered her eyes across the scratches on Claire's skin. "How long were you lying in the dyke?"

Claire drew her knees up to her chin and shrugged but said nothing.

"He knew, didn't he?" Freya said, and Claire's expression faded. "He worked it out before we did. He obviously loved your mother more than you thought."

"What will happen to him?" Claire asked.

"That all depends on you," Freya replied. "How long did you lay there for?"

"A few hours," she replied, then gazed into space, recalling the haze that so often follows rage. "I was running. It was all a blur. I didn't mean to do it. But I was fed up with her lies. Her..."

She stopped as if she was searching for the right word.

"Manipulation?" Freya suggested, and she nodded.

"I was on the lane. I know that much. I saw Kevin's van, just up near the car park. I couldn't face him. I couldn't let him see me. He'd know what I'd done. He's good like that. He's a good man. I just dived in and lay there, hoping everything would go away, wishing I could turn back the clock."

Freya said nothing, letting the pressure of guilt force the story from her.

"He is a good man. Kevin, I mean, despite his shortfalls. He had nothing to do with this. She tried to break us up. She's been trying to do it for years, opening the crack at any given opportunity," she said softly. "It was inevitable, I suppose, that one of us would break sooner or later. I hadn't planned it, you know?"

"I know," Freya said.

"I just wanted to catch her out. I wanted to make her realise that she couldn't keep on lying to me."

"You followed her?" Freya said, and Claire nodded.

"I knew she was lying. I just knew it. I knew I'd catch her out, and she'd try to lie her way out of it. It had to stop. She was destroying lives. They were destroying lives. Not just his and hers, but his wife's too. Now I know how she must have felt."

"He told us about the other woman," Freya said, and Claire's head fell forward onto her knees. "It was a business meeting. Did you know that?"

She raised her head slowly. "Is that what he told you?"

"He had to sign a contract to say he wouldn't disclose the details," Freya said. "His books are going to be made into a TV series."

"TV?"

Freya nodded, and the news seemed to be the final weight that crumpled her. Her shoulders jolted with every sob, and she hugged her legs in as tight as she could.

"He was onto her, you know? Your mother. He'd worked out what she was up to. We think that after the argument on Saturday, he visited your mother. He took a document from her house and kept it with Trevor Copeland. At first, I thought he did that to protect himself. Or to give himself some kind of ammunition against her in case he ever needed it. But do you know what? I actually think he did it to protect her in a weird kind of way. To somehow put a spanner in the works. I suppose we'll never know."

"That sounds like something he would do," Claire said.

"Did you know he sent your mother a copy of his book?"

"Dance With Death, by any chance?" she asked, and Freya nodded.

"He sent it on Monday."

"On Monday?"

"The day after you killed your mother, Claire," Freya said. "He had no idea any of it had happened until we picked him up at the cathedral, did he?"

Again, Claire shook her head, softly.

"Your mother was already dead when he gave the document to Trevor Copeland, too."

"He keeps everything with Trevor," Claire whined. "Mum was quite nosy and extremely overbearing. Always cleaning when she visited. Always looking through his things in his office. It used to drive him mad."

She looked up from the space on the floor she had been staring at and met Freya eye to eye.

"Is that how you knew it wasn't him?"

"That and the ending of the story," Freya said, and Claire looked up at the ceiling as if she trying to recall the twist.

"He was innocent," she said. "The suspect in the book was innocent, and the killer was the last person you'd expect it to be."

"The suspect wasn't just innocent, Claire. He was trying to save his mother-in-law."

"How poetic," Claire said, allowing a hint of bitterness to escape.

"Somebody once told me, that when an investigation gets too complex, that it's often the simplest of choices," Freya said. "It's not often I listen to advice, but in this instance, it seemed to have paid off."

Footsteps on the stairs interrupted Freya, and Claire pulled the towel down to cover her legs. A few moments later, Ben appeared in the doorway.

"Are you okay?" he asked Freya.

She nodded, but Claire edged away from him, holding the towel over her chest.

"We've got Steel," he said. "We found him running down the road. What do you want us to do with him?"

"Claire?" Freya said. "Are you going to press charges."

Claire shook her head.

"Like you said, he obviously loved mum more than I thought," she said. "What happens next?"

"You'll be taken to the station and charged," Freya told her. "From there, I imagine you'll be held on remand until the hearing."

The news took a few moments to sink in, and Claire looked around her bathroom for the last time in what would be a very long time.

"Do you have a dressing gown, Claire?" Freya asked.

"On the back of the bedroom door," she replied.

Ben took the hint and went to get the dressing gown, reappearing a few moments later, holding it open for her to slip into whilst averting his eyes.

Claire gave Freya a look of concern, steeling herself for an uncertain future as she tied the gown around her waist and found Ben's grip on her upper arm.

"It's okay. He's one of the good ones," Freya said, peering up at Ben. "In fact, he's one of the best."

CHAPTER FORTY-NINE

It was already late when Freya climbed from her bath. The steam had long since dispersed and the water was now just on the wrong side of comfortable. But that was okay; she still had her glass of wine. She sat on the edge of the bath, wrapped a towel around her, and studied her wrinkled fingers.

One day, they would look like that permanently, she thought, which led her mind into a rabbit hole of where she might be living, if she would still be lonely, and if she would still be a DI.

In her bedroom, she slipped into her finest lingerie, taking a few moments to find the angle in the mirror she enjoyed the most, or rather, the angle that showed her age the least.

The dress she had selected before her bath and had laid out ready to wear was one of her favourites. It wasn't the green, stylish number she had worn a few days before; that was far too formal for such an occasion. For what she had planned, she would need far more seductive qualities – a plunging neckline and a slit that allowed an intriguing glimpse of flesh yet still retained her modesty. It was, in her opinion, as sexy and as seductive as a dress could be without forgoing dignity. It was the epitome of a little black number, the very pinnacle of evening dates.

Sitting on the edge of her bed, she slipped into her shoes and ran her hands along her legs, feeling for areas she may have missed. There were none, of course.

Her makeup took the longest, and then her hair. The trick, she had learned, was not to do too much, which ironically somehow took longer than applying a full face. The only area that required some extra attention was the slight bruising on her neck.

Her hair, still blonde with a hint of her mother's red, just needed some volume. Then with a few careful adjustments, it was exactly how he liked it.

She sprayed a cloud of her new perfume from their Paris trip and walked through it, adding a touch more to her wrists for good measure.

Finally, she donned her mother's necklace, a simple topaz that complimented her reddish hair set in eighteen-carat gold with matching earrings.

The mirror portrayed an image of hope and guilt, exactly as intended, and she imagined his expression when he saw her. It could go one of two ways – success or complete failure.

From her kitchen, she collected the bottle of wine she had bought for the occasion, a Louis Latour Pino Noir, one of the finest red wines Freya had ever tried, and the same wine they had shared on that fateful Parisian evening on their hotel balcony overlooking the city's rooftops.

She grabbed her keys and opened the front door, aware that should she stop to check her reflection or procrastinate in any way; the voice in her head would convince her to stay, to slip into something comfortable and drink the wine alone. It was a risk-free option, but one that offered no future, no opportunity. And opportunities were to be taken when they were offered.

A dust cloud formed in her wake, as she idled along the narrow track that led from her little cottage to his. She passed the little junction that led to the main road and approached the trio of Savage houses. Ben's was the first of the three, with his father's in the middle and his brothers' house at the end, all of them forming a neat, welcoming arc.

She parked beside Ben's car and checked her reflection briefly.

There would be no turning back now. Tonight was a night for making amends.

With the bottle in her hand, she strode up to Ben's door, contemplating letting herself in. She imagined his surprise when she kissed him, forcing him back into that quaint, little lounge of his, and taking control over him and their future.

But that would never do. That, her father would have said, was not how a lady was to conduct herself, and even that glimmer of her father's memory doused the fire that burned inside her.

She knocked then stepped back, taking a moment to straighten her dress and prepare herself for his reaction.

Freya heard the footsteps on the other side of the door and her heart thumped like thunder inside her chest.

Then the door opened, and whatever embers of that fire had yet to be doused, were well and truly quenched.

"Freya?"

She was speechless, mortified, heartbroken, and defeated all at once. A melee of emotions rocked her, and she dizzied, stumbling backwards a little at the sight.

"Michaela?"

The two stared at each other in complete shock, until Ben appeared at the top of the stairs, with just a towel to protect his modesty.

He said nothing. There was nothing to say. There was nothing to do. Not now.

Except to turn around, hold her head up high, and for the second time in under a year, walk away, towards uncertainty.

The End

IN DEAD WATER - PROLOGUE

The moonlight cast deep shadows across the sand and mudflats, but barely lit the tall marsh grasses, that seemed to reach for Hayley's legs as she ran. Twice she stumbled and barely stayed upright, but never did she stop. She couldn't stop.

Because he was out there somewhere, mad as hell.

In daylight, she could have outrun him with ease. She could be home and dry.

In the darkness of the night, however, she had only her memory to find her way.

But it was all so different. The little streams seemed to have moved. The patches of soft sand were the same shade of grey as the dry sand, and the grasses seemed to have sprouted everywhere. Only the reflections from the brackish streams that spread like arteries throughout the mud, provided any real contrast against the night, and her thudding heart was the beat to which her bare feet pounded.

She launched herself across one the mirror-like obstacles, time seeming to stand still for the fragment of time she was airborne. Then she landed with a thud. Her feet sank deep into the sand and she fell flat on her face in the wet slime.

It took a moment or two to regain her senses. No bones were

broken. She took the opportunity to gain control of her breathing, listening hard for the sound of his footsteps behind her somewhere.

From where she lay, she had a clear view of where she had run. The tall marsh grasses, the arterial streams, and the beach beyond, framed by two large sand dunes. And beyond that, the inky mass of the North Sea, capped by the pale horizon, where somewhere, the sun graced some other land with its light. Somewhere in Europe, she thought. Germany, or Holland, maybe?

Surely if he was out there she would see him against the sky? Like some wraith from hell trudging through the stinking mud and sand with a methodical purpose.

But there was no sign of him. No shape against the horizon, no sound of sucking mud, there was only that smell. That smell she would never ever be rid of.

How she wished she had just stayed at home. Why did she have to go out alone? Why didn't she listen to the others?

A shiver ran through her, marking her time there. The cool evening breeze licked at the layer of sweat on her back, and the idea of running seemed beyond her remaining strength.

She could just sleep here.

He wouldn't find her. Not here.

She glanced at the horizon again. An hour. Two at the most.

What if she crawled to the dry sand a few metres away? She could lie between the grasses out of the wind.

She scanned the desolate ground behind her again finding nothing but stillness.

Then she made her move, or tried to at least.

Her feet seemed to be stuck in the mud. She had laid there too long. Panic set in and she struggled again the vacuum that held her there, only to find that she sank further.

She reached for a tuft of those hardy grasses, but it pulled free, allowing the ground to inhale another few inches.

The temptation to call out was overwhelming, but he was out there somewhere. Maybe he was watching? Maybe he knew the marshland better than her, and had found a way to overtake her. Inland was a mass of black. She could just make out the ramp that emergency vehicles used to access the marshes. She had seen them once before when a girl from her school had become stuck in the mud and died out here, alone.

And then it dawned on her.

She was that girl from school. Her's was the name that would be on people's lips.

Have you heard about Hayley Plant? Did you hear about the girl from Salt-fleet? You'd have thought she'd have known better. Her parents must be devastated.

She reached for another tuft of grass, and this time its roots held fast. She fell forward, to dig her elbows into the mud, to give herself every chance.

But it was no use.

A sob came from nowhere, a quiet whimper that somehow seemed amplified in the still of the night. She sniffed, no longer caring if he found her. No longer caring what he might do.

"Help," she called out, crying now, openly venting her fears. "Please, help."

She laid the side of her face down in the mud, staring out at the horizon. She could have sworn it was brighter now.

She remembered her dad saying that everyone should see at least one sunrise and one sunset every year, just to remind them f their insignificance. She had seen the sunset in Cornwall only a few weeks ago.

And now she was watching the sunrise, as insignificant as could be.

The sunset had been beautiful. She remembered how fast the sun seemed to fall below the horizon. She remembered the hues of orange like watercolour paints across the sea.

And now she stared at the onset of day. There were no orange hues. The sea was not calm and inviting.

And his black shape lurched into view, like death himself emerging from the shadows, braving the looming sunrise.

She could call out for help, but nobody would hear. She fought harder to free her legs, but she only sank further. What would be worse, death by his hand, or drowning in the thick mud?

He moved closer, and she cried freely, no longer caring for silence or stealth, and praying for there to be some remnant of a heart inside of him.

But he stopped a few metres away, seeming to peer at her with a childlike curiosity.

"Please," she said. "I'm stuck. Please, help me. I won't say anything."

But he said nothing. Instead, he stepped closer, and his broad, black body blocked the promise of the glorious last sunrise she would ever see.

ALSO BY JACK CARTWRIGHT

The DCI Cook Murder Mysteries

A Winter of Blood

A Secret to Die For

The Wild Fens Murder Mysteries

Secrets In Blood

One For Sorrow

In Cold Blood

Suffer In Silence

Dying To Tell

Never To Return

Lie Beside Me

Dance With Death

In Dead Water

One Deadly Night

Her Dying Mind

Into Death's Arms

Join my VIP reader group to be among the first to hear about new release dates, discounts, and get a free Wild Fens novella.

Visit www.jackcartwrightbooks.com for details.

VIP READER CLUB

Your FREE ebook is waiting for you now.

Get your FREE copy of the prequel story to the Wild Fens Murder Mystery series, and learn how DI Freya Bloom came to give up everything she had, to start a new life in Lincolnshire.

Visit www.jackcartwrightbooks.com to join the VIP Reader Club.

I'll see you there.

Jack Cartwright

AFTERWORD

Because reviews are critical to an author's career, if you have enjoyed this novel, you could do me a huge favour by leaving a review on Amazon.

Reviews allow other readers to find my books. Your help in leaving one would make a big difference to this author.

Thank you for taking the time to read *Dance With Death*.

COPYRIGHT

Milton Keynes UK
Ingram Content Group UK Ltd.
UKHW030659151124
451186UK00014B/402/J